Dear Reader,

Welcome to Parable County, Montana, whether you're new in town or not.

Big Sky Summer is the story of Walker Parrish, rodeo stock contractor and all-around cowboy in the "sexy" division, and Casey Elder, country music superstar and red-hot redhead! These two have a history, but it's a tumultuous one, that's for sure, including a couple of rapidly growing secrets. And you know how the truth is—it **will** come out, for better or worse.

Can these two hardheaded independent types make it work? A lot of people wouldn't give their on-again, off-again love, tough and durable as it is, the proverbial snowball's chance. But, as you and I both know, there's magic in Parable County, and love is its favorite trick.

In addition to this brand-new story, I'm delighted to announce that I have teamed up with Montana Silversmiths, the legendary makers of championship belt buckles and fabulous Western jewelry, to create a piece I call "Casey's necklace." You'll read all about it in the book, and might even find yourself wanting one of your own. Just go to www.montanasilversmiths.com/two-hats-one-heart. And know that 100 percent of my share of the profits will go toward establishing perpetual funding for my Linda Lael Miller Scholarships for Women, in the hope that generations of deserving ladies of all ages will continue to benefit from the program.

Meanwhile, stop on by www.lindalaelmiller.com for my (almost) daily blog, excerpts from my books, videos of some very sexy cowboys, scholarship news and fun contests, along with a few surprises now and then.

Happy trails, and thanks for the listen.

With love,

Linda Lael Miller

LINDA LAEL MILLER

BIG SKY Summer

DOUBLEDAY LARGE PRINT HOME LIBRARY EDITION

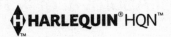

HARLEQUIN® HQN™

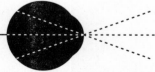

This Large Print Book carries the
Seal of Approval of N.A.V.H.

For Larry Readman, aka the Canadian Wrangler. Thanks for taking such good care of my horses.

CHAPTER ONE

Walker Parrish, wedged into the middle of a third-row pew, with old ladies wearing gauzy hats and floral dresses packed in tightly on either side, risked a glance up at the church ceiling, just to make sure it wasn't fixing to fall on his head. He resisted a nervous urge to loosen his tie—for him, like churchgoing, tie wearing was reserved for funerals and weddings. This occasion, fortunately, fell into the latter category.

The small sanctuary seemed charged with excitement; folks chatted in whispers, the organist was tuning up for the wedding march, and the groom, Sheriff Boone Taylor, stood tall up front, just to the right of the simple altar, looking eager and scared shitless, both at the same time. Like the majority of men around Parable, Montana, Boone lived in jeans, cotton shirts and boots most of the time, and he looked a few degrees past uncomfortable in his rented tux.

Hutch Carmody and Slade Barlow, half brothers and Boone's closest friends, stood up with him, hardly recognizable in monkey suits of their own. Both married men, and cowboys to the core, they kept an eye on Boone, as if ready to catch him by the elbows if his knees buckled, but wry grins twitched at the corners of their mouths, too. They were enjoying this, most likely figuring that if they'd had to get up in front of the whole county and plight their troths, Boone shouldn't be spared the ordeal, either.

Walker fixed his gaze on Hutch, remembering the last time he'd set foot in this tiny church—a June day, much like this one, with birds chirping in the trees and warm breezes sweeping up the aisle from the open doors of the entryway— and felt the hinges of his jaws lock down. Back then, almost two years ago now, Hutch had been the bridegroom, not best man. And Walker's kid sister, Brylee, the only blood kin he could—or would— rightly claim, had been the bride, shiny-eyed and full of bright hopes, wearing the kind of gown women start dreaming about when they're little girls.

Just when the organ cue sounded, on that other day, the bridesmaids having already taken their places up front, as endlessly rehearsed, and Walker had swung one foot forward to march Brylee between the rows of pews jammed with people, Hutch had suddenly broken rank with Boone and the minister and walked midway down the aisle, where he stopped.

"Hold it," he'd said in a sheepish but nonetheless determined tone.

He'd stopped the wedding, called it off, right then and there, shattering Brylee's fairy-tale dreams and maybe souring her forever on the subject of marriage.

While a part of Walker had been relieved—he'd never thought Brylee and Hutch Carmody were a good fit—the memory of his sister's humiliation still stung like a thistle stuck in his hide. If he hadn't been so busy trying to keep Brylee from doing something stupid, he'd have punched Carmody in the mouth, church or no church.

Which was part of the reason he didn't trust the rafters to hold. He tossed another wary glance toward the ceiling.

The Reverend Walter Beaumont was officiating, and he took his place, book in hand, resplendent in maroon robes and a long gold scarf of some kind. Most times, the preacher dressed Western, like most everybody else, but today he looked as serious as an Old Testament prophet about to lower the boom on a gathering of unrepentant sinners. He looked like Morgan Freeman and sounded like James Earl Jones, so everybody got ready to listen.

Beaumont cleared his throat.

The organist struck the first rousing chord, and the congregation settled in to watch the show. Walker suspected some of them were, like him, wondering if history was about to repeat itself. The thwarted Carmody-Parrish wedding was, around Parable County, anyhow, the stuff of legend.

Tara Kendall's twin stepdaughters, now living with her, were barely teenagers and served as flower girls, happily scattering rose petals in their wake as they fairly danced up the aisle, both of them beaming and obviously enjoying the attention of the guests.

Joslyn Barlow, married to Slade and in a noticeably advanced state of pregnancy, soon followed, wearing an elegant lavender maternity dress and carrying a bouquet of multicolored flowers in both hands.

Walker noted the electric look that passed between Joslyn and her husband as she took her place opposite the three men dressed like tall, rangy penguins.

Kendra Carmody, Hutch's beloved—the woman he'd thrown Brylee over for—came next, sleek and classy in pale yellow and also carrying the requisite flowers. Hutch winked at her when she came to a stop beside Joslyn, and a fetching blush pinked her cheeks.

Next to join the march were Boone's two young sons, wearing suit jackets and slacks and little bow ties. Each of them carried a satin pillow with a gold wedding band nestled in the hollow, and the smaller boy stopped a couple of times along the way, seeming to forget the procedure. He showed the ring he was carrying to Opal Dennison, and she smiled and gently steered him back on course.

This brought an affectionate twitter from the assembly, and the clicks of several phone cameras slipped in between the notes of organ music.

Walker grinned as the older boy finally backtracked and herded his little brother the rest of the way.

Then it sounded, the loud, triumphant chord signaling the imminent approach of the bride. Walker felt a pang, again reminded of Brylee's ill-fated wedding, but the truth was, he was glad for Boone and glad for Tara Kendall, too.

Widowed several years before, Boone had been one of the walking wounded for a long time, doing his job but clearly unhappy. He was a good sheriff and a fine man, and Walker liked him.

The bride, a glamorous city slicker hailing from the Big Apple, had come to Parable some time before, reportedly to reinvent herself after a nasty divorce. It had been a while before Boone and Tara got together, considering that they'd evidently disliked each other on sight, but they'd finally gotten past all that. And, wisely, Walker thought, they'd agreed on a fairly long courtship, just to make sure.

And now their big day was finally here.

There was a churchwide shuffle as the guests rose, turning to watch the bride start what probably felt like the longest short walk of her life.

Boone's brother-in-law, Bob, escorted Tara, but he was pretty much lost in Tara's glow. She looked like an angel bride in her billowing lacy dress, and her smile was clearly visible behind the rhinestone-studded netting of her veil, as were the happy tears sparkling in her eyes.

Walker felt a catch in his throat, wishing her and Boone well without reservation, but at the same time wanting that kind of joy for his disillusioned kid sister. She'd been invited to this shindig, right along with him, but Brylee stayed away from weddings these days. She stayed away from too many things, in his opinion, working crazy hours, too worn-out to say much when she did turn up, long after all her employees had called it a day and gone home. Even then she immediately retreated to her apartment in the main ranch house, her rescued German shepherd, Snidely, following devotedly at her heels.

Realizing he'd gone woolgathering, which was unlike him, Walker was a little startled when Casey Elder appeared beside the organist, music sheet in hand. She wore a blue choir robe and almost no makeup, and her shoulder-length red hair, usually tumbling around her face in spirals, had been pinned up into a sedate knot at her nape.

Inwardly, Walker allowed himself a grim, silent chortle.

This was a side of Casey he'd rarely if ever seen, despite the tangled and chaotic history they shared. She could still pack arenas and major concert halls, even after fifteen years as a professional entertainer, and she'd never recorded a song that hadn't gone straight to number one on all the charts and ridden there for weeks on end. Her videos were legendary, full of fire and smoke and color, and she was as famous for her flashy style as she was for her voice, always astounding in its power and range. A thing that spread its wings and took flight, soaring like a soul set free.

Onstage or on camera, she wore custom-made outfits so bejeweled that she glittered like a dark Montana sky full of stars, a one-woman constellation, and between her looks and the way she sang, she took every member of every audience captive and held them spellbound until the moment she retreated into the wings after the last curtain call. Even then, the magic lingered.

Walker wondered if Casey's legions of fans would even recognize her the way she looked today, all prim and well scrubbed. He shook off the riot of reactions he felt whenever he encountered this woman, up close or at a distance, and kept his face impassive when she started to sing.

She'd written the song, all about promises and sunrises and sticking together no matter what, especially for Boone and Tara. The organ played softly in the background, a gossamer thread of sound supporting that amazing voice.

By the time she finished, the old ladies on either side of Walker were sniffling happily into their lace-trimmed hankies, and Walker felt the need to blink a couple of times himself.

Casey retreated as swiftly and silently as a ghost, and the ceremony began.

The truth was, most of it was lost on Walker. He sat there in a daze, Casey's song reverberating inside him like a sweet echo.

Boone moved to stand tall and proud beside his bride, and the reverend began his speech.

Vows were exchanged, promises made, and the light of Boone's and Tara's separate candles bonded into a single flame, strong and steady, barely flickering. They slipped rings onto each other's fingers, their faces shining.

Walker, a man in a daze, took it all in, like a dream, with Casey's remarkable voice for a sound track.

The reverend pronounced them man and wife in a tone of rumbling jubilance, and Boone gently raised Tara's veil, smoothed it back and kissed her with a tenderness that struck even Walker's tough cowboy heart like the plucking of a fiddle string.

The organ erupted again, joyous thunder, startling Walker out of the spell Casey had cast over him, and Mr. and Mrs. Boone Taylor came down the aisle together, both of them beaming, cheers breaking out all around them.

Patiently, Walker waited for the guests to file out into the afternoon sunshine, scented with flowers and new-mown grass and fresh asphalt, glad the wedding was over and equally glad he'd put on scratchy duds and shown up.

Now all he had to do was put in an appearance at the reception, eat a little cake, shake Boone's hand and kiss Tara's cheek, nod to this person and that one, and make a subtle escape. The to-do, which would probably resemble a small circus, was to be held in Casey's massive backyard, about the last place Walker wanted to hang out, but there was no avoiding it, since he was representing Brylee as well as himself. If he was lucky, he might manage to steal a moment or two with Clare and Shane while steering clear of their mother.

Clare and Shane. Casey's children.

His children.

Finally reaching his truck, a big rig with an extended cab and plenty of horsepower for hauling trailers loaded with rodeo stock, Walker swung up into the driver's seat and immediately dispensed with his tie, which was starting to feel like a noose.

The road in front of the church was plenty crowded, and it took a while to get into the flow of traffic, all headed toward Casey's mansion on Rodeo Road.

Walker spotted the nuptial limo up ahead and smiled in spite of his increasing case of the jitters, because Boone's and Tara's heads and shoulders were sticking up through the open sunroof, and both of them glowed as if they'd had sunshine for breakfast. It was good to be reminded that that kind of happiness was possible, short of heaven itself. With one broken marriage behind him, besides his long and tempestuous relationship with Casey, Walker tended toward skepticism when it came to love and romance. The kind that lasted, anyhow.

A mild glumness overtook him as he drove at a parade pace, and he was tempted, more than once, to zip out of the procession onto a side street, head home to his horses and his bulls and his regular clothes, and skip the whole second act. If only he hadn't been cursed with a single-minded—some would say cussed—nature, the kind that compelled a man to do what he thought was right, whether that happened to be his personal inclination at the time or not.

So he endured, pushing on until the line of cars and trucks finally snaked onto Rodeo Road, and Casey's house loomed ahead, big as a mountain. He found a parking spot—no small feat in itself—and walked two blocks to the mouth of the long white-gravel driveway, blending in with the wedding guests and the throng of new arrivals who wouldn't have fit inside the church.

Everybody was dressed up in their best, toting wrapped presents and covered casseroles and flowers cut from their gardens.

Walker felt a little self-conscious, showing up empty-handed, but that passed quickly. Brylee had taken care of the gift-giving end of things, signing his name and her own to the card, and whatever she'd sent was sure to be just right for the occasion.

Rounding the side of the house with the others, Walker was amused to see that he'd guessed right—Casey's yard did indeed have a carnival-like atmosphere, with paper lanterns strung on every branch of every tree, a silver fountain flowing with chocolate instead of water, a massive canvas canopy arching above a couple of dozen tables. There was a bandstand, too, a temporary dance floor, an open bar and, incredibly, a genuine carousel for the little ones.

Obviously, this party would go on long after Boone and Tara had cut the cake, posed for the pictures, danced the customary waltz and lit out on their weeklong honeymoon. Rumors varied as to the destination—Vegas, Honolulu and Cabo were all in the running—but the bride and groom were keeping that information to themselves.

In a town where almost everybody knew everybody else's business, folks kept what secrets they could.

Walker was taking in the Casey-like spectacle of the whole setup when Shane turned up, handsome in his slacks and white dress shirt, though he'd gotten rid of his tie and suit jacket at some point. At thirteen, the boy was growing up fast—every time Walker saw him, he was a little taller, or his feet were a size bigger, or both.

"Hey, Walker," Shane greeted him, grinning. While his sister resembled Casey, with her auburn hair, milky complexion and green eyes, Shane looked pretty much the way Walker had at his age. Strange that nobody seemed to notice that and put two and two together.

"Hey," Walker replied. "Looks like this is going to be quite a party."

Shane nodded. "Mom's going to sing later," he said, "and the whole town could live for a year on the food the caterers are setting out."

Walker's throat tightened. He was tough, raised a ranch kid, no stranger to hard work **or** hard knocks, but hearing Casey sing at the wedding had nearly dropped him to his knees, figuratively, anyhow. Listening to her repertoire of greatest hits might just kill him.

"I can't stick around too long," he said, his voice coming out gruff. "I've got things to do out at the ranch—" He fell silent then, because of the way Shane's face fell. Although the kid probably had no clue that Walker was his biological father—Casey had made sure of that—there had always been a bond between him and Shane just the same. Walker was the avuncular family friend, the guy who usually turned up for Thanksgiving dinners, birthdays and sometimes Christmas. Casey refused to accept child support, but Walker had been putting away money for his son and daughter for years just the same.

"Oh," Shane said, looking bleak. Familiar with the operation, he knew what it took to run a spread the size of Timber Creek, where Walker raised cattle, along with bulls and broncos for the rodeo circuit.

He'd spent a week or two on the ranch most summers, along with Clare, and he knew there were plenty of capable ranch hands to take up the slack when Walker wasn't around.

Walker, aching on the inside, grinned and laid a hand on Shane's skinny shoulder. "I guess I can stay for a while," he conceded. Clare and Shane had had tutors, growing up on the road as they had, and attending school in Parable for the past year had been a new experience for them. Adaptable and confident, used to traveling from place to place in a well-appointed tour bus or a private jet, they'd thrived, even before the move to Montana.

Shane lit up. "Good," he said, and he

stuck pretty close to Walker for the next fifteen minutes or so before he noticed the flock of giggling girls watching him from the sidelines. "My public," he quipped, making Walker laugh.

"Go for it," Walker told him.

He meandered toward the bar, stopping every few feet to speak with somebody he knew, and finally scored a cold beer. Boone and Tara and the rest of the wedding party were busy posing for pictures, both amateur and professional, and he watched for a while, envying his friends a little. Between them, the newlyweds had four children: a ready-made family. What would it be like if he could claim Shane and Clare publicly as his own? If they called him Dad?

Never gonna happen, cowboy, he reminded himself silently. **So get over it.**

Walker took another long pull on his beer. How, exactly, did a man "get over" not being able to acknowledge his own flesh and blood?

He felt a stab of annoyance at Casey for insisting that Shane and Clare were **her** children, and hers alone, as though she'd somehow managed not just one Virgin Birth, but two. Heat climbed his neck and made his collar feel tight, so he set the bottle of cold beer on a side table, half-finished. Maybe it was the alcohol that was causing this fit of melancholy; best leave it alone for the time being.

He'd barely made his way through the crowd of thirsty wedding guests clustered around the bar when he came face-to-face with Kendra Carmody.

"Hello, Walker," she said. She was a Grace Kelly blonde, classy and smart and soft-spoken, and Walker could certainly see why Hutch loved her, even though his sympathies were, of course, with Brylee.

"Kendra," Walker said with a polite nod. He had nothing against the woman; she was no home-wrecker, and even Brylee knew that. When it came to Hutch, though, neither Walker nor his sister was quite so broad-minded.

"I'm sorry Brylee couldn't be here," Kendra told him, and he knew by the look in her pale green eyes that she meant it. Parable and Three Trees, just

thirty miles apart, were the kind of com-
munities where people just naturally included everybody when there was
something to celebrate, put right or
mourn.

Walker sighed. "Me, too," he said honestly. He wasn't about to make excuses
for his sister; Brylee was a grown woman,
and she had her reasons for avoiding
social occasions—specifically weddings—that made her uncomfortable.

Kendra smiled, touched his arm. "Anyway, it's good to see you," she said.

After a few polite words, they parted,
and Kendra went on to greet other
guests. Once, the big house had been
hers, but a lot had changed since then.
She and Hutch lived on Whisper Creek
Ranch, had two daughters and planned
to add several more children to their
family.

Once again, Walker put down a swell
of pure envy. Okay, so maybe he didn't
have everything he wanted—kids, a
wife, a home instead of just a house.
Who did? He liked his life for the most
part, liked breeding and raising rodeo
stock and ranching in general, and be-

sides, nothing good ever came of complaining. For him, it was all about keeping on.

Casey Elder wiggled her toes in the soft grass, glad to be barefoot after spending most of the day in high heels and pantyhose, both of which she hated. Her blue cotton sundress felt airy and light against her skin, too—a big improvement over that heavy choir robe she'd been talked into wearing when she sang at the wedding.

She smiled and nodded to passing guests, keeping to one side of the moving current of people, sipping champagne from a crystal flute and indulging in one of her favorite activities—watching Walker Parrish from a safe distance.

He was one fine hunk of a man, in her opinion; tall, with broad shoulders and a square jaw, movie-star handsome with his green-gray eyes and that head of glossy, deep brown hair, always a mite on the shaggy side. He was completely unaware of his effect on women, it seemed, which only made him more intriguing.

Casey's feelings for Walker were complicated, like everything in her life. She knew she could fall in love with him without half trying—hadn't she done precisely that numerous times over the years, only to talk herself out of it later? She was practical to the bone—**too** practical to open her heart to the one man on earth with the power to break it to bits.

As if he'd felt her gaze, Walker turned his head and their eyes met.

She nodded and lifted the champagne glass slightly. **Here we go,** she thought, wishing he'd walk away, hoping against hope that he'd weave his way through the crowd toward her instead.

Her breath snagged on a skittering heartbeat when Walker started in her direction. A sudden dizziness struck her, as though she'd stepped onto the rented merry-go-round only to have it start spinning fast enough to blur.

Once they were face-to-face, Casey tried hard to keep her cool, though part of her wanted to tumble right into those solemn, intelligent eyes of his and snuggle into a warm corner of his heart for the duration. "Hello, handsome," she said softly.

He didn't smile. "You did a real nice job with that song," he told her. "The one you sang at the wedding, I mean."

Casey raised one shoulder slightly, let it fall again. "I've had lots of practice," she said. Just for a moment, she let her eyes stray toward the wedding party, still posing for pictures over by the gazebo, and felt a tiny pinch of sorrow at the base of her throat.

When she looked back at Walker, she saw that he'd been watching her face the whole time, and hoped he hadn't guessed that, happy as she was for Boone and Tara, both of whom deserved the best of everything, she happened to be feeling just a tad sorry for herself at the moment.

"They're lucky," Walker observed quietly, inclining his head toward the bride and groom, who were clowning for the cameras now.

"Yes," Casey agreed, barely suppressing a sigh. She knew her friends had traveled some twisting, rocky roads to find each other, and she was ashamed to admit to herself that she envied Tara all that was ahead—not just the wedding night and the honeymoon, but the solace and shelter of a committed marriage, the sex and the laughter, the babies and the plans. Fiercely independent though she was, Casey sometimes longed to be held and loved in the depths of the night, to share her joys and her worries and her children with a man who loved her, instead of always playing the brave single mother who could more than manage on her own. "Very lucky."

To her surprise, Walker cupped a calloused yet gentle hand under her chin and lifted her face so he could look straight into her eyes. For one dreadful, wonderful moment, she actually thought he might kiss her.

He didn't, though.

His expression was so serious that it bordered on grave. Whatever he was about to say was lost—probably for the best—when fourteen-year-old Clare bounded up, beautiful in her peach-colored dress chosen especially for the wedding. She was still coltish, horse crazy and ambivalent about boys, but the woman she would become was clearly visible in her poise and lively personality just the same.

Faintly, Casey heard a few of the local musicians tuning up, but the sight of her daughter, so beautiful, beaming up at Walker in pure delight, almost stopped her heart in midbeat. **Don't turn into an adult,** Casey pleaded silently. **Not yet.**

"You **have** to dance with me," Clare told Walker. The child didn't have a shy bone in her body, and anyway, both Clare and Shane had always been close to this man, and to Brylee, as well.

Boone and Tara, with the photo session finally behind them, were standing in the middle of the dance floor, looking like the figures on top of some celestial wedding cake.

Walker smiled down at the daughter who thought of him as a beloved uncle, and in that moment Casey caught a glimpse of a place deep inside him, that part of his soul where he was this child's father, not just a loyal and trusted friend of the family.

"Let's wait a couple of minutes," he

said, taking Clare's hand and squeezing it lightly.

Somehow, Casey found her voice. "The bride and groom always have the first dance, honey," she told Clare. "It's tradition."

Clare's emerald eyes sparkled with mischief and spirit. "Okay," she agreed good-naturedly, still looking up at Walker with something like hero worship. She bit her lip, then blurted out eagerly, "When I get married, will you give me away? Please, Walker? I wouldn't want anybody else to do it except you."

Casey lifted her chin, swallowed. "That's a ways off," she said somewhat weakly. "Your getting married, I mean."

"I'd be proud to walk you down the aisle," Walker told his daughter, "when the time comes." He paused, eyes twinkling, and one corner of his mouth crooked up in a grin, the way it did when he was teasing. "Of course, it all depends on whether or not I like the yahoo you choose for a husband."

Clare laughed, clinging to his arm and clearly adoring him. "If I like him," she reasoned with confidence, "you will, too."

Walker chuckled and kissed the top of the girl's head. "You're probably right about that, princess," he agreed.

Boone and Tara owned the dance floor, waltzing slowly, closer than close, lost in each other's eyes.

Casey's own eyes scalded, and she looked away quickly, afraid Walker or Clare would notice, but they, like everyone else, were watching the newlyweds.

As prearranged—Casey knew her showmanship—hundreds of snow-white rose petals drifted down on Boone and Tara like a velvety, fragrant first snow, spilling from a net strung up in the high branches of a venerable maple tree.

The guests were impressed, gasping in delight, and Boone and Tara looked up, smiling, Tara putting her hands out to catch some of the petals in her palms.

Casey started the applause, her throat thick with emotion, and the rest of the company joined in.

In the interim, the makeshift band launched into a twangy ballad that opened the dance floor to all comers, while Boone beckoned for others to join them. Clare practically dragged Walker onto the floor, and seeing how happy Clare was to have his full and laughing attention, Casey felt the starch go out of her knees. She made her way to the porch steps and sat down, willing herself not to blubber like a sentimental fool.

There, in the shade, amid all that celebration, she thought of the lies she'd told, right from the beginning. Sure, she'd been young and scared, wanting Walker a lot but wanting her then-blossoming career even more, back then at least. She'd told Walker the baby she was carrying belonged to another man, someone he didn't know, and at first, he'd believed her. They'd broken up, as she'd planned, because Walker was a proud and decent man, but the grief she felt after losing him was something she hadn't reckoned on, consuming and painful as a broken bone.

Casey had done what she always did: she'd carried on. Barely showing even when she was near full term, she'd been able to camouflage her pregnancy, from the fans and the media, anyway, by wearing flowing gowns and big shirts.

But a year later, she and Walker had met up again, and they'd both lost their heads and conceived Shane.

Knowing Walker wouldn't buy the same story twice, Casey called him from the road when the second pregnancy was confirmed.

Nobody's fool, Walker had soon figured out that the redheaded baby girl, just learning to toddle around on her own, was his, too.

All hell had broken loose, and the battle was on.

Walker wanted to get married immediately, but his cold rage was hardly conducive to romance. They'd wrangled back and forth over the children for a couple of years, though they never got quite as far as the courtroom, and finally, they'd forged a sort of armed truce.

Unwillingly, Walker had agreed to go along with Casey's story—that both Clare and Shane were test-tube babies, fathered by an anonymous sperm donor—as long as he was allowed regular visits with both children.

For a long time, it worked, but now— well, Casey could feel the framework teetering around her, and she was scared.

Kendra sat down beside her on the porch step just then, touched her arm. Her friend was the only person on earth, besides Casey and Walker, of course, who knew the truth about Clare's and Shane's births. Oddly enough, it had been Walker who'd told her, possibly out of frustration, rather than Casey herself.

"It's not too late to fix this, you know," Kendra said gently, bumping her shoulder briefly against Casey's. She was watching as Clare persuaded Walker to dance with her just once more, her gaze soft with understanding.

"Has anybody ever told you that you're too damn perceptive sometimes, Kendra Carmody?"

Kendra smiled. "I might have heard it once or twice," she replied. Then her smile faded and her expression turned serious. "Things like this have a way of coming out, Casey," she said, nearly in a whisper. "In fact, given how famous you are, it's a miracle the story hasn't broken already."

Casey wiped her cheeks with the back of one hand, sat up a little straighter. "What if they don't understand?" she asked, barely breathing the words. "What if Clare and Shane never forgive me?"

Kendra sighed, then countered with a question of her own. "Do you want them to hear it from somebody else?" she asked.

CHAPTER TWO

Though it wasn't quite dark, lights glowed yellow-gold in the kitchen windows of the ranch house when Walker pulled in, and that raised his spirits a little, since he was grappling with a bad case of lonesome at the moment. Leaving Clare and Shane and, okay, Casey, too, had that effect on him, especially at that homesick time around sunset, when families were supposed to gather in a warm and well-lit room, laughing and telling each other all about their day.

Not that long ago, his ancient, arthritic black Labs, Willie and Nelson, would have been waiting in the yard to greet him, tails wagging, gray-muzzled faces upturned in grinning welcome and the hope of a pat on the head, but they'd both passed on last fall, within a few weeks of each other, dying peacefully in their sleep as good dogs deserve to do. Now they rested side by side in a special spot near the apple orchard, and Walker never got through a day without missing them.

He swallowed hard as he left the truck behind, heading for the house. He'd raised Willie and Nelson from pups, and Brylee had been urging him to replace them, but he wasn't ready for that. For the time being, he'd rather share his sister's dog, though Snidely went everywhere with his mistress, which meant he wasn't around home much.

Walker let himself in through the side door, which opened into the spacious, old-fashioned kitchen, his suit jacket slung over one shoulder, and was heartened to find Brylee there. Blue-jeaned and wearing a T-shirt with the motto Men Suck on the front, her heavy brown hair pulled back in a ponytail, she was splotched with flour from head to foot.

Snidely kept watch nearby, curled up on a hooked rug.

"Hey," Walker said, addressing both of them, draping his jacket over the back of a chair.

Snidely lifted his head, sighed and rested his muzzle on his forelegs again.

"Hey," Brylee said, careful not to look at Walker. She'd been baking bread, probably for hours. The air was scented with that homey aroma, and pans full of rising, butter-glistened dough waited, assembly-line fashion, on the counter nearest the stove. "How was the wedding?"

Walker wanted a beer and a quiet chat with his sister, but he had to get out of his suit and head for the barn and stock pens, to make sure the chores had all been done. With six ranch hands working the place year-round, though, the task was more habit than necessity. "It was a wedding," he said, pausing. He wasn't being flippant; the church variety was always pretty much the same, that's all—white dress and veil for the bride, nervous groom, preacher, organ music, crowded pews, tons of flowers.

Every line of Brylee's slender body looked rigid as she absorbed his reply, and she kept her back to him. Whenever somebody got married, she folded in on herself like this, keeping frenetically busy and pretending it didn't matter.

"So it went off without a hitch, then?" she asked, her tone so falsely airy that a crack zigzagged its way down the middle of Walker's big-brother heart. Brylee wouldn't have wished what had happened at **her** wedding on anybody, but she always asked that same question after every new ceremony and she always seemed to be braced for the worst.

"I'd say it was perfect," Walker answered gently. He'd retrieved his jacket from the chair back, but beyond that, he hadn't moved. His feet seemed to be stuck to the kitchen floor.

Brylee looked back over one flour-coated shoulder, offered a wobbly smile that didn't quite stick to her wide mouth. "That's good," she said, blinking once and then turning to the dough she was kneading.

"What's with all the bread?" Walker asked.

"Opal Dennison and some of the other ladies from her church are holding a bake sale tomorrow, after the second service," she replied with brave good cheer, though her shoulders slumped slightly and she was careful to keep her face averted. "To raise more money for the McCulloughs."

Young Dawson McCullough, seriously injured in a fall from the now-demolished water tower in town, had worked on the ranch since he was big enough to buck hay bales and muck out stalls, after school and during the summer, and he was practically a member of the family.

"And you're the only woman in the whole county who signed up to bake bread?" Walker asked lightly.

Brylee stopped, stiff along her spine again and across her shoulders. She kept her head up, but it looked like an effort. "Don't, Walker," she said softly. "I know what you're trying to do, and I appreciate the thought, but, please—don't."

Walker sighed, shoved a hand through his hair. He opened his mouth, thought better of saying more and closed it again, went on through the kitchen, along the corridor, past the dining and living rooms, and into his spacious first-floor bedroom, where he peeled off the suit and kicked off the dress shoes and put on worn jeans, a lightweight flannel shirt and boots.

The relief of being himself again was enormous.

Brylee was lining up what looked like the last of the doughy loaves on the oven racks when Walker came back through, on his way to the door. She didn't acknowledge him, but Snidely got to his feet and lumbered along after him, outside, across that wing of the porch that wrapped around the house on three sides, down the steps.

"Women," Walker told the dog in an exasperated undertone. "Brylee could have her pick of men and what does she do? She pines after the one that got away."

Tongue lolling, Snidely wagged his tail as he ambled companionably alongside.

Walker was glad to have the company. "The worst part is," he went on, relieved that nobody on two legs could hear him prattling away to a German shepherd, "she's just being cussed, that's all. Deep down—but not all **that** deep down—Brylee knows damn well that she and Hutch weren't right for each other. By now, the honeymoon wouldn't just be over, they'd have crashed and burned."

Snidely offered no insight, but, in that way of faithful dogs, his mere presence was soothing. He paused to lift one hind leg against a pillar of the hitching post, then trotted to catch up with Walker at the barn door.

Walker flipped on the lights lining the long breezeway and stepped inside, pausing to check on each horse in each stall, making sure the electronic watering system was working and there was hay in every feeder.

Mack, his big buckskin gelding, occupied the largest stall, the one across from the tack room, and he nickered a greeting when Walker stopped to offer a quiet howdy. All the horses, Mack included, had been properly looked after, but Walker had had to see that with his own eyes if he expected to get any sleep. Same with the bulls and the broncos, some in the pastures and some in the holding pens behind the barn.

He sighed again, rubbed the back of his neck, still itchy from the starch in the collar of the dress shirt he'd worn earlier, and adjusted his hat, even though it didn't need adjusting. With his head full of Casey Elder and the two children they should have been raising together, he'd probably toss and turn the whole night and wake up cranky as an old bear with a nettle between its toes.

Snidely, standing close, thumped the back of Walker's right knee with his swinging tail, as if to remind him of the here and now.

Walker chuckled and leaned down to ruffle the dog's ears, and then the two of them went on to check on the bulls snorting and pawing the ground in their steel-girded pens, the broncos grazing in the nearby pasture. Across the Big

Sky River, the lights of the ranch hands' cabins and trailers winked in the shadows of early evening, casting dancing reflections on the water. Voices drifted over—children playing outside, determined to wring the last moment of fun from a dying day, mothers calling them inside for baths and bedtime, men smoking in their yards while they swapped tall tales and laughed at each other's jokes.

The sounds were ordinary, but they lodged in Walker's chest like slivers that night. He tilted back his head, looked up at a sky popping with stars and wondered how a man could live square in the middle of a busy ranch like Timber Creek and still feel as though he'd been exiled to some faraway planet with a population of one.

Snidely lingered, but it was plain that he wanted to head back toward to the house and Brylee, and Walker figured the dog had it right. God knew, standing out here by the river, listening in on all those family sounds, wasn't doing him any good.

"Let's go," he told Snidely, and started back.

By the time they reached the house, Brylee had the kitchen cleaned up, about two dozen loaves of bread wrapped up in foil and ready for tomorrow's bake sale, and was actually sitting down at the table, sipping from a cup of tea while she waited for the stove timer to ring so she could take out the last batch.

She'd pulled herself together while Walker was out, and he was grateful, because he never knew how to comfort her when she got into one of these jilted-bride moods.

"I kept back a few loaves for you," she told her brother, smiling a genuine Brylee smile when Snidely walked over and laid his chin on her lap so she could stroke his long, gleaming back. "One in the breadbox, two in the freezer."

"Thanks," Walker said, hanging his hat on its peg next to the door and proceeding to the sink to roll up his sleeves and wash his hands the way he always did when he'd been outside. He remembered their father doing the same thing in the same way, and their granddad, too. There was a certain reassurance in that kind of quiet continuity.

"I guess you must have seen Casey and the kids today," Brylee said easily.

"I saw them," Walker said.

"And?"

"And what?" Walker grabbed a dish towel and dried his hands, his motions brisk.

Brylee chuckled. "Whoa," she exclaimed. "Touchy."

"You're a fine one to talk about being touchy," Walker pointed out, frowning at her.

Brylee held up both hands, palms out. "Okay, fair enough," she conceded. "It's just that I'm allergic to white lace and promises." Her hazel eyes, set wide above high cheekbones, twinkled, and she reached back to free her hair from the rubber band that had held it in place, shaking her head a couple of times so her curls flew around her face. Before the wedding-that-wasn't, Brylee's hair had tumbled past her waist, but she'd had it cut to shoulder-length afterward, which was better, Walker supposed, than getting a tattoo or having something pierced.

"You might want to get over that," Walker remarked, walking over to the fridge, opening the door and taking out a can of cold beer.

"Are you going to make a speech?" The question was mildly put, but it had an edge to it nevertheless. Brylee narrowed her eyes, her cheeks flushed from an afternoon spent baking bread in a hot kitchen. "Because you're the **last** person on earth, Walker Parrish, who has room to lecture anybody about their love life."

He hooked one foot around the leg of a chair at the table, scraped it back and sat, plunking his can of beer down on the red-and-white-checked cloth and regarding her steadily. "Who said I was fixing to give a lecture?" he asked coolly.

Brylee flashed him one of her wide, toothy grins. The woman was a walking advertisement for orthodontia now, but as a kid, her pearly whites had gone every which way but straight down. "It isn't as if we don't have this conversation every time there's a wedding anywhere in Parable County."

"What conversation?" Walker took a long, thoughtful draft of his beer. "You said you were allergic to white lace and promises, and I said you might want to think about getting over that. Where I come from, that doesn't qualify as a conversation."

Brylee rolled her eyes. For somebody who'd probably been down in the mouth all day, she'd certainly perked up all of a sudden. "I come from the same place you do," she reminded him. "Right here on this ranch."

"Is this discussion going anywhere?" Walker asked, suddenly realizing he was hungry. The only food he'd had since lunch, after all, was a slice of white cake, a few pastel mints and a handful of those tiny sandwiches held together by frilly toothpicks.

She reached out then, rested her hand briefly on his forearm and then withdrew it. "I know you worry about me, Walker," Brylee said softly. "But I'll be all right. I really will."

"When?" Walker wanted to know.

"Things take time," she hedged, making her big brother wish he'd left well enough alone and talked about things like the price of beef or the weather or, better yet, nothing at all.

"How much time?" he asked, because they were already knee-deep in the subject and wishing he'd kept his mouth shut in the first place wouldn't help now. "It's been a couple of years since you and Hutch parted ways and, far as I know, you haven't so much as looked at another guy since then, let alone dated."

Brylee propped one elbow on the table and rested her chin in her palm, regarding him with a sort of tender amusement. "I'm running a business, Walker—a **successful** business, in case you haven't noticed—and that keeps me pretty busy."

"Too busy, if you ask me," Walker grumbled.

"I didn't ask you," Brylee reminded him sweetly. Her brow furrowed in a slight frown, quickly gone, and another twinkle sparked in her eyes. "Are you afraid I'll wind up an old maid, and you'll be stuck with me for good?"

An image of Brylee sitting on the front porch in a rocking chair, her hair gray and pinned back in a bun, wearing a church-lady dress and knitting socks, flashed into Walker's mind and made his mouth twitch upward at one corner. "Heck, no," he teased. "I'd just park you in some nursing home and get on with my life."

Brylee didn't laugh, or even smile. Her expression was sad, and she gazed off into some unseeable distance. "What if we **do** end up all alone when we're old?" she murmured. "It happens."

"I reckon I'll wait a decade or two before I start worrying about that," he said. There had to be things he could say that would encourage Brylee, get her off the sidelines and back into the rough-and-tumble of life, but he was damned if he knew what those things were.

Like quicksilver, Brylee's mood changed again. The timer on the stove made a chiming sound, and she pushed her chair back to stand, dislodging Snidely's big dog head from her thigh. All hustle and bustle, she picked up a couple of pot holders and started taking tinfoil loaf pans out of the oven and setting them on the waiting cooling racks. "You're right," she said, as though there had been no lag in their verbal exchange. "Let's wait twenty years and figure it out then."

Remembering that he was hungry, Walker stood, went to the breadbox on the counter, a retro thing coated in green enamel, took out a loaf and set it on the counter while he rummaged through a nearby drawer for a knife. "It's a deal," he agreed, proceeding to open and close cupboard doors until he found a jar of peanut butter and one of those little plastic bears with honey inside. The bottle was sticky and the cap was missing, and honey went everywhere when he squeezed too hard.

"Honestly," Brylee scolded, elbowing him aside, constructing the sandwich and shoving it at him, then wiping up the mess with a damp sponge.

Walker grinned at her efficiency. "You were born to pack lunches for a bunch of little kids," he observed.

"Gee," Brylee said, **"thanks."**

"I only meant—"

"I **know** what you meant, Walker," she broke in crisply.

He bit into the sandwich, chewed, swallowed. "Well, **excuse** me," he said, pretending to be wounded.

"Shut up and go to bed," Brylee told him.

"I'll do that," Walker replied, thinking that they must have slipped into a time warp and been transported back to their teens, when they couldn't be in the same room without needling each other.

She made a disgusted sound and thumped the tops of a few loaves with one knuckle. She'd be up for a while, waiting for the last batch of bread to cool off so she could wrap it.

Walker saluted her with a lift of his sandwich and headed for his room, shaking his head as he went. He wondered when he was going to learn. Ninety-five percent of the time, reasoning with a woman, especially when that woman happened to be his kid sister, was a waste of breath.

*　*　*

It was almost midnight when the last guests took their leave and the carousel finally stopped turning.

Surveying her backyard, empty except for the caterer's helpers and the guys taking down the big canopy and dismantling the dance floor, Casey was reminded of her childhood and the feeling she got when the carnival moved on after its yearly visit, leaving a bare and somewhat forlorn patch of ground behind.

"Mom?" Clare stood at her elbow, barefoot but still in her party dress. She was already taller than Casey, and so was her brother, and she had the elegant carriage of a young woman. "You okay?"

Casey turned her head, smiled at her daughter, thinking that if she loved her kids even a smidgeon more, she'd burst. "I'm fine, sweetheart," she said. "Just a little tired." She paused, enjoying the night air and the sky full of stars and the bittersweet remnants of a happy day. "Speaking of which—shouldn't you be in bed by now?"

Named for Casey's late grandmother,

Clare resembled the woman more with every passing year. Now she made a face. **"Mom,"** she said, "I'm almost **fifteen** and, anyway, it's Saturday, so I can sleep in tomorrow."

"We're going to church," Casey reminded the woman-child. "There's a bake sale after the eleven o'clock service, and I promised Opal I'd help out. And you won't be fifteen for another eight months."

With a dramatic sigh, Clare turned and started across the darkened sunporch, toward the kitchen, and Casey followed with some reluctance, turning her back on that big sky full of stars.

"Well," the girl argued, since teenagers couldn't go more than ten minutes, it seemed to Casey, without offering up some kind of back talk, "you didn't promise Opal that **I'd** help, did you?"

Shane stood at one of the sleek granite-covered counters in that gleaming, cavernous kitchen, eating leftover wedding cake with his fingers. He gave Casey a look of good-natured guilt, shrugged once and reached for another slice.

"You're disgusting," Clare informed him.

Shane stuck out a crumb-covered tongue and made a rude noise.

"Yuck," Clare wailed, drawing the term out to three times its normal length. "**Mother,** are you just going to stand there and let him act like a baboon?"

Casey pretended to consider the question. "Yeah," she said finally, with a little grin. "I guess I am."

Shane laughed in obnoxious triumph, snorting more crumbs. The three dogs, clustered around him, waited eagerly for scraps.

Clare made a strangled, screamlike sound of truly theatrical proportions and stomped off toward the rear stairway, bound for the sanctuary of her upstairs bedroom, a private preserve where Shane was not allowed.

"That's enough cake," Casey told her son. "Have the dogs been outside?"

Shane nodded, his mouth full, and dusted frosting-sticky hands together. Once he'd swallowed again—actually, it was more of a gulp—he answered, "Only about five times. Rockford ate a crepe paper streamer and part of a balloon."

Rockford, the baby of the chocolate-Lab trio, gave a mournful little howl of protest, as though objecting to being snitched on.

Casey walked around, took a gentle hold on the dog's ears and looked him over closely. "He seems all right," she said.

"He'll be okay," Shane confirmed nonchalantly. "He already barfed. That's how I knew what he ate."

"Ewwww," Casey said, taking her son by the shoulders and steering him toward the stairs. "Be sure to wash up before you turn in for the night," she added as he followed the trail blazed by his older sister.

The dogs trooped after him, the way they did every night.

Doris, the cook and housekeeper, poked her head out of her apartment off to the side of the kitchen, wearing face cream and curlers and a pink chenille bathrobe. "Is the party over?" she asked pleasantly. It was, of course, a rhetorical question; Doris had to have heard all the goodbying and the slamming of car doors and the crunch of gravel in the driveway. She'd stayed until nearly ten, socializing, then retired to shampoo and set her hair so she'd look good at church the next morning.

"Yep," Casey replied with a smile. She locked the back door, set the alarm and padded over to the counter to brew a cup of herbal tea. The stuff helped her sleep—usually.

Doris nodded a good-night and retreated back into her nest, shutting the door softly behind her.

Casey lingered in the kitchen for a few minutes, sipping tea and listening to the familiar sounds overhead—the dogs' nails clicking on the hardwood floor of the upstairs corridor, Shane laughing like a villain in a melodrama, Clare calling him a choice name and slamming her bedroom door hard.

With a sigh, Casey crossed the kitchen—it seemed to cover two acres, that room—and, reaching the foot of the stairs, flipped off the lights.

Shane was still baiting Clare from the hallway when Casey reached the second floor, and Clare made the mistake of opening her bedroom door and calling him another name, which, of course, only egged him on.

Casey whistled shrilly through her teeth, the way Juan, her grandparents' gardener and all-around handyman, had taught her to do when she was eight. The sirenlike sound was an attention-getter, all right, and it had served Casey well over the years, not only with the kids, but with the band, the road crew and every dog she'd ever owned.

"The fight is over, and I'm calling it a draw," she announced with authority when both Clare and Shane stared at her, startled, along with all three of the dogs.

"Dickhead," Clare said to Shane in an undertone.

"Pizza face," Shane shot back.

Casey put her hands on her hips and puckered up to whistle again.

The mere threat made them both retreat into their rooms, the dogs ducking in ahead of Shane, probably keeping a low profile in case they were in some kind of trouble themselves.

"My sweet children," Casey said wryly, and went on to her own room.

Actually, the word **room** fell a little short of accurate description—the place was the size of a small gymnasium, or one of those swanky penthouse hotel suites that take up a whole floor all by themselves.

Again, she had that sense that things had shifted. Everything **looked** the same—the fancy antique bed rescued from some crumbling Italian villa and sporting a museum-quality painting of nymphs frolicking with various Roman gods on the gilded headboard, the massive dresser, the couch and chairs and elegant marble fireplace, the expanse of floor-to-ceiling windows specially made to give her a sweeping view and, at the same time, ensure her complete privacy.

It was just plain too big a space for one lone woman, but at least it didn't have wheels, like the tour bus, or a reception desk downstairs, like a hotel. This was the home she'd hungered for all her life.

Oh, yes, she'd wanted this house, she reminded herself, wanted to park herself and the children somewhere solid and real and finally put down some roots. So what if she and Clare and Shane sometimes seemed to rattle around in the place like dried beans in a bucket? She hadn't bought the mansion because it was grand, so she could play lady of the manor or live in the style to which the public probably believed she was accustomed; she'd bought it because it was **big,** with room for the band and the backup singers and the roadies and a host of other staffers who came and went. Downstairs, there was a soundstage for filming videos **and** a recording studio, both of which she used constantly.

Try fitting all **that** into a three-bedroom, split-level ranch, she thought, glancing at her reflection in the big three-way mirror, encircled with lights, above her vanity table.

Vanity was certainly the operative word for that setup, Casey reflected with a shake of her head as she turned away and set her course for the bathroom. Like the rest of the house, the room was almost decadently luxurious—the shower stall could have accommodated a football team, and she'd seen back-yard hot tubs smaller than the mosaic-lined pool she bathed in.

Shutting the door—it was a habit one developed after years of living in a bus—Casey washed her face at one of the three gleaming brass sinks, brushed her teeth and finally pulled her dress off over her head, tossing it dutifully into the laundry hamper, along with her under-wear, before pulling on flannel boxer shorts and a T-shirt commemorating her most recent European tour. Once again, she faced her own reflection.

Wearing the shirt should have made her feel nostalgic, she supposed, since that tour had been a record breaker, ev-ery concert sold out months before she and the gang had flown over a dark ocean in a jet with her name embla-zoned on its sides to visit the first of twelve cities. She'd loved singing in front of huge audiences—thrived on it, in fact—and instead of wearing her out, those performances had energized her, flooded her system with endorphins, provided a high no drug could have matched. Unlike some of her colleagues in the music business, she'd never burned out, had a breakdown, played the home-wrecker or floated into rehab on a wave of booze and cocaine.

So why didn't she miss all that excitement and attention and applause? She supposed it was because, for her, life was and had always been all about singing and plucking out new tunes on her favorite guitar, the scarred and battered one her grandfather had given her for Christmas when she was around Shane's age. She'd done what she'd set out to do, pursuing her goals with near-ruthless resolve, but somewhere along the line, she'd noticed that her children were growing up faster than she'd ever thought possible. All too soon, she'd realized with a road-to-Damascus flash of insight, they'd be heading off to college, starting careers of their own, getting married and having children.

Figuratively blinded by the light, Casey had finished the tour, called Walker and asked him if he knew of any houses for sale in his part of Montana. Suddenly, she wanted her children attending a regular school, saluting the flag every morning and making friends their own age. And she'd wanted Clare and Shane to see a lot more of Walker, too, though she hadn't been sure why and still wasn't, considering the effort she'd gone to to keep the truth under wraps.

If he'd been surprised by this turn of events, Walker hadn't given any indication of it. He'd said he knew a real estate broker—who turned out to be Kendra, now a dear and trusted friend to Casey, like Joslyn and Tara—and before she could say **Jack Daniels,** she'd found herself smack-dab in the middle of Parable, Montana, taking one good look at this house and promptly signing on the dotted line.

Since then, Casey had had plenty of second thoughts, though she'd never actually regretted the decision to settle in a small town where it was still safe for kids to go trick-or-treating on Halloween, where everybody knew everybody else and people not only went to church on Sundays and then had breakfast over at the Butter Biscuit Café, but voted in every election.

It was living in close proximity to Walker Parrish that made her question this particular choice. By doing so, she'd put the secret she'd guarded for years in obvious jeopardy.

Frowning thoughtfully, Casey left the bathroom, crossed to her big, lonely bed and switched out the lamp on the nightstand.

Was it possible that, on some level, she'd **wanted** the truth to come out?

CHAPTER THREE

Irritable after a restless night, Walker spoke briefly with his longtime foreman, Al Pickens, leaving the orchestration of yet another fairly routine workday on the ranch to him. Climbing into his truck, the backseat jam-packed with boxes of Brylee's homemade bread, each loaf carefully wrapped in shining foil and tied with a ribbon for the church bake sale, it occurred to Walker—and not for the first time—that he was more of a figure-head than a real rancher.

Sure, he ran things, made all the major decisions, personally hauled badass

bulls and even badder broncos to rodeos all over the western United States
and parts of Canada, led roundups and
rode fence lines here at the homestead,
signed the paychecks and paid the bills.
But, in point of fact, his crew was so
competent that they could manage without him, any day of the week.

He headed for Parable, a thirty-mile
drive, with his windows rolled down and
a worn Johnny Cash CD blaring out of
the dashboard speakers, tapping out
the familiar rhythms on the steering
wheel with one hand as he drove. There
were some days, he thought wryly, when
nothing but songs like "Folsom Prison
Blues" and "A Boy Named Sue" could
keep a man's mind off his problems.

When he reached the same small
clapboard church he'd sat in the day
before, watching Boone and Tara tie the
proverbial knot, the Sunday services
were still going on. He found a parking
place in the crowded gravel lot, and not
without difficulty, as the Reverend Walter Beaumont was a popular preacher.

Since the day was warm and the congregation wouldn't spring for air-condi-

tioning, the doors were propped open, and the voices of those gathered to make a joyful noise before the Lord spilled out into the sunshine, curiously comforting simply because the words of the old hymn were so familiar.

Spotting the booths set up in back of the church—members who had probably attended the early service were out there lining up goods for the bake sale—Walker briefly recalled the Sundays of his youth. His mother had branded the whole idea of religion as pure hypocrisy—and, in her case, that was certainly true—but their dad had carted him and Brylee off to a similar place of worship over in Three Trees every single week until they reached the "age of reason," that being, by Barclay Parrish's reckoning, twelve.

Life had its rough patches, the old man had quietly maintained, and, in his opinion, a person could take the dogma or leave it, but over the long run, they'd be better off believing than **not** believing. If nothing else, he'd figured, Walker and Brylee would lead better lives just for trying.

Brylee had continued to attend services, on and off, but Walker had gone his own way when he was given the option. He wasn't a believer **or** a nonbeliever—it seemed obvious to him that nobody really knew what the celestial deal was—but he was grateful for the training and the Bible verses he'd had to memorize for Sunday school just the same. Those lines of Scripture had a way of popping into his mind when he needed them.

Opal Dennison, soon to be Opal Beaumont since she was engaged to the preacher, beamed at him from behind one of the booths. A tall, handsome black woman, Opal carried herself with an easygoing dignity and served as matchmaker and mother confessor to half the county. Rumor had it that she'd been directly involved in hooking up not only Boone and Tara, but Hutch and Kendra Carmody, and Slade and Joslyn Barlow, as well.

A part of Walker tended to turn nervous whenever he encountered Opal— he might suddenly find himself married if he wasn't careful.

She approached as he was opening the back door of the truck and reaching in for the first box of Brylee's homemade bread.

"Mercy," Opal marveled, her eyes widening a little at the sheer bounty. "Talk about the miracle of the loaves and fishes. Without the fishes, of course."

Walker grinned at her. "Brylee got a little carried away," he said, recognizing this as an understatement of no small consequence. "Where do you want this?"

Opal pointed out a nearby booth, consisting of a portable table covered with a checkered vinyl cloth and shaded by an old patio umbrella with its pole held in place by a pyramid of cinder blocks. A charitable frown creased her forehead as she walked alongside Walker, subtly herding him from here to there in case he got lost between the truck and the backyard bake sale. "I didn't see Brylee at the wedding yesterday," she said before adding in a confidential whisper, "I worry about that girl."

Walker set the first box down on the appointed table and started back for another. Opal stuck with him, marching along in her sensible shoes and her flowery dress, which she'd probably sewn herself.

"Me, too," he admitted, thinking admissions like that one came all too easily with Opal. She did have a way about her.

Picking up the second of three boxes brimming with wrapped and beribboned loaves, Walker raised an eyebrow and grinned. "You keeping attendance records at weddings these days, Miss Opal?" he asked.

She laughed. "I've got what you might call a photographic memory," she explained, sunlight glistening on the lenses of her old-fashioned eyeglasses. "It's a God-given gift—if anybody's missing from anywhere, I know it right away." She paused, ruminating. "It's time that sister of yours got her act together, as far as love and marriage are concerned. And **past** time she put what happened with Hutch Carmody behind her once and for all and moved on."

"I couldn't agree more," Walker said on the return trip to the booth.

"Not that you're doing all that great in the love department yourself," Opal observed, benignly forthright. "You're not getting any younger, you know. Living out there in that big house, all alone except for your sister and her dog—haven't you noticed just how happy your good friends Slade, Hutch and Boone are these days?"

"It would be hard to miss that," Walker allowed with another grin, this one slightly wicked, "what with Joslyn and Kendra coming a-crop with new babies and all."

Opal smiled widely, and mischief danced in her eyes. "That's just the way it should be," she said with confidence.

Walker set down the box of bread and returned to his truck for the last one.

Again, Opal accompanied him every step of the way, there **and** back again.

"I wouldn't dream of arguing with you, Miss Opal," Walker said as they covered the final leg of the journey.

"Good," she answered, "because you wouldn't win."

He laughed, tugged at the brim of his hat, intending to bid her farewell and get out of there, reasoning that if he headed straight for the Butter Biscuit Café, he might beat some of the after-church rush, especially since it was safe to assume a large portion of folks from the other local denominations would gravitate to the bake sale.

Opal caught hold of his shirtsleeve. "Don't you go rushing off. These other ladies and me, we could use some help setting up extra tables."

Walker suppressed a sigh. He couldn't turn Opal down—that would go against his grain and she knew it—but he did narrow his eyes at her so she'd know he had his suspicions concerning what she might be up to.

She just laughed and pointed him toward a half-assembled booth with boxes of fresh strawberries stacked all around it. It was no big surprise when Casey Elder came out of the church kitchen carrying a tray loaded with shortcake to go with the strawberries. Seeing Walker, she stopped in midstep, rummaged up a smile and then marched straight toward him.

"Hello, Walker," she said sweetly.

Walker had set his hat aside and crouched to wrestle with a table leg that refused to unfold. That put him at a physical disadvantage, the way he saw it. "Casey," he replied with a brief nod and no smile. After all, this woman and her stubborn streak had cost him the better part of a night's sleep—and not just this once, either.

Her mouth quirked up at one corner, and she cast a glance in Opal's direction before meeting his gaze again. "This must be some kind of record," she said. "Walker Parrish setting foot on church property twice in two days, I mean."

He got the table leg unjammed with a hard jerk of one hand, straightened, hat in hand. Walker rarely made small talk—there wasn't much call for it on a ranch, working with a bunch of seasoned cowboys—and he didn't have a quip at the ready.

He felt heat climb his neck and throb behind his ears.

Opal whisked over and, with a billowy flourish, spread a cotton cloth over the rickety table before vanishing again. Casey set the tray of shortcakes down with a knowing and possibly annoyed little smile.

"I'm sorry," she murmured without looking at Walker.

The interlude gave him time to recover some of his equilibrium, and he was secretly grateful, though he wasn't sure to whom. "For what?" he asked calmly. Oh, yeah, Mr. Suave-and-Sophisticated, that was him.

"Giving you a hard time just now," Casey answered, meeting his gaze but keeping her hands busy fussing with the cellophane covering all those little yellow rounds of shortcake. "It was nice of you to help with the table and everything."

Walker felt his Adam's apple travel the length of his throat and back down again, like mercury surging in a thermometer, and hoped his ears weren't glowing bright red. He was a confident man, at home in his own hide and stone-sure of his own mind, but something about this ordinary exchange made him swear he'd reverted to puberty in the space of a few moments. "That's all right," he managed, apropos of whatever. The appropriate answer, of course, would have been something along the lines of **You're welcome.**

Everything seemed to go still around him and Casey as they stood there, looking at each other in the shade of half a dozen venerable oak and maple trees, the new-mown lawn under their feet. Birds didn't sing, and the voices of the bake-sale ladies and the congregation inside the church faded to a mere hum. Right then, Walker would have bet the earth had stopped turning and the universe had ceased expanding.

There was so much he wanted, needed, to say to this woman, but his throat was immovable, like a cement mixer with its contents left to dry out and form concrete.

Fortunately—or **un**fortunately, the jury was still out on that one—church finally let out and people spilled into the yard, streaming colorfully along both sides of the building and through the rear doors, too.

It was Shane who broke the spell, jarring the whole of Creation back into a lurching motion with a happy "Hey,

Walker—can you have breakfast with us, after the bake sale is over? Doris is making stacks of blueberry pancakes, and there are always too many—"

Clare appeared at her brother's side, equally insistent. "Please?" she added. "Mitch will be there, too, and he's probably planning on bugging Mom about going on the road again. You could run interference!"

Mitch Wilcox, Walker knew, was Casey's longtime manager. He'd never really liked the man, though there was no denying Wilcox was the best at what he did. Whatever that was.

Casey had regained her composure— if she'd ever lost it—while Walker was still trying to get his vocal cords to come unstuck.

"You'd be welcome," she said, gently amused, her smile making Walker feel light-headed and very much off his game. "And you **don't** have to 'run interference.' I can handle Mitch Wilcox just fine." With that, she sent a mildly reproving glance in Clare's direction, but the girl was undaunted, all her attention focused on Walker's face.

"Say you'll be there," Clare wheedled, guilelessly wily.

"Yeah," Shane put in. "'Cause if I have to eat your share of the pancakes on top of mine, I'll probably puke or something."

"Shane," Casey warned sweetly, "this is no place for that kind of talk."

"Sorry," Shane said, clearly unrepentant.

Walker knew it would be better to refuse the invitation, especially since it hadn't been Casey's idea, but, looking into the hopeful faces of his children, he couldn't bring himself to say no. "All right," he said gruffly, finding that his voice had gathered some rust in the past few minutes.

"The bake sale will wind up in an hour or so," Casey said. "After that, we'll be heading for home, and Doris will be ready to put brunch on the table." She checked her watch, the plastic kind sold from kiosks in shopping malls. "Stop by around one-thirty?" she concluded.

Walker nodded and was just turning to walk away when he nearly collided with a smiling Patsy McCullough. Her young daughter wasn't in evidence, but Dawson was beside her, seated in his wheelchair, grinning up at Walker. Just behind Patsy's right shoulder stood Treat McQuillan, Parable's chief of police and most irritating citizen.

The look that passed between Walker and Treat was deadly, though brief.

Once upon a time, when he was still working as a sheriff's deputy, Treat had crossed a line by putting a hand on Brylee in the Boot Scoot Tavern, demanding that she dance with him.

She'd indicated that she'd rather not, but Treat hadn't taken no for an answer. He'd made the mistake of trying to drag Walker's kid sister onto the small dance floor, really just a table-free space in front of the jukebox, since the establishment was nothing fancy, and Walker had clocked him for it. For a while afterward, Treat had made a lot of noise about pressing assault charges against an officer of the law, but in the end, he and Walker had come to a gentlemen's agreement, the details of which Walker couldn't exactly recall. Treat hadn't filed a complaint with his boss, Boone Taylor, and he'd mostly kept himself out of Walker's way.

None of which meant he wasn't as sneaky as a rattlesnake curled up in a woodpile, ready to strike when the right opportunity presented itself.

Dawson, a handsome kid with dark hair and inquisitive blue eyes, broke the silence by asking, "When can I come out to Timber Creek and ride a horse again?"

Out of the corner of his eye, Walker saw a stricken look cross Patsy's thin face.

"You just say the word, cowboy," Walker said to the boy, hoping his smile covered the sorrow he felt whenever he thought of the way Dawson had been before he'd climbed that damn water tower and fallen nearly fifty feet, doing permanent damage to his spine.

"You know he can't ride a horse," Treat growled. As always, he was on the peck, beating the brush for something he could get all riled up over.

Patsy, a plain, hard-worn woman in a cotton dress, eased herself between Treat and Walker and offered up a feeble smile. "What Treat means is," she warbled nervously, "we wouldn't want Dawson to get hurt—"

Dawson groaned angrily.

"Patsy," Walker said, ignoring McQuillan the way he ignored flies when he was shoveling out stalls, "I wouldn't let anything happen to your boy. You can be sure of it."

"I know," Patsy allowed after a fleeting glance over her shoulder to gauge the heat of her escort's temper, followed by a longer, softer look down at her son. It was clear that she loved the boy, felt torn between protecting her child and letting him spread his wings as far as their limited span permitted. "I guess it would be all right," she went on, still focused on Dawson. "As long as Mr. Parrish was right there with you the whole time and all."

Dawson's face, cloudy before, busted loose with a dazzling smile. **"Yes!"** he said, punching the air with one triumphant fist.

Walker, who had been holding his hat until then, carefully placed it on his head, gave the brim a slight pull for Patsy's benefit, a tacit signal that he was done here and he'd be going on his way now. Treat simmered behind her, but for once he had the good sense not to offer an opinion.

"I'll be in touch in the next few days," Walker said, grinning down at Dawson.

"Thanks," Dawson replied, almost breathless. "I'll be waiting to hear from you."

Walker said goodbye and meandered through the milling congregation, making his way back to his truck. He had just short of ninety minutes to kill before turning up at Casey's place for the pancake feed, but he wasn't about to pass them hanging around a bake sale.

Casey smiled and served strawberry shortcake to a long line of eager customers, Clare obligingly squirting canned whipped cream on each plateful before handing it over, Shane making change from a cigar box balanced on the seat of a folding chair.

By the time the sale was over—the men of the congregation had been volunteered by their wives to clean up af-

terward and stow away the folding tables and other gear, since the women
had done most of the baking and selling—Casey was more than ready to go
home, have a few unhurried cups of coffee and enjoy another of Doris's incom-
parable Sunday brunches.

And never mind that the pit of her
stomach felt jittery, hungry as she was,
because Walker would be joining them.

It was crazy—she'd had two children
by the man, after all, and though they
hadn't been intimate in a long time, there
was no part of her body Walker Parrish
didn't know his way around—but she
was as jumpy as a wallflower suddenly
elected prom queen.

Walker had that effect on her, even
now.

"So what's this about needing somebody to keep Mitch from talking me into
booking another concert tour?" she
asked when she and the kids were buckled into their respective seats in her un-
assuming blue SUV and rolling in the direction of Rodeo Road. "In the first
place, I gave you two my word I'd stay
off the road until further notice, and, in

the **second** place, I've never, in my whole entire life, had any trouble standing up to Mitch Wilcox or anybody else."

Clare, whose turn it was to ride shotgun, flicked a glance at the rearview mirror, the next best thing to making eye contact with her brother, seated in back. The exchange wasn't exactly guilty, Casey noted with some amusement, but there was clearly some collusion going on there. Considering last night's row in the upstairs corridor, by no means an unusual occurrence, unfortunately, it was almost a relief that brother and sister seemed to be on the same page, however briefly.

Neither of them spoke, though.

Casey sighed, keeping her eyes on the road ahead. By now, she knew every street in Parable and most of the ones in Three Trees, too, to the point that she could have driven them in her sleep, but you never knew when somebody might run a stop sign, or a dog might dash out into the road.

Careerwise, Casey was a card-carrying risk taker, but when it came to her children, she didn't take chances.

Unless you counted lying to them for their whole lives, she thought with a slight wince.

"Fess up," she said. "What's going on here?"

"Walker looked like he might say no," Clare finally answered. "To breakfast, I mean."

"Ah," Casey said knowingly. The knowing routine was sometimes an act; her kids were smart, and they confounded her more often than she'd have liked to admit. This time, though, she would have had to be in a coma not to pick up on their motivation.

"You could have invited him yourself," Shane put in, addressing his mother and sounding slightly put out, as though he thought she'd been remiss. "It wouldn't kill you to be nice to Walker, you know."

Casey waited, sure there was more and unwilling to share her suspicion that being too nice to Walker Parrish might **well** kill her, because he had the power to break her heart.

"Did you see Walker talking to Dawson McCullough?" Shane asked, still fretful. "I heard him say Dawson could come out to the ranch and ride horses with him."

A pang struck Casey's heart. Did Shane envy the attention Walker had paid the other boy?

"I saw," Clare told her brother, none too sympathetically. "Get over it, dweeb. Dawson's in a **wheelchair,** in case you missed that, and he used to work for Walker sometimes, before he got hurt. They're friends."

Casey let the "dweeb" remark pass, and Shane maintained a glum and resentful silence the rest of the way home.

When they pulled into the driveway, Mitch Wilcox's rental car, a white compact, was parked beside the guest cottage, and he was already lugging suitcases over the threshold.

How long, Casey wondered, was her manager planning to stick around? He'd called to say he'd like to "drop by," and once he'd emailed his arrival time— Mitch had flown in from Nashville— Casey had replied that she and the kids would be out when he got to Parable, but she'd leave the key to the cottage under the doormat. He was to go ahead and make himself at home.

Evidently, he'd taken her at her word. From the looks of his luggage, he wasn't just making himself at home; he was moving in.

Yikes.

Twenty years older than Casey and several times divorced, Mitch was still an attractive man, with his tall, graceful frame and full head of silver-gray hair. It would be easy enough to figure him for a catch, Casey supposed, provided you didn't know him the way she did.

He set his bags down and waved as Casey parked the SUV. The kids got out of the rig immediately. Shane sprinted toward the house so he could let the dogs out to run in the yard for a while. Clare approached Mitch with one hand gracefully extended, like a princess welcoming a visiting dignitary.

Casey walked slowly behind her daughter, nervous now that Mitch had actually arrived. Most of the time, when he made plans to visit, he had an agenda—an offer to appear in a TV movie, perhaps, or some other "huge" opportunity she'd be a fool to turn down, but he was also prone to canceling his travel plans at the last minute. She'd hoped this would be one of those times, and for all the bravado she'd shown in the car, for the kids' benefit, she was uneasy.

Mitch wasn't one of the most successful managers in the music business because he wasn't persuasive. The man could sell sand in Morocco or mosquitos in Minnesota. And she was feeling oddly vulnerable just now.

"Try to contain your enthusiasm," he teased, planting a light kiss on Casey's cheek. "I'm the bearer of good news."

Casey smiled and folded her arms, then wished she hadn't. Folded arms were classic body language for **Don't convince me, I'm feeling too convincible,** and Mitch was more than shrewd enough to read her. In fact, he was a master at it.

"Get settled in," she said cordially. "Doris is back from church by now, and she's about to start stacking serious numbers of pancakes."

Mitch laughed. "Wonderful," he said.

"I'm starved. They served three peanuts, two broken pretzels and a cup of bad coffee on the plane—and that was in first class."

"Poor you," Clare said, linking her arm with Mitch's. During the years on the road, he'd been like a grandfather to Casey's kids, and they were both fond of him, though not in the way they were of Walker.

Another tide of guilt washed through Casey's beleaguered soul with that thought. What would her children say, what would they think of her, if they ever found out that Walker, the man they adored, was their father? On one level, they'd both be thrilled, she surmised, believing, as they did now, that they didn't have a dad at all. And then they'd be furious—with her. She'd been the secret keeper, the villain of the piece, the one who'd raised them on lies, however well-intentioned. The one who'd robbed them of what they probably wanted most—a father.

She must have turned a little pale just then, because Mitch narrowed his wise blue eyes at her and asked with concern, "Are you feeling all right?"

Clare was already tugging Mitch toward the house. Mostly, she was eager to get out of her church clothes and into shorts and a T-shirt.

The three dogs clamored across the sunporch floor and shot down the steps like fur-covered bullets, overjoyed by the heady return of freedom and the presence of their significant humans.

"I'm fine," Casey said, moving to head off the dogs. If she hadn't, they'd have knocked poor Mitch to the ground in their exuberance.

Mitch looked skeptical, but he didn't refute her statement.

Doris, who attended a different church, was back in her regular clothes and all smiles and bustling busyness. She'd set the big table on the sunporch with fine china and the best crystal, and well-polished silverware gleamed at each place.

"Walker's coming to breakfast, too," Clare said happily. "I'll get another place setting."

With that, she zipped into the kitchen,

and Casey indulged in a proud moment, because her children hadn't been raised to expect Doris or anyone else to wait on them or do their bidding. They cleaned their own rooms and washed their own clothes, for instance, though Shane was admittedly less of a laundry expert than his sister.

Doris said hello to Mitch and gave Casey a wry look. "Walker, is it?" she asked. "Imagine."

Casey wondered, not for the first time, how much her cook/housekeeper had guessed over the years, and looked away quickly, pretending to straighten the perfect bouquet of spring flowers in the center of the table.

"Do my eyes deceive me," Mitch inquired, "or did I actually see a genuine merry-go-round in the yard?"

Doris had already hurried back to the kitchen, and Clare returned with a plate, silverware and a glass for Walker, which she carefully placed, Casey noted, opposite the place where she normally sat.

"We had a wedding reception here yesterday," Clare chirped in explanation. Miraculously, in the short time she'd been out of sight, she'd swapped out her dress for denim shorts and a tank top—probably raiding the laundry room and changing there. "Mom likes to make sure the little kids have something fun to do whenever she entertains."

Outside, wheels ground up the gravel driveway. The dogs barked out a happy chorus, and Shane called out his usual "Hey, Walker!"

Clare abandoned the table to rush out and join the welcoming party.

Mitch, meanwhile, arched one neatly trimmed gray eyebrow and remarked quietly, "I **wondered** if he wasn't part of the reason you decided to settle in Podunk, Montana."

Casey blushed. "He's a friend," she said, sounding more defensive than she might have wished. "A **good** friend."

Something sad moved in Mitch's eyes, there for a millisecond and then gone again. "Yes," he said, almost sighing the word.

Casey watched through the screen enclosing the sunporch on three sides as her children and the dogs ushered Walker toward the house, surrounding him like an entourage. Both Clare and Shane chattered fit to wear off his ears, but he didn't seem to mind. In fact, he looked as happy as they did.

Casey's stomach clenched, a not entirely unpleasant sensation but an alarming one nonetheless.

If—**when**—the secret was out, Clare and Shane wouldn't blame Walker for the deception. They'd place the onus on Casey herself, and rightfully so. Dread filled her, even as the old, ill-advised excitement sang in her veins and made her nerve endings crackle. Had she been lying so long that she didn't recognize the truth when she encountered it?

She **wanted** Walker Parrish, and not just as a friend, either. She wanted him as a man, as a lover. Heat surged through her as she remembered their times together, alone and lost in each other while the world flowed on past, like some oblivious river.

Walker looked up just at that moment—luck wouldn't have had it any other way, Casey figured sadly—and when their glances connected, the planet slipped off its axis for the length of a heartbeat.

She went to the screen door, opened it and smiled her most cordial smile, the one she wore for guests and special fans. "You made it," she said, that being country for **hello.**

Walker's smile, slow and cowboy-confident, made her heart skitter. "Good to see you again, Casey," he said, as though it had been days or even years since they'd last met, instead of an hour and a half.

The kids and the dogs and Walker all spilled onto the sunporch, forming a crowd.

Walker looked at Mitch.

Mitch looked at Walker.

And, finally, the two men shook hands.

Was she imagining it, Casey asked herself, or had she just heard the sound of antlers locking in combat?

CHAPTER FOUR

Casey felt as jumpy as a cat crossing a hot griddle, with Walker seated across the sunporch table from her, consuming a respectable stack of Doris's pancakes, Shane at his left elbow, Clare at his right. Both kids actively jockeyed for his attention, and he managed to strike a remarkably diplomatic balance, taking in every word of their chatter and weighing it all, somewhere behind those calm green-gray eyes of his.

Poor Mitch might have been invisible, at least as far as Clare and Shane were concerned, and they didn't spare their mom a whole lot of notice, either.

Casey wasn't bothered by this—she understood their yearning to connect with this man they didn't know was their father—but the guilt was another matter. She'd always been able to rationalize keeping the secret, out there on the road, far from Walker and the place he called home, but now she didn't have a constant round of concert tours and other distractions to serve as buffers. The reality of what she had cost these children, and this man, all the while thinking she was doing the right thing, keeping them safe, was now up close and personal, in her face, a table's width away. Denial, she realized, required distance—in close proximity to Walker, she might as well have been trying to spin plates on top of long sticks.

Once, amid the chatter of his children, Walker looked over at her, caught her gaze and held it, somehow making it impossible for her to look away. And what she saw in his eyes only reinforced the conclusion she'd already reached: that there was a crisis coming, an inevitable collision of deception and truth, and there **would** be casualties. That she stood directly in the line of fire was a given—and the least of her worries. Casey's greatest concern was the havoc this revelation would wreak in the lives of her children and, yes, in Walker's, too.

Yet again, the question pealed in her heart like sorrowing church bells announcing a funeral: **What have I done?**

Exhibiting surprising sensitivity, Mitch, sitting beside Casey at the table, reached over to squeeze her hand lightly. Another person, she thought with a stab of regret, who hadn't been fooled. Mitch—and how many other people?—must have known all along that Walker was more than a family friend. Very possibly, her longtime manager had merely been pretending to believe Casey's claims that the children's fathers were anonymous donors. He'd been willing, for whatever reason, to play a small part in her private soap opera.

An achy warmth enfolded her heart just then, and she gave Mitch a grateful glance, which he acknowledged with a wink.

"So can we, Mom?" Shane's eager voice jarred Casey back into the present moment. "Please?"

Flustered, Casey felt color bloom in her cheeks. She'd missed whatever had been said before, and now everyone at the table would know she hadn't been listening.

Walker came to her rescue in a way so offhand and easy that she could have kissed him—which, of course, was something she'd already been obsessing about anyway, for very different reasons. "We'll head out to the ranch and do some horseback riding," he recapped, "and I'll bring the kids back here after supper, if that's okay with you."

Casey swallowed, offered a wobbly smile and a nod of assent. If she'd heard the original request, she might well have refused it, if only to avoid being alone with her manager for a while longer. She wasn't afraid of Mitch, far from it, but she didn't feel like her usual scrappy self, either. Whatever he planned to propose—Mitch never showed up when she was off the road without a specific reason, generally one that would fatten his fee—she would honestly consider, and probably refuse. She knew her mind, and she was certainly no push-over, but the exchange was going to take more emotional energy than she could spare at the moment.

Both Shane and Clare cheered up-roariously now that she'd given her per-mission, drowning out any possibility of conversation, and all three dogs got to their feet, suddenly alert, barking out a chorus of canine excitement.

"Can they come, too?" Shane asked Walker, big-eyed with hope, referring, of course, to the Labs.

"Sure," Walker said gruffly. How could anyone miss the love in his face, in the roughness of his voice, as he returned his son's gaze? And how had **she** man-aged to ignore the wide-open spaces of Walker's heart—a heart big-sky expan-sive enough to hold not just his children, but a trio of chocolate Labs clamoring to join the festivities?

By comparison, Casey thought sadly, she was the Grinch, with a ticker the size of a walnut.

Chaos reigned as the meal ended and Clare and Shane rushed to clear the table and load the dishwasher—always their shared responsibility—each racing to be the first one finished, evidently, laughing and elbowing each other out of the way, good-naturedly for once. The dogs, clueless but wild with delight, only increased the mayhem.

"This is giving me a headache," Mitch said, quickly retreating to the guest-house.

On the one hand, Casey was glad he'd gone, because it was hard enough to think with Walker sitting there looking so unspeakably good, the dogs barking, the kids carrying on. On the other, though, she was, however briefly, alone with Walker.

And that sparked a kind of delicious terror inside her.

"You and I need to talk," he told her quietly, in a tone that held regret as well as finality. "Soon."

Casey's heart had shimmied up into the back of her throat and lodged itself there, beating so hard that she felt sub-merged in the sound of blood pumping in her ears. She merely nodded, unable to speak.

Walker's expression was not unkind, but it was obvious, from his tone of voice, that he wasn't going to give an inch of ground, either. He'd reached critical mass, the proverbial hundredth monkey, and this time there would be no going back, no reasoning with him, no changing his mind.

He meant to claim Clare and Shane as his own, once and for all, and publicly, whether she wanted him to or not.

Once the children and the dogs had all been loaded into Walker's pickup truck, the figurative floodwaters slowly subsided, and Casey could, at last, hear herself think.

She brewed a cup of tea and went downstairs to the soundstage, turning on a single lamp, the only light in the huge room besides the green, blue, yellow and red LEDs blinking back at her from various pieces of high-tech equipment.

Casey opened the battered guitar case she'd first glimpsed under a glittering Christmas tree when she was still a child herself, reverently lifted out the instrument on which she'd played her first, stumbling chords, picked out the initial uncertain notes, made her earliest attempts at composing songs. Eventually, after many incarnations, some of those tunes had become hits, catapulting her to fame.

Remarkable.

The guitar fit comfortably in her arms, and she smiled sadly as she looked down at the open case—both Clare and Shane had taken backstage naps in that unlikely cradle, as tiny babies, bundled in denim jackets on loan from the band or the roadies, nestled among rolled-up souvenir T-shirts or blankets brought in from the bus.

Remembering, Casey's heart turned over again.

She began to play softly, feeling her way into the sweet flow of music that had always been her solace, her hiding place. Even before she'd learned to play the guitar or any other instrument, she'd sung along with the radio or her grandparents' stereo system. According to family lore, she'd tackled singing first, and talking later on.

There, in the music, her private refuge, if only for a little while, she lost her fears and her worries and her doubts, and her everyday self with them.

The truck was a rolling uproar—both kids talking at once, the dogs scrambling to change places every few minutes, like some canine version of the Keystone Cops—the wind whipping past open windows and swirling inside to jumble it all into primordial chaos.

Walker loved it, but his delight in Shane and Clare's company was bittersweet, too. In a few hours, it would be time to say goodbye and take them back to their mother and her world, the one they knew so well—and he had no place in.

It was something of a relief to see Brylee's rig parked in the driveway when they pulled in at the ranch house— Walker, grimly independent all his life, suddenly felt the need for his sister's moral support.

She stood on the steps of the side

porch, blue-jeaned and wearing a flannel shirt over a T-shirt, battered boots on her feet, her smile as wide as the Big Sky River that flowed through Parable, through the middle of Three Trees, and rolled on by Timber Creek Ranch, in a hurry to reach the distant coast. Her dog sat obediently at her side, tilting his large head to the right, ears perked in curiosity as he took a silent roll call and found himself up two kids and three dogs from the norm.

Walker had no more than stopped the truck when Shane and Clare both tumbled out, hitting the ground running like just-thrown riders racing for the fence at the rodeo, with a pissed-off bull hot on their heels. The Labs, quieter now, followed, probably trying to gauge Snidely as friend or foe.

Brylee met the kids halfway, and the three of them ended up in a huddle hug, laughing and jumping around like happy fools on a trampoline.

Walker hung back, taking it all in. It was a scene he wanted to remember, etch into his heart and mind, so he could come back to it when he felt the need, and savor the sight and the sounds.

Snidely greeted the Labs with some sniffing and some cautious tail wagging and, as quickly as that, the dogs were all friends. They dashed off to explore the wonders of a genuine barnyard on a genuine ranch, Brylee's faithful German shepherd leading the pack.

Brylee's eyes were gleaming with happy tears when the hugging and jumping finally subsided long enough for everybody to catch their breath.

"What a terrific surprise!" She beamed, apparently crediting Walker with the working of this particular miracle.

Brylee loved Clare and Shane; she considered them her honorary niece and nephew—if only she knew—kept their most recent pictures taped to the refrigerator in her apartment kitchen, was forever sending them texts or emails or small gifts.

"Opal said to thank you for all that bread," Walker told his glowing sister, oddly uncomfortable in the face of all that joy.

"Every single bit of it got sold!" Clare

put in. "Mom said the bake sale took in a small fortune."

"Good," Brylee said, slipping one arm around Clare's shoulders and one around Shane's and giving them each a squeeze. Her eyes were full of questions, though, as she studied Walker's face.

"We're going riding," Shane said to Brylee. "Will you come with us?"

Brylee, still looking at Walker, raised one eyebrow in silent question.

"Absolutely," Walker said. When, he wondered, was the last time he'd seen Brylee looking so happy?

Anyhow, they all ended up in the barn, choosing which horses they wanted to ride—Walker steered the kids toward the gentler ones—saddling up, leading the animals out into the penny-bright sunshine of a Sunday afternoon in summer.

Brylee, like Walker, had been riding since before she could walk or talk, but as far as he knew, she hadn't done more than groom her trusty black-and-white pinto gelding, Toby, in months. She'd told Walker once, in a weak moment, that some things, like certain kinds of music and the company of her horse, touched places so raw inside her that she had to back away.

Recalling this, Walker was heartened to watch his sister instructing Clare and Shane, who were fair riders but lacking in experience, as easy in the saddle as if she'd been born there. This was the old, spirited, devil-take-the-hindmost Brylee, the one Walker knew best and loved without reservation.

With Brylee leading the way, Clare alongside on Tessie, the four of them headed for the foothills rippling at the base of Big Sky Mountain like ruffles on a fancy skirt. Walker followed on Mack, while Shane bounced cheerfully beside him, riding chubby, mild-mannered Smokey.

The four dogs brought up the rear, behaving themselves and sticking close to the band of horses and riders, though not so close they were in danger of being kicked or trampled.

"This is great!" Shane said enthusiastically, his backside slapping hard against the saddle as Brylee eased Toby into a slow trot and the other horses followed suit.

Walker laughed. "You're going to be mighty sore tomorrow if you don't get in rhythm with that horse," he told his son.

His son. He wanted to shout it from the mountaintop: **my daughter, my son, my children.**

"I'm **trying,**" Shane answered, smiling fit to light up the whole county.

Walker showed him how to stand up in the stirrups—sometimes that helped a rider get in step, so to speak, with his mount—but the boy's legs weren't quite long enough to reach.

When they got to the creek, some fifteen minutes later, Walker got off Mack, walked over to Smokey and adjusted the stirrups to suit Shane.

"I guess I'm sort of out of practice," Shane said, keeping his voice low so Brylee and Clare, who were having a fine old time girling it up, wouldn't overhear.

"That'll be easy to fix," Walker assured him. "It's been a while since you and your sister came for a visit, after all, and my guess is, you haven't had many opportunities to ride horses in the meantime."

Shane studied him solemnly, swallowed once. "I wouldn't mind being here more often," he said, choosing his words with such obvious care that Walker's heart hurt a little. "If you wanted me—us—Clare and me, I mean, hanging around and stuff."

Careful, Walker counseled himself, because his most powerful instinct was to gather the boy in his arms, tell him how much he wanted Shane and Clare to play bigger parts in his life. How very much he wanted to tell them they were his, try his damnedest to make up for lost time, hear the world call them by their rightful surname, which was Parrish, not Elder.

"You can hang around as much as your mom will allow," Walker finally replied. "How's that?"

"She'll say you're busy and we'll be underfoot," Shane answered with bleak certainty.

Walker's throat hurt. He cleared it, in order to speak. "I reckon that part of it is my call," he said cautiously. Then, after a long pause, he added, "Suppose I have a talk with her?"

Shane brightened, but his delight faded as quickly as it had appeared. "You can try," he said. "Mom's pretty hardheaded, though. Everybody says so."

Walker chuckled, a rusty sound, saw-toothed enough to draw blood, the way it felt coming out. "That's true," he allowed gently, "but I reckon she's had to be a bit on the hardheaded side to raise you and your sister into the people you are, and build a world-class career at the same time."

Shane appeared to consider this, but in the end, Walker suspected, the finer points went over his head. He was only thirteen, after all, in that in-between place, neither boy nor man, an ever-changing sketch of the person he would become as he grew to manhood. "I guess," he said, sounding unsure.

"Are we going to ride or stand around and yammer?" Brylee interceded, the smile on her face seeping into her voice. She hadn't dismounted, and neither had Clare.

Walker laughed, shook his head and swung back up into the saddle, the reins resting loosely across his right palm. "You ready?" he asked Shane in a quiet aside.

Shane nodded, proud and determined. "Ready," he confirmed.

They rode for another hour, until the dogs started lagging behind, tongues lolling, signaling that, as Walker's dad used to say, they'd had about all the fun they could stand for one afternoon.

Back at the barn, Brylee and Clare continued to chatter while they unsaddled their horses and put them away in their stalls. They talked while they brushed the animals, too, and the whole time they were feeding them.

"How come women talk so much?" Shane asked innocently. He and Walker had been performing the same tasks as Brylee and Clare right along, but only a few words had passed between them. It wasn't that there wasn't anything to say—working together, side by side, was its own kind of communication, rendering speech unnecessary.

"I have no idea," Walker answered in

all honesty. "I guess females are just wired that way."

"Maybe," Shane agreed. "Mike— that's my mom's lead guitarist—says girls think if things get too quiet, some-body's mad at them."

Walker weighed the pros and cons of that theory. "That's a little on the sim-plistic side, I think," he said. "My guess is, strong women—like your mom and Brylee and Clare—don't worry too much about whether or not anybody's mad at them. They're too busy doing the things they figure they ought to get done."

Shane nodded thoughtfully, and Walker would have given a lot to know what was going on in the boy's mind just then. What had it been like for him, on the road with Casey and the band for most of his young life? Had he ever felt scared, facing new places and new people at every turn? Did he ever wish he could just light somewhere, attend regular school, make friends and play on the softball or soccer team?

He didn't really know Shane, or Clare, for that matter, and that realization, oft-visited though it was, shook him, made him feel wistful and pissed off and a whole passel of other things, too. He clamped his jaw down tight so he wouldn't say it, wouldn't blurt out the facts. While it was probably right, the claim that the truth set people free, it was **equally** true that it could scorch the earth, destroying everything in its path, leaving nothing but rubble in its wake. It could break hearts.

Maybe, he reflected glumly, it was already too late to rectify the situation without doing more harm than good.

He was fairly sure Casey believed exactly that—and she might be right.

"Spaghetti for supper?" Brylee asked when the horses were taken care of. Two ranch hands were already busy feeding the rest of the livestock and attending to other end-of-the-day chores.

The kids approved of the suggestion loudly and with vigor, but Walker remained pensive, thinking of all the time they'd wasted, he and Casey and the kids. And while he figured he could love the woman if he was ever fool enough to trust her that much, right about then, if she'd been handy, he'd have read her the riot act from start to finish, and then started all over again just in case she'd missed anything.

Whatever happened between him and Casey, Walker thought, he was through playing games, through watching from the sidelines while his children grew up, through with the lies and the pretending and all the other bullshit.

If the four of them—he and Casey, Clare and Shane—couldn't be a family, well, so be it. It wasn't an uncommon problem, in the modern world—folks dealt with it, did the best they could.

All Walker could have said for sure as he fed and watered all four dogs on the side porch, the sounds of laughter and cooking and table-setting rolling out through the screen door between there and the kitchen, was that he was **done** doing this Casey's way.

Yes, there would be consequences. He'd just have to find a way to work through them, the way a man worked through a hard winter or a long-term heartache.

*   *   *

Mitch found her, eventually, probably drawn by the faint strains of her guitar and a song that wouldn't quite come together.

Companionably, Casey's manager sat down on the bottom step, rested his elbows on his knees and his chin in one palm.

"You and the cowboy," he began. "Is it serious?"

Casey stopped playing, placed her guitar gently back in its case, lowered the lid and snapped it closed. "By 'the cowboy,'" she replied, "I assume you mean Walker?"

"Don't try to throw me off, Case," Mitch said with a note of sadness in his voice. "We've known each other too long for that."

Casey looked away. "Walker is a— friend," she said, because the first person she told about her relationship with Walker was **not** going to be Mitch Wilcox, no matter how much she respected him and appreciated all he'd done for her over the years. No, Clare and Shane had to hear what she had to say before anyone else and, after them, Brylee. This was, after all, a family matter.

"If you say so," Mitch agreed, still seated on the stairs. Out of the corner of her eye, Casey saw him spread his hands in a gesture of helpless acceptance. "I'm not here to talk about Walker Parrish."

"You could have fooled me," Casey replied sweetly, though the joke fell a little flat, flopping between them like a fish out of water.

"I care about you, Casey," Mitch went on in a concessionary tone. "And about the kids, of course." With Mitch, Clare and Shane were always an afterthought. A logistical problem. "That's why I'm here—in Parable, I mean."

She looked straight at him then, dread leaking into her soul through the holes in her heart. "What?" she asked, somewhat stupidly.

"I care about you," Mitch repeated.

A silence fell, very awkward and pulsing with all sorts of nebulous meaning.

"I care about you, too," Casey finally replied.

Mitch seemed to relax slightly, and a

grin spread across his face. "Then maybe there's a chance," he said.

"A chance for what?" Casey had no clue, though later she would reflect that she ought to have known where this conversation was headed. In some ways, she'd always been aware of the undercurrent in her association with Mitch.

He looked affably hurt. "I know you're not in love with me," he said carefully, "but I'm proposing all the same. You're tired and burned out, Casey. You need someone to take care of **you** for a change."

She blinked, unable to believe what she was hearing. Yes, she'd suspected once or twice that Mitch had a "thing" for her, but it came and went. Every few years, he got married, then divorced, then married again. Each time that happened, she'd shaken her head in confused concern, but she'd never entertained the idea of joining the lineup.

"You're a good friend, Mitch," Casey said, trying to be gentle and, at the same time, firm. "I'm grateful for all you've done for me, careerwise, but you're right, I don't love you."

"Love is overrated," Mitch offered with a casualness she knew he was putting on for the sake of his pride. "Where has the fantasy of happily-ever-after gotten you so far, Casey? Two children, no husband—all the money and fame in the world can't make up for the loneliness you're bound to feel when Clare and Shane grow up and go off to live their own lives."

Casey blinked. **Where has the fantasy of happily-ever-after gotten you so far, Casey?** Was Mitch implying that she'd been in love before and wound up with a broken heart? True or not, that was private turf—no trespassing allowed.

"Where has **what** gotten me so far?" she demanded, feeling testy and dizzy and very disoriented, as though she'd wandered onto the set of a play with a worldwide audience and didn't know her lines. This was the stuff of her nightmares—going onstage, finding herself unable to sing or play her guitar or even think.

"Let's take the gloves off," Mitch said with a lightness that made her want to cross the room and slap him across the face—hard. "I know Walker Parrish is the father of your children, Casey—" He paused, raised both hands, palms out. "Don't deny it, please. Shane looks just like him, and Clare bears a resemblance, too, though you have to look more closely to see it."

"I don't believe this," Casey said, although she **did** believe it. Like Job, the thing she had most feared had come upon her. "That's just—speculation, Mitch. **Dangerous** speculation. What do you think gossip like that could do to Shane and Clare?"

Mitch simply looked at her for a long moment, his expression maddeningly tolerant and even gentle. "Stop," he said. "I'm not going to blow your cover, Casey—I love you, and I love the kids. But after all the years we've worked together, I think I deserve the truth."

"I think you need to leave now," Casey said evenly.

"I'm not going anywhere," Mitch replied flatly and without rancor. "Not before you agree to marry me, anyway."

She gaped at him. "Marry you?"

"It's not as if I'm the Elephant Man or the Incredible Hulk," Mitch pointed out. "I've been your partner, Casey. Your mentor and your advisor and, most important, your friend. Maybe I can't offer passion and all that other fairy-tale malarkey, but I understand you. And I can give you companionship, security, a good name—"

"A **good name?**" Casey broke in, incensed. She'd come in for her share of trash talk, having two children without benefit of marriage, but she was damned if she'd apologize for doing her honest best. Besides, this was **her** business, not Mitch's. Friend or not, he didn't have the right to pry or make judgments—especially not with **his** marital track record.

"Maybe I could have been more tactful," Mitch allowed.

"I doubt it," Casey observed sharply. She was glad she'd put her cherished guitar away, because if she hadn't, she might have been tempted to smash it over Mitch's head. "No, Mitch. That's my answer. **No.** And, furthermore, I'd appreciate it if we could pretend this conversation never took place."

"In that case," Mitch said, looking broken, "perhaps this is the time to offer my resignation as your manager."

"That might be for the best," Casey said, shaking on the inside, solid on the outside. If it hadn't been for Mitch, she might never have gotten past playing in cheap bars and opening for loser bands in third-rate venues, yet while she certainly owed him a debt of gratitude, she did **not** owe him her soul.

Mitch said nothing after that. He simply set his jaw, got to his feet and headed back up the stairs. Fifteen minutes later, after she'd crept into the vast kitchen to brew another cup of tea with shaky hands, Casey heard the rental car start up and saw her old friend driving away— probably for good.

"Oh, hell," she told the two cats curling around her ankles. They kept a low profile when the dogs were around, but invariably appeared when Casey needed comforting.

Doris opened her apartment door. "Did you say something, dear?" she asked.

Chagrined, Casey shook her head, managed a lame smile. "That was a lovely breakfast you prepared for us," she said. "Thank you."

Doris looked benevolently suspicious. "Are you all right?"

"Why do you ask?" Casey retorted, teasing. "Because I complimented you on your cooking skills?"

"No," Doris said, "because Mitch Wilcox just drove out of here like the devil himself was on his tail, and I haven't seen hide nor hair of Clare or Shane since breakfast. The dogs, either."

Casey felt her shoulders slump a little. "The kids are with Walker," she admitted, "and the dogs went along for the ride."

"I see," Doris replied, her tone and expression annoyingly cryptic.

No, you don't see, Casey wanted to argue, knowing all the while that she didn't have a leg to stand on. **I'm about to lose the two most important peo-**

ple in my life, possibly forever, and I've got nobody to blame but myself.

"I'm **fine**," she said instead.

"Of course you are, dear," Doris agreed charitably and without a shred of sincerity. "Do you need anything? Because if you don't, I'll just watch my Sunday-night programs and then turn in early. Mondays are always crazy around here."

From Casey's viewpoint, **every** day was crazy around Casa-Too-Grande, but it was a good kind of crazy.

"Good night," Casey said.

Doris replied in kind and ducked back into her private quarters, closing the door softly behind her.

Casey stood in the middle of her massive kitchen, in the heart of her massive house, and felt as bereft as a lone polar bear on an ice floe. Was this what it all came down to—after all her work and her struggles, all her hoping and believing, all her trying and failing and trying again?

Loneliness was loneliness, after all, even in the midst of luxury.

Basically, it was the story of her life.

As a child, she'd rattled around in her grandparents' stately pile, haunting the vast, echoing rooms like a little ghost searching for the doorway to heaven. If it hadn't been for Lupe, the housekeeper, and Juan, the gardener as well as Lupe's devoted husband, he of the whistling expertise, she might have gone days without anyone saying a word to her.

How was it that she'd come so far, only to wind up right back where she'd started?

CHAPTER FIVE

The critter, sitting forlorn and slat-ribbed in front of the supermarket, well away from the automatic doors, looked like a wad of dryer lint with legs and eyeballs. Walker, parking his truck, considered the dog as he shut off the engine and got out, noticing how people came and went without so much as a glance in the animal's direction. Even in a good place like Parable, some folks had a tendency to look the other way, pretending they didn't see a problem when they didn't have a solution handy.

Walker Parrish, for better and sometimes for worse, was constitutionally incapable of turning his back on trouble— the old man had seen to that, not by preaching, but by saying a few well-placed words and setting an example. **When you see trouble, boy,** Barclay always said, **don't you walk away thinking someone else will deal with it. Roll up your sleeves, put some steel in your spine and wade in.**

So, having no other choice—at least, not one he could live with—Walker approached the stray slowly, careful not to startle it. From the looks of him, this fella had already experienced his fair share of trouble, and more besides.

"Hey, there, lintball," he said affably, keeping his distance.

The dog scooched—Brylee's word, apt in this instance—backward on his skinny hind end, as if trying to hide himself in the shadows between the blue-metal mailbox and the DVD vending machine, probably expecting to be kicked or chased off, or both.

"You sure are ugly," Walker commented, still as a pond on a windless day, his gaze fastened on the dog's upturned and patently sorrowful face. A few minutes earlier, as he was leaving Casey's place, Brylee had called him on his cell phone and asked him to stop by the store for milk, some lightbulbs and a certain brand of flowery shampoo, and he'd agreed. He hadn't been looking forward to setting that ultrafeminine bottle of shampoo on the counter—the brand that apparently inspired orgasms in the models in the TV commercials—for the checker to ring up and maybe even run a hold-it-up-and-yell price check, but he supposed he ought to be grateful she hadn't asked for tampons.

The dog made a throaty, whimpering sound and moved, ever so slightly, toward Walker.

Walker crouched, put out a hand. "Come on over here, boy," he said. "I won't hurt you."

Meanwhile, people went into the store, and others came out. Walker and the dog remained invisible, it seemed.

Tentatively, the critter crept forward and gave Walker's knuckles a wary sniff, then a brief lick, before retreating again.

Though saddened to see any living

thing in such a fix, Walker was also glad to have a distraction. Before making the stray's acquaintance, he'd been all churned up on the inside, full of things he intended to say to Casey the first chance he got. Of course, there hadn't been an opportunity when he took the kids and the dogs home, mainly because they'd sort of hovered, his son and daughter, like reporters waiting outside a courthouse for a big verdict to be handed down by the grand jury.

Between Brylee's shopping list and this hard-luck dog, Walker had other things to think about, and that was a good thing.

"Wait here," he told the critter, standing up straight again, scouting around for anybody who looked as though they might have dumped a helpless animal in the last little while. Considering the sorry shape the dog was in, it had probably been at least a month since he'd been run off or abandoned or simply wandered away from home and gotten lost.

Hoping the latter was the case, Walker went inside the store, tracked down the lightbulbs and the milk and the embarrassing shampoo, adding a large bag of kibble, a couple of plastic pet bowls and a toy skunk with a squeaker inside to his cart just before taking his place in the express-checkout lane.

The woman in front of him surreptitiously counted the number of items in his cart and seemed disappointed to discover that he was under the limit.

When Walker's turn at the register came, he asked the twentysomething clerk about the dog out front. Did she have any idea who it belonged to?

The clerk, someone he didn't know since he lived closer to Three Trees than Parable and generally did whatever shopping he couldn't avoid there, shook her head and sighed. She had a strange haircut, some kind of Mohawk, and wore too much eyeliner, giving her the look of a beleaguered raccoon, though he figured she was probably a nice enough person on the whole.

"You could take him over to Marti Wren—she runs Paws for Reflection, the shelter," the clerk suggested. "She'll take him in if she's got the kennel space."

Walker absorbed this information as if

it were new, nodded, handed over a bill and accepted change. "Thanks," he said, noncommittal. He knew Marti— she was a good woman with a generous and caring heart—but somehow leaving the lintball with her or anybody else didn't sit well. Just how many times could a creature be dropped off someplace without giving up all hope?

Outside, he noted that the dog was still in his hiding place. The animal's brown eyes glowed luminous in the gathering darkness, patient as those of a suffering saint.

Walker stowed his purchases in the truck, drove it up close to the front door and got out, leaving the engine running.

"I reckon you'd better come with me," he told the dog.

Miraculously, the dog seemed to agree. He low-crawled out of his shadowy nook, like a soldier hauling himself through a hail of gunfire on forearms and elbows, dragging the rest of his body along with him.

Walker opened the passenger door, and the four-legged saint eyed the interior of the truck, rummaging up his last shred of faith in human nature to take one more chance.

Hoping the creature wouldn't bite off one of his ears, Walker lifted him off his unsteady feet and set him inside, to ride shotgun.

The dog trembled, but if he had any fight left in him, he held it in reserve.

No collar, Walker noted after double-checking, which meant no tags or other visible identification and almost certainly no microchip.

"You're gonna be fine from now on," Walker told his newly acquired sidekick. In this small thing, if not the larger terrain of his life—namely, the realm occupied by Casey and his unclaimed children—he could make a pronouncement like that one, without qualification, and know he'd be able to follow through.

It was something, anyway.

The newcomer rode quietly all the way to the ranch, though Walker wasn't sure whether he was glad to find himself in safe company or simply resigned to a whole new kind of nothing-much.

Twenty minutes later, Brylee put a hand to her mouth when Walker carried his quivering protégé into the kitchen in both arms, like a shepherd bearing a lamb back to the flock. Snidely, snoozing in a corner of the room, looked up, yawned and went back to sleep.

"What on earth happened to that poor thing?" Brylee asked, quietly alarmed, eyes full of compassion and a fair portion of righteous indignation, going by the way she jammed her hands onto her hips and jutted out her elbows.

"That's anybody's guess," Walker answered mildly. He passed Brylee to head into the laundry room; she shuffled ahead to turn on the water in the big sink next to the washer and search the cupboards for Snidely's grooming supplies.

Gently, Walker soaked the dog with the sprayer and scrubbed him repeatedly, unable to raise any suds at all until after the third rinse. Brylee, meanwhile, crooned to the dog as the animal huddled shivering in the laundry sink, enduring.

Once most of the dirt was gone, the critter looked less like a lintball and more like an actual dog, a midsize mixed breed of questionable lineage. He was black, it turned out, floppy-eared and slightly cross-eyed, with no visible injuries or illness, and no spare meat on his bones, either.

While Walker toweled the dog dry, Brylee went back to the kitchen, where she could be heard explaining this new turn of events to Snidely and asking him to be nice.

Walker smiled at that, but when he and the former lint-wad joined the others, he would have sworn Snidely had understood Brylee's kindly lecture and decided to abide by her suggestions. He sniffed at the painfully thin wayfarer; then, amazingly, walked over to his bed, one of several placed at various household locations in case of sudden dog exhaustion, picked up his favorite toy, a red plastic fire hydrant, with his teeth, brought it back and set it carefully at the black dog's feet.

"Isn't that sweet?" Brylee marveled.

"It's weird, that's what it is," Walker commented, wondering if he was hallucinating or something. In his experience, dogs might tolerate each other's presence, but they tended to be territorial about their possessions and their food.

Brylee dismissed Walker's remark with a wave of one hand. "What's his name?" she asked.

"Damned if I know," Walker said. "I just found him outside the supermarket, remember? And he hasn't shared any information."

Brylee made a wry face, then shook her head once, in case the face hadn't expressed her low opinion of his intelligence clearly enough. "You're being deliberately obtuse," she cried with despairing good humor. "This dog needs a **name,** so he knows there's a place for him in the scheme of things. He'll need a veterinary checkup, too, and maybe some special vitamins to build him up."

"Thank you, Dr. Doolittle," Walker said.

Brylee's whole face lit up. "That's it!" she cried jubilantly. "We'll call him Doolittle!"

Walker chuckled. "Whatever," he said, studying the dog's unimpressive countenance. "It's probably a pretty apt handle, considering what he's likely to contribute around here, which won't be much."

"Wrong," Brylee argued on a swell of conviction. "Doolittle might not herd cattle or guard against marauding intruders, but he'll be **excellent** company, and that's worth something, isn't it?"

"I reckon it is," Walker concluded as the dog gazed up at him in wary adoration.

"Did you get the shampoo and the other things I asked for?" Brylee asked. So much for the greeting-card moment.

"In the truck," Walker said, starting for the side door, meaning to bring in the small bag containing the items he'd bought at the supermarket.

Doolittle, he soon learned, wasn't about to let his new master out of his sight. As Walker left the house, that dog stuck to his heels like a gob of chewing gum on a hot sidewalk.

Walker brought the dog food in first, then the bowls and the toy, but Doolittle, hungry though he surely was, wouldn't be distracted by the offer of a square meal. He clearly intended to go wherever Walker went, period.

Laughing, Brylee said she'd get the last bag herself and left the house.

Walker opened the kibble bag, scooped some into one of the plastic pet bowls and set it on the floor. While Doolittle sniffed the food suspiciously, as though it might be booby-trapped, Walker filled the water bowl and put that down, too.

Doolittle was thirstier, it turned out, than he was hungry. He lapped up that whole bowl full of good country well water and looked up at Walker, asking for more as clearly as if he'd spoken in plain English.

Walker refilled the bowl and Doolittle drank most of that, too, before turning to the kibble.

Snidely watched the whole scene with quiet interest for a few moments, then ambled over and casually reclaimed his fire hydrant.

Brylee came in with the small shopping bag, set it on the counter. Watched fondly as Doolittle munched away on his supper.

Walker, remembering that the front of his shirt was soaking wet from washing the dog in the laundry sink, held the fabric away from his chest and frowned with distaste.

Brylee laughed, not in the halfhearted, forced way that had become a habit with her, but for real. Until they'd gone horseback riding with the kids earlier that same day, Walker hadn't heard her let go. It was about time.

"Give me the shirt," she said, holding out one hand. "I'll wash it next time I run a load of whites."

Walker undid a few buttons, then got impatient and peeled the garment off over his head, mussing up his hair in the process. Then, bare-chested and mildly self-conscious about it, he went to his room to find a T-shirt.

Doolittle immediately stopped eating and followed.

In his bedroom, Walker rummaged through the antique blanket chest and made a square, tidy pile for Doolittle to sleep on, over by the fireplace. While the dog checked out the bed and all corners of the room, Walker pulled on an old T-shirt.

When he went back to the kitchen, Doolittle accompanied him.

Brylee and Snidely had retreated to Brylee's apartment by then, so Walker locked the side door—nobody came to the front entrance except for the UPS man and those hell-bent on spreading the Good News, whatever reception they might receive.

"Looks like it's just you and me," Walker told the dog.

He got a can of beer out of the fridge, popped the top and turned one of the kitchen chairs around to straddle it, resting an arm across the top of its ladder-back.

Doolittle returned to his bowl of kibble and resumed his supper.

And thoughts of Casey and the kids, held at bay for a short time, flooded back into Walker's mind, like rising waters taking out a flimsy dam. He took a long drink of beer, swallowed and waited for the foam to settle in his stomach.

"Beware of redheaded women," he told Doolittle, who paid no discernible attention to the advice.

* * *

"Where's Uncle Mitch?" Clare asked long after she and Shane and the motley crew of dogs arrived home. She stood on tiptoe, peering out the kitchen window, having noticed, finally, that the guesthouse was dark and the rental car was gone.

Casey, seated at the table in her flannel pajama bottoms and a band shirt, her legs curled beneath her on the chair, tossed off her answer. "He got called back to Nashville," she said. **Liar,** accused her conscience, which refused to be suppressed for another moment. "Or something like that."

Shane, sitting across from her and sipping hot chocolate, made a snorting sound. "Good," he said. "He wants to marry you, Mom, and that would be a serious bummer."

Casey's mouth nearly dropped open. "What would make you say such a thing?" she practically gasped.

Clare turned around at this, all ears, but she kept her face expressionless. She looked like a hurricane trapped in a barrel, full to bursting with opinions that were bound to bust loose.

"He **asked** me," Shane said, pausing to pretend he was gagging, "for permission to propose. Said I was the 'man of the house,' and it was only right to consult me before he made his pitch."

"He asked me, too," Clare put in, looking indignant, "even though I'm not the **man of the house.**"

Casey was aghast—and furious with Mitch. She tried to speak, but all that came out was a sputter reminiscent of a lawn mower failing to start when the cord was pulled.

"**Did** Mitch propose, Mom?" Clare pressed.

Casey closed her eyes. A headache flashed across her brain and then rolled back and forth between her temples. "Yes," she said. "After a fashion, he did."

Both kids were staring at her when she opened her eyes again.

"And you said—?" Shane prompted, pale except for the circles of defiant red splotching his cheeks.

"I said no, of course," Casey informed her children, somewhat indignant that her answer to such a question wasn't perfectly obvious.

Clare beamed and punched the air with one fist, like a cheerleader celebrating a Hail Mary score on behalf of her team, with only seconds to go before the final buzzer sounded.

"Now I won't have to run away," Shane said matter-of-factly, and with measurable relief.

"You were planning to run away?" Casey demanded. That was one of her worst fears, that Clare or Shane would take off on their own sometime, in a fit of adolescent angst, and she wouldn't know where they'd gone. Running away from home was dangerous enough for any kid, but for the children of a celebrity, it was asking to be abducted, held for ransom and God only knew what else. The mere idea made her queasy.

"Only as far as Timber Creek Ranch," Shane replied lightly. Then his expression changed, in the blink of an eye, and he looked thoughtful. "Do you think Walker wishes Dawson McCullough was his son?"

The question struck Casey like a bolt of lightning from a clear blue sky. She couldn't have answered to save her soul.

Clare did it for her. "No, dork brain," she told her brother, her tone and manner none too charitable. "Walker's a realist. He's into what is, not making stupid wishes that have a snowball's chance of coming true."

Casey spent a few moments groping for her lost equilibrium. It wasn't what Clare had said that troubled her so much as the **way** she'd said the words **stupid wishes.** She'd sounded so jaded, so cynical.

Was this the same child who, as a little girl, wished on stars and believed unquestioningly that the tooth fairy and a legion of guardian angels and Santa Claus always kept tabs on her and her brother, whether they were rolling along some highway in a tour bus or calling yet another hotel suite home?

Casey wanted to weep for that long-ago Clare, confidently hanging up her stocking wherever Christmas Eve happened to find them, assuring her younger brother that it was dumb to worry. Hadn't Santa Claus always caught up with them before?

"I'm not a dork brain," Shane told his

sister heatedly. "And you're not supposed to call names, horse face!"

"That's enough," Casey said wearily. "Off to bed, both of you. Tomorrow's a whole new day."

"It's only nine o'clock, Mom," Clare protested.

"It feels like midnight," Casey responded, briefly closing her eyes again and squeezing the bridge of her nose between a thumb and forefinger. The headache wasn't letting up.

"Can I cruise the net for a while at least?" Shane asked, shambling to his feet, which seemed to be growing twice as fast as the rest of him, and causing all three dogs to leap to attention, ready for adventure.

Casey had employed experts to keep track of the sites Clare and Shane visited on their computers, blocking the unsavory ones, but, compared to her, the kids were superhackers. They could probably sail right past any barrier they came across online.

"Watch TV instead," she said. "Or, here's an idea. Read a book."

Shane groaned like a prisoner sentenced to solitary confinement, though he, like Clare, was an avid reader. He'd devoured all the Harry Potter books, not to mention **The Hobbit** and the **Lord of the Rings** trilogy and a lot of similar tomes.

"Take the dogs out first," Clare commanded her brother. "If you don't, they'll pee in the house—or worse."

Shane scowled at Clare, but he took the dogs outside.

"When did you stop believing that wishes can come true?" Casey asked her daughter, the moment they were alone in that vast kitchen. She hadn't consciously decided to raise the question—it had simply popped out of her mouth.

Clare looked too skeptical for someone so young. "Every year when I blow out the candles on my birthday cake," she answered, "I wish for a dad." She paused and spread her hands, apparently indicating the absence of said father. "Obviously, I've been wasting my breath, at least on the wish front, since I was five."

Casey willed back the tears that would

have filled her eyes if she'd allowed them to get that far. **Bucking up,** that had been her grandfather's term for overriding inconvenient emotions.

Sometimes, it was hard to do.

"Oh, honey," she said when she could manage even that much.

Clare lifted one slender shoulder in an offhanded semblance of a shrug, then crossed to Casey, leaned over and kissed her on top of the head. "Everybody has to grow up sometime," she said, and vanished up the back stairs, bound for her bedroom.

Forty-five minutes later, when the kids and the dogs were finally showing signs of staying put behind their doors, Casey drew a deep, quavering breath, picked up the phone and scrolled until Walker's number appeared.

She speed dialed before she could back out, and waited through one ring, then two, then three. Her heart pounded the whole time, and a little voice in her head repeated, **Hang up, hang up, hang up . . .**

Finally, Walker answered, his voice a sleepy rumble. "Casey?" he muttered.

"Were you asleep?" Casey asked.

"No," he said. "Which isn't to say I wasn't trying."

She carried the cell phone into the cavernous living room, spoke in a whisper. If ever there had been a time when privacy was vital, this was it.

"You were right," she forced herself to say. And, man, it wasn't easy.

Walker was silent for a long moment, then he let out a slow, quiet whistle of exclamation. "Who is this, really?" he joked.

"You know damn well who it is," Casey retorted, unamused. "And there's no need to make this any harder for me than it already is."

"Say your piece," Walker said generously. "The part that comes after **You were right,** I mean."

He was loving this, Casey thought, tight-jawed. "We have to tell Clare and Shane the truth."

"Babe, you're not going to get any argument from me on that score."

Casey scrubbed away tears with the back of one hand. **Buck up,** she told herself sternly, but it didn't help much. "The question is, how?"

"In plain words," Walker said.

"What if they hate me?" Casey fretted, pacing.

"They might be angry for a while," Walker told her, gruffly gentle. "But hate you? That'll never happen."

"I thought I was doing the right thing," Casey lamented.

"I know," Walker replied, tough and tender at the same time, like any cowboy worthy of the name. "In time, I think Clare and Shane will understand that."

"In time," Casey echoed, miserable.

"Don't build this up into more than it is, Case," Walker advised. How different it was, when he called her by that shortened version of her name from when Mitch did the same. "I'm not going to hang you out to dry by putting all the blame on you. I just want my kids to **know** they're my kids, and that I love them. They don't have to take sides, like this was some kind of war."

"That doesn't mean they won't," Casey said in anguish as she paced the darkened living room. "Take sides, I mean. You'll be the hero, and I'll be Darth Vader."

"Not if I don't play the hero, and **you** don't play the villain."

Casey frowned, working her way through that somewhat-cryptic sentence. "You'll stand up for me?" She hardly dared hope for that.

"Of course," Walker said without hesitation. "You're their **mother,** Case. And you've been a good one. Clare and Shane will get through this. We all will."

"Do you really think so?" It was lame, but Casey couldn't help asking.

"Have I ever told you about **my** mother?" Walker countered.

"Not really," Casey said. Whenever she and Walker had been alone together, back in the early days anyhow, they hadn't talked about anything or anybody. They'd been too busy making love.

Making babies.

"Remind me to do that sometime," Walker said. Something about the masculine timbre of his voice wrapped itself around Casey like an invisible caress.

Casey agreed that she would, but the

fact was, she couldn't think that far ahead, couldn't think beyond the expressions on her children's beloved faces when she dropped the bomb.

Oh, by the way, she imagined herself saying, **Walker is your biological father. Sorry I didn't mention that sooner.**

"How are we going to do this?" she asked in a frantic whisper. Just then, she missed old-fashioned phones, the kind with cords you could twist around your fingers.

"Very carefully," Walker answered. "Did it ever occur to you that Clare and Shane might be **happy** to find out they were conceived in the usual way, instead of in a test tube?"

Casey recalled what Clare had told her in the kitchen, about all those ungranted birthday wishes, and felt such a stab of painful regret that she nearly doubled over. "I'm so scared," she confessed.

"You don't have to do this alone," Walker promised.

"When?" Casey was pacing again.

"When are we going to tell them, I mean?"

"I think you and I ought to discuss it first," Walker said reasonably. "In person. So we can present a united front and all that."

Casey felt a rush of purely unfounded relief. "Walker?" she ventured.

"What?"

"Thank you."

"For what?" He sounded honestly puzzled.

"For not using this situation as a weapon to beat me over the head with," Casey answered. "Some men would, you know."

"I'm not 'some men.' And you'd do well to remember that, Casey."

As if she'd ever been able to forget, for as much as a second, how unique Walker Parrish really was. He was a passionate man, with a strong body and stronger opinions, but, for the sake of his children, he'd kept a secret he didn't want to keep. Now, after years of dutifully playing the avuncular family friend— he'd never made any bones about his misgivings—he wanted to "present a united front." He was willing to defend her, to take on as much of the blame as necessary.

And that was no small thing.

"Good night," she said.

"I'll be by tomorrow," he replied.

"What about the kids?" Casey worried. "They'll be around—"

"They can stay with your housekeeper or that manager guy, if you trust him."

"Mitch is gone," Casey said, without meaning to offer up the information in the first place. "He and I had—words."

Walker was quiet for a long moment. Casey could tell he wanted to pursue the subject further but, to his everlasting credit, he didn't. "Well," he finally said, "that leaves the housekeeper."

"Right," Casey said. "That leaves Doris."

"I'll pick you up before breakfast," Walker finished up. "We'll have something to eat over at the Butter Biscuit, and then we'll head out here to the ranch, saddle up and ride."

"It's been a while," Casey reminded him.

He chuckled. "A while since what?"

he asked, his voice raspy and so thoroughly male that it made her nerve endings sizzle.

Casey blushed. "Since I rode a horse," she said with emphasis.

"Glad we cleared that up," Walker teased. "I might have thought you meant it's been a while since we made love."

Casey had no reply. What could she say, after all? That her whole body burned for his touch? That, after two pregnancies and a load of heartbreak, she'd probably fall under his spell all over again, given half a chance?

"See you in the morning," Walker said after a few beats of eloquent silence.

"See you in the morning," Casey confirmed, all but sighing the words.

"Walker's here," Shane announced, peering out through one of the sunporch windows as the familiar truck rolled up the driveway.

"He is?" Clare asked breathlessly, hurrying over to see for herself.

Casey, seated at the table with a cup of coffee in front of her, sighed. "He and I are going out for breakfast," she said.

Both kids turned their heads, stared at her over their shoulders.

"Can't we go along?" Shane wanted to know.

"Not this time," Casey said mildly.

"What are we supposed to do?" Clare inquired dramatically. "Starve?"

Casey stifled a chuckle, which would have come out sounding more like a sob, the way her emotions were behaving. "Doris will feed you," she said as Walker's truck door slammed and the dogs, a beat or two behind the times, uttered a few tentative woofs. "And, anyway, it's not as if you're helpless."

Clare folded her arms and looked stubborn. "What's going on here?" she demanded.

"Nothing you need to worry about," Casey replied lightly. **Yet.** "The people from that rental place are coming to pick up the carousel today. If they show up while I'm gone, make sure they don't trample any of the flower beds like they did when they delivered the thing."

Clare blinked. "What kind of answer is that?" she persisted.

"The only kind you're going to get,"

Casey answered. Walker was almost to the porch steps by then, looking unfairly handsome in his usual getup of jeans, boots and a starched Western shirt.

The kids didn't lobby Walker to override Casey's decree and let them come along on the outing, which surprised her a little. She hadn't spoiled Clare and Shane, but she hadn't raised her children to give up easily when they wanted something, either. They were scrappers, as she was, and they rarely kept to the sidelines.

Walker greeted them quietly, then patted each of the eager dogs in turn.

"I brought Doolittle along with me," he told Casey solemnly when the dogs and the kids backed off a little. "He's kind of mulish when it comes to being left behind."

"Doolittle?" Casey asked.

"My dog," Walker said with a tilted grin and a note of pride in his voice. "He did consent to ride in the backseat," he added. "But it took some fast talking."

CHAPTER SIX

Walker parked directly in front of the Butter Biscuit Café. Casey, riding in the passenger seat, was turned halfway around, reassuring Doolittle that he'd be just fine waiting in the truck until they got through eating.

Doolittle had warmed to Casey right off, and he proved to be surprisingly tractable over the issue of temporary separation. It must have been Casey's celebrated charisma.

"See?" Casey said to the dog, pointing toward the broad window, through which tables, part of the counter and quite a few customers were clearly visible. "We'll sit right there, where you can see us the whole time."

Walker was not a fanciful man, but the gentle way Casey talked to Doolittle, and the way the dog seemed to respond, moved something inside him—something that had been rusted over and stuck fast for a long, long time. "You're talking to a dog," he pointed out reasonably, pushing open the driver's side door.

"What's wrong with that?" Casey asked, just as reasonably, sitting tight while Walker rounded the truck to open her door.

Facing her now, Walker shoved his hat to the back of his head and grinned. "Nothing, I reckon," he said, thinking that he might have to grip the metal doorframe just to keep from falling right into Casey Elder's impossibly green eyes.

She smiled back at him, a little wistfully, he thought, unsnapped her seat belt and squeezed past him to stand on the sidewalk. That fiery red hair of hers, pulled back into a ponytail, gleamed in the morning sunshine, and she looked like a teenager in her jeans, ordinary boots and blue cotton top.

Walker moved Doolittle from the backseat to the front so the critter could put his paws up on the dashboard and peer through the windshield, should he choose to do so. He left a window rolled down partway, too, so there would be plenty of air, and he and Casey walked toward the entrance to the restaurant, side by side but not quite touching.

Looking back, a little confounded because he'd expected some whining and carrying on, Walker saw Doolittle gazing placidly out at him, forefeet resting on the dashboard of the truck, as he'd imagined the scenario moments before, but without the yowling, droopy ears and long-suffering countenance.

"He'll be all right," Casey told Walker with a soft smile as he opened the door to the Butter Biscuit and held it for her. He'd told her all about finding Doolittle outside the supermarket while they were making the short drive over to the café, and she'd gotten all misty-eyed listening to the story.

Inside, Essie, the portly proprietor, seated them immediately, directly in front of the main window, as Casey requested. They settled into the booth across from each other, fiddling with their menus, suddenly shy now that they were inside, with folks sliding curious and furtive glances their way.

Casey looked out the window and waggled her fingers at Doolittle, who was watching them from the truck, just as she'd instructed him to do.

"I guess he believed you," Walker said, having decided on the special, whatever it happened to be that day. He had enough on his mind, thanks to this woman, and didn't need even one more decision to make, however mundane it might be.

Casey turned to face him. "Of course he believed me," she said with a little grin. "Would I lie?"

The next moment, one of awkward silence, reminded Walker of a mammoth caught off guard by the Ice Age and freezing so fast that it never got a chance to chew the grass in its mouth.

Casey looked mortified, and somehow smaller than she was.

Walker, deciding to spare her the obvious answer to her question, cleared his throat diplomatically and said, "I hope you're hungry. The portions are big here at the Butter Biscuit."

Casey swallowed visibly and, for a moment, her eyes shone emerald behind a sheen of tears. She blinked rapidly as Essie approached with the coffeepot in one hand, her order book in the other and a stub of pencil riding above her right ear.

"What'll it be?" Essie asked. She probably thought she was being subtle, but Walker knew the woman was about to bust a gasket with the effort of keeping a whole passel of nosy questions to herself. Everybody in Parable County knew Walker and Casey were friends—that was old news, like Casey being famous, and the movie stars that came and went like ducks in a carnival shooting gallery—but to Essie, this probably looked a lot like a date. Maybe even a morning-after kind of deal.

If only.

"I'll take the special," Walker ground out, willing himself not to go red behind the ears. He could feel the other diners looking on, speculating. They'd be lucky if they got out of there, he and Casey, before the buzzing commenced.

"With or without gravy?" Essie asked, going all twinkly.

Walker, who hadn't the first idea what the day's special actually was, replied simply, "With." To his way of thinking, there were very few foods that couldn't be improved with a dollop of Essie's epicurean gravy.

Casey ordered something—Walker didn't hear what—and Essie swept them both up in a knowing smile, gathered the menus with a flourish and pranced off toward the kitchen.

Spoons clattered in coffee cups all around as the clientele took up wherever they'd left off when Walker and Casey came strolling in, bold as you please, like they were a couple or something.

Casey smiled at him over the rim of her coffee cup. "It's reassuring to know

I'm not the only one here who's nervous," she said.

Walker wasn't about to admit to the jitters. He was calm, perfectly calm. Not that he was going to reach for his own coffee anytime soon, since he didn't quite trust his grip.

He laced his fingers together, hands resting idly on the tabletop. Throwing in breakfast before they got down to business had seemed like a good idea at the time, but now he wasn't so sure.

Casey's green eyes widened mischievously. "Walker," she said, "you look ready to jump out of your skin." A pause. "I don't bite, you know."

This time, he couldn't resist. He raised one eyebrow and asked, "Don't you?"

Casey went as red as the vinyl bench she was sitting on. Leaning in a little, clearly flustered, she replied in a terse whisper, "Nipping and biting are **not** the same thing."

That was when the tension broke, and Walker couldn't help it—he laughed. Right out loud and with all those nosy locals there to hear.

Casey glared at him. "It isn't funny," she said.

Walker pulled himself together. "Whatever you say, Casey Jones," he replied, falsely gracious.

"Dammit," Casey shot back in a furious undertone, "I **hate** it when you do that!"

"When I do what?" Walker asked innocently. "Call you 'Casey Jones'?"

"No," Casey bit out, "when you say things like 'Whatever you say.' It's placating, it's condescending—it's a way of dismissing my feelings! 'Pay no attention to the little lady, she gets like this sometimes.'"

"Whoa," Walker said. "Hold it. It seems to me you're reading a whole lot into a few simple words."

Casey sat back, hard. If it wouldn't have meant she'd have to make a scene, she probably would have stormed out of the café right then and marched herself home to Rodeo Road without a backward glance.

"Right," she snapped. **"Whatever you say,** Walker."

"Look," Walker said, catching her

gaze and holding it, "if you're trying to pick a fight so we don't have to talk about—well, what we're fixing to talk about—give it up, because I'm not **about** to get sucked into an argument."

Casey put both of her hands up, palms out, conceding the point, or so it would seem. "Okay," she said, plainly begrudging him even that much. **"Okay."**

Nothing more was said until after Essie brought their food—a poached egg on wheat toast for Casey, biscuits, sausage and eggs swimming in gravy for Walker.

All of a sudden, he didn't have an appetite—he'd been ravenous as a bear after a long winter earlier—but leaving his food untouched would have let Casey know she'd gotten to him, and he wasn't having that. He picked up his knife and fork and got ready to eat.

Casey stared down at her meal with a kind of low-key horror, as if it was an eyeball looking back at her instead of an ordinary chicken egg riding a raft of toasted bread. "Why does this always happen?" she asked in a voice soft so that Walker barely heard it, even though the Butter Biscuit Café was unusually quiet.

Walker could have pretended he didn't know what she meant, tossed the question back at her as he had the one before it, but his personal code of honor wouldn't let him do that a second time.

Once had been pushing it.

"I'm not sure," he admitted. "But in the past, it always ended well."

Casey tried hard to look sour, but she ended up giving a little snort of laughter. "You're awful," she said. Then, in a whisper, she added, "It **ended** with a baby, and then **another** baby."

"I wondered what was causing that," Walker teased, making her laugh again.

After that, things lightened up considerably.

They finished their meal—twice interrupted by passersby asking for Casey's autograph, which she cheerfully gave. Walker paid the check, left a tip on the table for Essie and looked squarely back at everybody who looked at him as the two of them left the restaurant.

Returning to the truck, Walker transferred a very happy Doolittle to the backseat, and Casey took the critter's place up front. Push, he realized grimly, had just come to shove, because they were alone now, except for the dog, and they could talk freely.

They didn't, though.

Casey rode in silence, seemingly lost in thought, and Walker just drove. When they reached the ranch house, Brylee's rig was gone, which meant she was working, and the hands were all busy elsewhere.

This was a relief to Walker, since he had his hands full dealing with one person—Casey—and any additions would have constituted a crowd.

"I don't suppose you remember how to saddle a horse," Walker ventured, getting out of the truck, going around to open Casey's door for her and then hoisting Doolittle from the backseat to the ground.

"I never knew how in the first place," Casey responded nonchalantly, jumping down from the running board. Walker wondered if she was scared, if it was a lamebrain idea on his part, having one of the most important discussions of their lives somewhere on the open range. Maybe they ought to go inside the house, like normal people, to have their say.

Except that, to Walker, the exchange was much too important, and too sacred, to take place anywhere but under the big sky. The house, spacious as it was, would close in around him, making it hard to breathe, let alone concentrate on the subject at hand.

"Allow me," he said with a grand gesture in the direction of the barn.

If Casey **was** scared, she wouldn't have let him know it. Chin high and shoulders back, she sashayed through the tall, open doorway of that barn like Annie Oakley about to perform a little trick riding and some fancy shooting in a Wild West show.

Whatever else a person might say about Casey Elder, Walker conceded silently, she had guts, no question about it. He saddled Smokey, the gelding Shane had ridden the day before, and then Mack, his own favorite. Casey trailed after him as he led both horses out of the barn.

Sunlight glistened on the animals'

well-brushed coats, and Doolittle wandered over, curious about the goings-on.

Cussedly independent, Casey mounted up on her own—somewhat awkwardly, though Walker pretended not to notice that—and he put down an urge to show off a little and simply put one foot in the stirrup and swung sedately up into the saddle. The fact was, he and Brylee had grown up riding bareback, often using halters instead of bridles, and when it came to getting on or off a horse, they were as agile as a pair of Apaches.

"You can come along if you want to," he told Doolittle, who stood looking up at him, head tilted slightly to one side as he pondered this new development.

Instead of following, though, the dog turned away, walked slowly toward the porch, lapped up some water from Snidely's outside bowl and settled down for a nap in the shade.

"I'll be," Walker said.

"He knows you'll be back," Casey observed softly.

"So it seems," Walker agreed.

He looked back a couple of times as

they headed for the road—one of his favorite trails snaked up into the foothills from the other side—but old Doolittle didn't move a muscle. Maybe he'd had enough excitement for one morning.

Casey, it turned out, was a natural in the saddle. She held the reins correctly, instead of sawing on them as most greenhorns did, and as they climbed the hill just across the road, Walker and Mack leading the way, she knew to lean forward over Smokey's neck instead of grasping the saddle horn in both hands and holding on for dear life as he'd half expected her to do.

Walker was proud of her, in a quiet and private way that had little or nothing to do with her status as a world-famous singer. He resettled his hat, pleased, and rode on, slowing his pace when he figured Casey was having trouble keeping up.

After twenty minutes or so, they reached the high, wide pasture overlooking the valley where his cattle, the ones he raised for beef, grazed on sweet grass and drank from Timber Creek, an offshoot of the Big Sky River.

Dismounting in a copse of maple and oak trees—there had been a cabin here once, though only part of the chimney remained, along with a few weathered floorboards with wildflowers growing between the cracks—Walker looked up at Casey, stricken by the sight of her. For the umpteenth time since they'd met, years before, during some down-at-the-heels rodeo where she'd been asked to sing the national anthem and he'd been entered in the bull-riding competition, he thought how impossibly beautiful she was.

Casey got down off Smokey, stretched the small of her back and looked around. "Who lived here?" she asked, still holding the reins.

"My great-great-grandparents," Walker replied, and he could almost feel roots sprouting from the soles of his feet, reaching deep into the rocky but fertile ground. "This was the original homestead, where they parked the covered wagon, unhitched the oxen, dug a well and threw together a shack just before winter hit."

Casey approached a runaway thicket

of peony bushes, tall as trees and laden with red blossoms and buzzing with lazy bees. "These must have been her flowers," she said, her voice wistful. "Your great-great-grandmother's, I mean."

Walker nodded. "She brought them all the way from Kansas," he answered. "Planted them that first spring, as the story goes."

Casey turned to look at him, shading her eyes from the sun with one hand. "It's a happy sorrow," she said, "seeing them untended, in this lonely place, but growing like crazy just the same."

A happy sorrow. It was a phrase Walker wouldn't have thought up in a million years, but it sounded like poetry coming from Casey. He figured she'd eventually weave it into one of her songs. He secured the reins and left Mack to graze, and did the same for Casey's horse.

"It was a hard life," he said, remembering the small gravestone hidden in the tall grass, where his ancestors had buried their three-month-old daughter after she died of scarlet fever. "But they stuck it out, made it mean something."

Casey wandered farther afield, and bent to pluck something from the ground. It was a spear of asparagus, the stray remnant of a garden that had been gone for better than a century. "It's perfect," she said, pleased.

"Grows all over the place," Walker said, pleased himself, and a little hoarse with it. "Brylee and I used to gather asparagus by the bushel out here, take it home and boil it up for supper."

Casey stopped, gazing at him. "Is that a happy story?" she asked. "Or is it more like a tale of hard luck?"

Walker grinned, though something about her question made his throat thicken a little. "We were okay as kids," he replied. "Mom didn't take a whole lot of interest in us, but Dad was rock solid."

"I wish I'd known him."

"Me, too," Walker answered. "He'd have liked you."

Casey found a large, flat rock rising out of the grass, brushed away dirt and pine needles and sat down. "My folks died when I was a toddler," she said without a trace of self-pity. "I grew up with my paternal grandparents."

"Yes," Walker replied, joining her, since the rock was wide enough to accommodate both of them. "I think I read about that in **People** magazine."

Casey's smile was a little thin by then, but her lips quirked up at the corners for a moment. "You read **People** magazine?" she joked. "I had you pegged for a **Western Horseman** subscriber."

"I'm that, too," Walker admitted. "But when your face or your name is on the cover of a magazine—any magazine—I buy it and I read it."

That seemed to unsettle her slightly. She slid her palms along the thighs of her jeans, as though smoothing a skirt. "You know, of course, that there's a lot of hype out there. You can't believe everything you read, and all that."

Walker nodded, removed his hat, held it loosely between his hands. "Yep," he said. Then he grinned. "I admit I was intrigued by that tabloid story about your having a secret husband tucked away somewhere."

She drew a deep breath, let it out slowly, taking in the hardy antique flowers and the ruins of the cabin and the herd, way off in the distance. "You think that was bad?" she countered lightly. "What about the one that claimed I was abducted by aliens and my children are the result?"

Walker chuckled. "I might have believed it happened once," he joked. "But twice would stretch my credulity."

She laughed, but that was quickly followed by a barely stifled sob.

"Hey," Walker said awkwardly. "Don't cry."

For God's sake, don't cry.

She turned her head to look directly at him, her beautiful eyes moist. "I can't help it," she said. "Clare and Shane are the most important people in my life, and now I have to tell them I've been lying through my teeth since day one!"

Walker set his hat aside, took her hand, interlaced his fingers with hers. "If you need more time—"

"No," Casey broke in, glumly resolved. "I should have told them a long time ago. Putting it off would only make everything harder."

Walker was quiet for a long time, still holding her hand. Then he asked, his voice husky and pitched low, "Why **didn't** you, Casey? Why didn't you tell Clare and Shane that I'm their father? And why didn't you tell me the truth, right from the beginning?"

She swallowed hard, swiped at her eyes with the back of one hand, sat up a little straighter. Her chin wobbled, but she got the answer out, hard as it was to hear. "I thought you'd want us to get married."

"I did," Walker said, remembering. Hurting. "But I wouldn't have held a gun to your head, Casey. You could have said no."

"That's easy for **you** to say." She sniffled. "You wouldn't have needed a gun— you could have talked me into anything, including marriage, and it would have been all wrong because—because **dammit,** I wanted to sing, on a real stage, in front of a real audience. I had something to prove, and you, Walker Parrish, didn't need to prove a darn thing!"

"So you told me Clare was another man's child," Walker said evenly. After all these years, it still stuck in his craw, that memory.

"I'm sorry about that," Casey said. "I was young and I was confused and I just didn't know what else to do."

"You could have **trusted** me just a little, Case," Walker told her, sad through and through. "I might be a cowboy, and I might be a little old-fashioned, too, but I wouldn't have forced you to give up your career, move to this ranch and start ironing shirts, raising vegetables and cranking out more babies." He paused, dealing with old wounds that still hurt like hell whenever he acknowledged them, which wasn't often. "I knew how much your music meant to you, how talented you were. Knew even then, when you were singing for peanuts, that you had a big future. I would have done my level best to help you any way I could."

Casey started crying again then, in earnest. Even the horses noticed, looking up from their grass-munching as though catching the scent of trouble on the breeze.

Walker gathered Casey in his arms, not knowing what else to do. He held her close, feeling her hot tears soaking through the fabric of his shirt, propped his chin on top of her head and waited in silence for the storm to subside. Words wouldn't help now, even if he'd known what to say. He'd probably said too much as it was.

After a while, Casey recovered her composure enough to accept the clean cotton handkerchief he handed her. She swabbed her puffy cheeks and then blew her nose, foghorn-style.

"How are we going to tell Clare and Shane the truth?" she finally asked, her voice small and her shoulders drooping a little.

"I've been thinking about that," Walker said, not holding her quite so tightly but not turning her loose, either. "It'll have to be just the four of us, in a quiet place, but there's no way to make this easy, Casey. It's a hard thing to tell, and it'll be a hard thing to hear."

She nodded, sniffled again, started to hand the handkerchief back to him in a crumpled wad, decided against that and stuffed it into her bra, where it bulged comically. "I don't think I could do this alone," she said, looking away.

Walker cupped her chin lightly, turned her face toward him, looked into the Irish-green depths of her eyes. "You don't have to do it alone," he told her.

And then, without intending to, he kissed her, a mere brush of their mouths at first. Her lips felt damp against his, and tasted of salt.

She stiffened, then opened to him, sliding her arms around his neck, drawing him closer. Need rocked him, as powerful as an earthquake deep underground, the kind that starts tsunamis, far out to sea.

The kiss deepened.

Casey moaned softly, warm against him. Curvy and pliable, the perfect fit.

Walker pulled away, got to his feet, grabbing up his hat as he moved, breathing hard and keeping his back to Casey while he fought to regain control. He felt her approach, almost flinched when she laid her hands, fingers splayed wide, on his shoulder blades. Fire raced through his system and branded his soul.

"Walker," she said. That was all, just

his name, but there was a world of sorrow and regret in that one word.

"We'd better go," he said, still not turning to face her, his voice rough as gravel. "I don't know about you, but I'm on the ragged edge of doing something stupid right about now, and with our track record, you'd probably get pregnant."

She was silent for a few moments, then she slipped around in front of him, put her arms around his waist. Looking up at him with eyes full of tears, she gave a raspy chuckle. "I can see where that might be a problem for you," she confessed, "my getting pregnant, that is, but I kind of like the idea."

Of all the things Casey might have said at that moment, that was the last one he would have expected. Something inside Walker soared at the thought of Casey carrying and then bearing his child, but another part of him was downright pissed off. What part of **We're in a big fix here** did she not understand?

"I've already got two kids who are bound to think, at least for a little while, that they're mistakes we tried to cover up," he said coldly, "and I'm not about to let that happen to a third."

Casey looked startled, almost as though he'd struck her. She started to say something, then caught herself and clamped her mouth shut.

Moving stiffly, she strode over to Smokey, stuck a foot in one stirrup, grabbed the saddle horn in her right hand and hauled herself up onto the gelding's back.

Walker knew he could have stated his case in a more tactful manner, but he **also** knew he'd been speaking the God's truth, so he locked his jaws at the hinges and mounted Mack, and he and Casey rode all the way back down the hill, across the road and into the barnyard without a single word passing between them.

When they arrived, Brylee was sitting on the porch steps, Doolittle on one side of her, Snidely on the other.

Well, Walker fumed silently, that was just fine. Not only were he and Casey virtually at each other's throats—again— but there was an eyewitness to their folly.

Brylee stood, her wide smile fading as she sized up the situation. She slid her hands backward into the rear pockets of her jeans and came toward them.

The dogs, blessed with better sense, stayed where they were.

"Peace," Brylee said weakly, making the two-fingered hippie sign.

Walker dismounted, as did Casey, and the women remained behind while he led Mack and Smokey into the barn to remove their saddles and other tack and brush them both down. Doolittle kept him company, waiting sympathetically in the breezeway while Walker drew out chores he could have performed in his sleep for as long as possible.

Casey and Brylee had gone into the house; they were probably sitting in the kitchen, drinking coffee or tea, and talking about hardheaded men.

Though he would rather have avoided another encounter with Casey, however brief, that would have been an act of cowardice. He'd brought Casey to the ranch, and therefore it was his responsibility to take her back home. So he made for the porch steps, crossed to

the door and stepped over the threshold, hat in hand, dog at his heels.

Sure enough, the two women were at
the table, with steaming cups before
them, talking in quiet voices. Naturally,
they fell silent when they heard Walker's
footsteps on the porch.

Casey lowered her eyes when he and
Doolittle entered the kitchen, but Brylee
glared at him through narrow eyes. She
might as well have shouted the word
fool, her thoughts were so obvious.

Walker suppressed a sigh and hung
his hat on a peg. Then he ambled over
to the sink, rolled up his sleeves and
scrubbed his hands with the harsh yellow soap that was always waiting for
him there.

That done, he picked up Doolittle's
water bowl, rinsed it out under the fau-
cet and filled it again.

Still, nobody said anything, though
Brylee kept trying to wither him with her
stare.

He scowled at her, leaned back
against the counter while Doolittle
lapped up water and folded his arms.
"There are two sides to every story," he

said, and then wished he hadn't, because now he'd given away the fact that
the argument between him and Casey
was still stuck under his hide like a fish-
hook.

"Nobody said there weren't," Brylee
informed him coldly.

Casey finally met his eyes, squaring
her shoulders and jutting out her chin
as she did. "If you wouldn't mind," she
said, "I'd like to go home now."

"That's fine with me," Walker replied
without inflection. And he gestured
toward the screen door. "After you."

Casey scraped back her chair and
got to her feet. "Thank you for the tea,"
she said to Brylee, both of them rendering Walker invisible in that mysterious
way women have.

"I could take you back to Parable,"
Brylee offered. To look at her, a person
would have thought she was **Casey's**
sister, not his. She knew zip about the
situation, but she'd already thrown in
with Casey—that much was obvious.

Casey shook her head. "Thanks, but I
know you have to get back to work.
Walker can drop me off."

With that, Walker opened the screen door and held it for Casey, who blew through it like a redheaded wind.

He was a little stung when Doolittle decided to stay behind, with Brylee and her German shepherd, instead of coming along for the ride. Dammit, Walker thought, even the **dog** was against him.

He and Casey were both in the truck, buckled up and rolling down the driveway, before he spoke. "What did you tell Brylee?" he rasped after unsticking his jawbones.

"Nothing about Clare and Shane, if that's what you're thinking," Casey said, self-righteous as a fanatical Puritan. "I just told her you were impossible." She tossed off a mockery of a smile. "Turns out, she already knew that. Go figure."

That was the end of the day's conversation.

CHAPTER SEVEN

For a full week, nothing happened, nothing regarding the big reveal, at least. Walker didn't call or stop by, or even grace Casey's in-box with an email.

Clare and Shane remained clueless as far as their paternity was concerned. They swam in the community pool every afternoon, hung out with their friends, played tag with the dogs in the backyard and rarely sniped at each other. That last part was the tip-off, Casey figured. They were smart kids: they knew some kind of major change was imminent, and they'd formed an alliance, probably brief, probably tenuous, but an alliance nonetheless.

Casey was grateful for small favors.

Boone and Tara returned from their honeymoon, and Boone ran the sheriff's department again, but otherwise, both of them kept a low profile for a few days. Then, letting the local grapevine spread the word, they invited practically the whole county to a big Friday-night party at their place, complete with barbecued beef, washtubs full of potato salad, slow-roasted corn on the cob and biscuits the size of Frisbees. Those who knew Tara well, as Casey did, noticed right away that chicken wasn't on the menu, and were amused by the irony.

Tara, a former cosmetics tycoon, had been billing herself as a chicken farmer from the day she moved to Parable, but, as far as anybody knew, not one of her fine feathered friends had ever been beheaded, subsequently cleaned and plucked, cut to pieces and fried in bacon grease, let alone turned up crispy and delicious on somebody's dinner plate.

People were tolerant of this oddity—

in rural areas like Parable County, chickens weren't pets, and their purpose was clear: give eggs and eventually wind up in a skillet or a stewpot—reminding each other that, after all, Tara was from **New York City,** and therefore might be expected to have a few strange ideas rattling around in that pretty head.

Though she'd rather have continued hibernating and feeling sorry for herself, Casey spiffed herself up, put on black jeans, a long-sleeve T-shirt to match, shiny boots and a modicum of makeup and, to appease the part of her that wanted to hide, a baseball cap. She drove, with Doris and the kids, out to Boone and Tara's farm.

Ah, Boone and Tara, Casey reflected with a smile.

At first, they were feuding neighbors, that pair, Boone living, with his two young sons, in a double-wide trailer one step away from being condemned and surrounded by high grass and assorted junk—an annoying contrast to Tara's well-kept farmhouse, just across the little slice of river that separated their two properties.

Now the double-wide was long gone, and a beautiful barn and white-rail corral stood in its place, complete with horses. The newlyweds, along with Boone's boys, Griffin and Fletcher, and Tara's teenage twin stepdaughters, Erin and Elle, resided in Tara's house, since their doctor father was too busy to raise them. It was spacious, that august Victorian structure, the kind of place that would look perfect, with just a dusting of snow and a holly wreath at the door, on the front of a Christmas card. They were already adding on, making room for babies.

Babies. Ouch.

As she parked the SUV in a field, amid dozens of other vehicles, Casey recalled the brazen thing she'd said to Walker, up there at his great-great-grandparents' homestead the day they'd gone horseback riding, about how a baby might be a problem for him, but she kind of liked the idea. Just remembering that made her blush, never mind that it was completely true.

After all, she was still young, only in her thirties, and she wanted another child very much. Maybe several. But she'd been a fool to say as much to Walker, after the way she'd brought Clare and Shane up—wholly loved, but lied to, nonetheless.

What had she been thinking?

She sighed, trying to dodge the inevitable riot of emotions. She hadn't been thinking at all, and that was the trouble. She'd never been able to put two sensible thoughts together when it came to Walker Parrish. If she had been, everything would have been different. She'd either be a childless loner, still pursuing her career at full throttle, or married to Walker, living on the ranch and popping out brothers and sisters for Clare and Shane.

"Mom?" Clare prompted as they walked toward the Taylors' yard, which was already bursting with laughing visitors. "This is a **party,** not a funeral. Buck up, for Pete's sake."

Casey smiled while scanning the crowd for any sign of Walker. "You're right, honey," she agreed quietly, but part of her still wanted to turn tail and run like hell. They'd gotten into that stupid row, she and Walker, before they could agree on a time and a place for the powwow to end all powwows, and she'd been guiltily grateful for the reprieve. At the same time, the nearly unbearable dread had continued to build.

According to the kids, who kept track of him like a pair of private detectives staking out a cheating husband, Walker had been off hauling bulls and broncos to some distant rodeo over the past week or so, and, much to Shane's thinly disguised irritation, he'd taken Dawson McCullough along with him, wheelchair and all.

With any luck, Casey thought, he was still away.

She made her way through the throng of guests to Boone and Tara, who beamed like a pair of human lighthouses as people shook Boone's hand and hugged Tara and congratulated them over and over again.

When her turn came, Casey hugged both of them, first Tara, then Boone. Doris and the children, it seemed, had already been absorbed into their various circles of friends, because they were nowhere in sight.

"You look beautiful," Casey told Tara, meaning it.

Tara **did** look beautiful, glowing with happiness as Boone slipped a husbandly arm around his bride's shoulders and gave her a squeeze. "There's nothing like a honeymoon to perk a person up," Tara said, and then blushed.

Casey smiled. She couldn't have been happier for her friends, so why was her throat thick with unshed tears? Another pang of envy struck, too, shaming her. "And where did you go on this mysterious honeymoon, or is that still a secret?"

"Hawaii," Tara said with delight, stretching out her bare arms to show off her golden tan. "We had our very own grass hut."

Boone sighed cheerfully at the memory, and Tara gave him a light poke in the ribs with one elbow.

"It's good to have you back," Casey said, kissing Tara's cheek. "Let's get together soon."

Tara nodded. "Soon," she agreed.

Since other new arrivals were waiting to speak to Tara and Boone, Casey moved on, looking for Kendra or Joslyn much the same way a shipwrecked sailor might search the horizon for land.

In the process, she crashed right into a broad, hard and all-too-familiar chest, looked up and met Walker's eyes. The impact of **that** rocked her far more than the physical collision had, and that was saying something.

Well, she thought, trying to be philosophical while her heart flailed around in her chest like a bird trying to escape a cage, that settled one question, anyway. Walker Parrish was definitely back from his travels.

"Hello, Casey," he drawled, smiling down at her.

Did he know what that smile did to her? If he did, he was an unconscionable rake, taking unfair advantage.

"Walker," Casey croaked out in reply. Why hadn't she stayed at home, camping out in her room, watching the Soap Channel in her bathrobe and eating too much ice cream?

Because Tara and Boone were her

friends, that was why, she reminded herself sternly. And because, mostly, it wasn't like her to hide out.

"We didn't finish our conversation," Walker reminded her. His voice was gruff and low, but his eyes were gentle. He'd decided, in his infinite mercy, to make things easy for her, she concluded.

The arrogant bastard.

"No," she said sweetly. "You went off to some rodeo and left me to stew in my own juices, wondering what was going to happen next. Waiting for the proverbial other shoe to drop."

Walker rolled his shoulders, the only outward indication that he was tense, too. "It's my job. I had a contract. What was I supposed to do, Casey?"

"You could have called," she replied, smiling hard for the benefit of anybody who might be looking their way while she knew her eyes were shooting green fire. "Said you'd be out of town for a while. **Something.**"

He leaned in until their foreheads were almost touching. "You mean," he said, barely breathing the words, "the way **you** called **me** almost fifteen years ago and told me you were carrying my baby?"

Casey's cheeks flamed, and she was glad she hadn't been to the punch bowl yet, because she might not have been able to keep herself from flinging the contents of her cup in his handsome, self-righteous face. **That** would have been a fine how-do-you-do, with the whole of Parable County looking on.

"There's no need to be rude," she snapped rudely, folding her arms and letting the smile fall away, since it was too hard to hold on to, anyhow.

"Tomorrow," Walker said, and she couldn't tell whether that glint in his eyes was fury or amusement. "My place, at high noon. That's when the sh—mustard hits the fan, Casey Jones."

Casey, on fire moments before, went icy cold. Swallowed hard, looked away for a moment, forced herself to look back. He'd drawn a line in the sand, and she had no choice but to step over it if she wanted to make things right with her children.

"We'll be there," she said.

Walker had the gall to grin that wicked

grin, the one that always made her want to either slap him silly or tear off all her clothes and jump his bones on the spot.

Obviously, the latter wasn't an option, and, for that matter, slapping was off the table, too. Casey had taught Clare and Shane that hitting was wrong, and she could hardly go against her own rule, as badly as she might want to do just that. Especially not in public.

"Noon," he repeated, like Gary Cooper scheduling a showdown on the street in front of the old saloon.

Casey fairly snarled her response. "Noon," she agreed.

Then she turned on one heel and proceeded to put as much space between herself and Walker Parrish as she could.

Walker watched her walk away, smiling to himself and enjoying the way her shapely blue-jeaned backside swayed from side to side as she moved. She was wearing a baseball cap, pulled down low over her eyes, and her long ponytail jutted through the opening in back, swinging to the beat of her outrage.

Though nobody would have guessed it, Walker figured he was as nervous about tomorrow as Casey was—maybe more so, because Shane and Clare would probably be just as mad at him as they would be at their mother, and neither he nor the lady had a leg to stand on when it came to the right and wrong of it all.

A lie, however well-intentioned, was still a lie.

"Where's Brylee?" asked a feminine voice at his side just as Casey vanished into the mob.

Walker looked over and saw Joslyn Barlow standing next to him. She was pretty calm and collected, for somebody trying to smuggle a bowling ball under her dress.

"Why do people keep asking me that?" he asked calmly, but with a smile. He liked Joslyn, after all, liked her husband, Slade, too, and he knew she really cared about his sister.

Joslyn widened her eyes in a mockery of innocence and countered, "Because we'd like to get a straight answer?"

Walker, remembering the glass of beer he was holding for the first time since he'd nearly spilled it all over Casey in the collision, took a sip and savored it before offering a reply. "She's probably at home, or in her office or racing around on a forklift in the warehouse."

Brylee owned Décor Galore, a direct marketing company specializing mostly in home parties and online sales. She'd built it from nothing to a multimillion-dollar corporation in a few short years, and Walker worried that she'd die of overwork before she ever got a chance to enjoy the fruits of all those twelve- and sixteen-hour days.

Sipping punch, Joslyn smiled sadly. "It's only fair to warn you," she said, "that Opal's getting mighty concerned about Brylee, and she's thinking about stepping in."

Walker pretended horror. "Oh, no," he gasped, splaying his free hand on his chest, "not **that.**"

Joslyn laughed. "Never underestimate the power of Opal," she told him. "When she's on a mission, she's a force to be reckoned with."

"I thought she specialized in match-making," Walker said. Over the tops of people's heads, he caught a distant glimpse of Casey, talking with Kendra Carmody and none other than the great Opal herself.

For some reason, that made his shirt collar feel too tight, even though he'd left the uppermost snaps unfastened.

"That's true enough," Joslyn agreed. "Opal has uncanny instincts, particularly when it comes to romance."

"All that and a fantastic housekeeper, too," Walker said, trying to ignore Casey, especially now that Kendra had wandered away and left her alone to confer with Opal.

Joslyn smiled. "We'll be losing Opal soon," she said. "At least, as far as housekeeping goes. She's getting married."

"I heard," Walker said.

Casey and Opal seemed deep in conversation, earnest as all get-out. What the devil were those two talking about?

Joslyn said goodbye then and slipped away, and Walker remembered that he'd been on his way over to talk to Patsy

McCullough about Dawson when he got sidetracked talking to Casey. **Talking?** They'd been taking potshots at each other, the way they did everywhere but in bed.

It was downright discouraging. Looking around, he spotted Patsy once again, now sitting primly on a folding chair in the shade of a maple tree, a full paper plate balanced on her lap, though she didn't look all that interested in food.

Walker had dropped Dawson off at home on his way to Boone and Tara's place—the boy had had a fine time at the rodeo, but he'd declined the invitation to go on to the party, claiming, with all justification, that he was too tired.

It wasn't the tiredness that troubled Walker, though; he could have used twelve hours of uninterrupted sleep himself, right about then. No, it was what the boy had said about Doolittle, who went along on the trip—that he thought the dog used to belong to Treat McQuillan, his mother's current boyfriend. Dawson and his sister were getting attached to the critter when he just dropped off the radar—there one day, gone the next.

Dawson, who'd been spending a lot of time alone back then, having just gotten out of the hospital after yet another surgery, had missed the dog's company, so he'd asked Treat where he was. Treat had evaded the question repeatedly, finally saying that "the mutt" had run off, and good riddance, since he'd turned out to be more trouble than he was worth.

The last thing Walker had wanted to do was give up Doolittle—they were true partners now—but what's right is right, and he'd asked Dawson if he wanted the dog back. He'd been relieved, of course, when the boy shook his head no and said Doolittle was better off staying where he was.

Now, making his way toward Patsy, who smiled at passersby but didn't make any noticeable effort to join the festivities, being famously shy by nature, Walker considered the obvious fact that Patsy had every right to date whoever she wanted, and her relationship with Treat was none of his or anybody else's business. He didn't even know what he was going to say to the woman, but he'd made up his mind to say **something.**

By his reasoning, if McQuillan would turn out a helpless dog, leaving it to fend for itself, how kind was he likely to be to Dawson and his little sister? Would **they** end up being "more trouble than they were worth," as Doolittle had been? Would Patsy?

"Hello, Patsy," Walker said, very quietly, when he reached her.

"Walker," she replied with a cordial nod. "I guess you must have left Dawson off at home."

"He was tired," Walker said, affirming her assumption.

"It was good of you to take him with you," Patsy offered. "I haven't seen my boy so happy since before—before—" She fell silent, swallowed hard.

It was no wonder that the accident was hard for her to talk about, Walker figured. Most likely, the image of her son plunging off the water tower haunted her, waking and sleeping, and how did a person deal with the knowledge that Dawson would need more surgeries in the years to come, none of which would give him back the use of his legs?

Walker crouched, reached over and took Patsy's thin, work-worn hand. Things were better for the McCulloughs, at least financially—the community had been generous, Casey included—but all that trouble would have scratched the shine off just about anybody's spirit. She'd had a lifetime of it, even before Dawson got hurt.

"You holding up okay, Patsy?" he asked.

She didn't pull her hand free, but she did look a mite uncomfortable. Was McQuillan the jealous type? Probably.

"Most of the time," she answered. "Some days are harder than others, though."

Walker let go of her hand but remained where he was, sitting on his haunches and looking up into her weary, resigned face. He'd made a sizable donation to Dawson's medical fund, and he knew Brylee had, too, as well as the Barlows, the Carmodys, Boone and Tara, and others. Even the itinerant movie stars had sent hefty checks, though they rarely took part in anything that went on in Parable or Three Trees.

"Treat's good with the kids?" Walker asked.

Patsy's eyes immediately widened. "Who says he isn't?" she immediately retorted.

"Nobody," Walker said gently. "I was just wondering."

"Why?" It was a demand. Patsy Mc-Cullough, normally so docile, so beaten down by bad husbands and hard times, was riled.

Walker let out his breath. "Dawson said there was a dog—"

"That dog ran away," Patsy snapped. "They **do** that, Walker. It isn't Treat's fault."

Walker stood up, glad he was a Montana cowboy and not an ambassador of some kind. With his talent for diplomacy, he'd likely have started World War III just by pissing somebody off at a cocktail party.

Before he could think of anything to say—anything that wouldn't make matters worse, that is—Treat showed up, in uniform and obviously on the lookout for something to raise hell about. If the pompous-ass rent-a-cop didn't find any trouble handy, Walker thought, he was likely to **make** some.

Walker would have welcomed a confrontation in any other setting, but this was Boone and Tara's home-from-the-honeymoon party, and a brawl would not only spoil it, it would become the communal memory of the occasion, overriding everything good.

Patsy immediately leaped into the breach, shooting up from her folding chair and overturning her untouched food on the ground, her voice soft but nearly frantic. "Walker was just telling me that he and Dawson had a good time at the rodeo."

Walker frowned. Was she scared of McQuillan? He couldn't help recalling that night at the Boot Scoot Tavern, when the then-deputy had essentially manhandled Brylee after she refused to dance with him. Did Treat make a **habit** of pushing smaller, weaker people around?

"Isn't that nice," Treat said acidly.

"Now, Treat, don't—" Patsy protested lamely.

"I'll be on my way," Walker put in, ignoring the chief of police and focusing on the lady. If he didn't go, things were going to get ugly. "If you ever need anything, Patsy, call me. Dawson has my numbers."

Treat's color flared, as though there were an overheated engine inside his head, fixing to throw a rod. "If Patsy **needs** anything—" he seethed "—I'll be the one she calls."

People were starting to notice, turning toward them. Slade, Hutch and Boone, none of them fans of Treat McQuillan, started moving in their direction.

Patsy clutched Treat's arm. "Take me home," she pleaded, her voice quiet and quick. "Right now. My boy's been gone for a while, and I want to see him."

Treat's Adam's apple raced up and down the length of his neck like an elevator gone haywire, and his eyes bulged, but he finally gave in and, with stiff-spined dignity, squired Patsy toward the road, where his car was parked with lots of others.

Walker watched them go, troubled.

"Everything all right?" Boone asked, being the first one there. He might have been the bridegroom, but he was also the sheriff, and he took the job seriously.

"I hope so," Walker answered, finally turning to face his friend.

Slade and Hutch joined them. Slade had been the sheriff of Parable County before Boone took office, and Hutch was the type to go ahead and deputize himself whenever he thought there might be a need for reinforcements. Whatever their differences over Brylee, and the in-famous wedding-that-wasn't, Walker liked Hutch Carmody.

Treat and Patsy roared off in his fancy new police car, throwing up a plume of dust behind them.

Slade shook his head, quietly dis-gusted, and returned to the party.

Boone went back to his bride, as any sane man would have done in his place, which left Hutch and Walker by them-selves.

An awkward development, to say the least.

Hutch laid his hand briefly on Walker's shoulder, saying nothing, then turned and walked away.

Walker lingered a while, circulated among the other guests as best he could and kept one eye on Casey Elder the rest of the evening.

Casey couldn't even **think** about breakfast the next morning, so she sat at the table on the sunporch, her coffee untouched and her plate empty, watching Shane and Clare as they simultaneously bickered and consumed their oatmeal and fresh fruit.

So much for the brother-sister alliance.

Doris, in uniform and miffed because she prided herself on her cooking and got cranky when everybody didn't choose to eat it, came and went from the kitchen with her carefully powdered nose in the air, her mouth tight and her eyes averted.

"I suppose you'd eat if **Lupe** had

made breakfast," she said, sniffing, on one swing through with the coffeepot.

Casey smiled sadly, getting the reference. Lupe had been Casey's grandmother's housekeeper and cook, and Doris knew that Casey adored the woman. When she was younger, Lupe and Juan had been more like family than her well-heeled grandparents. Some of the happiest days of her childhood, in fact, had been spent on Lupe's father's truck farm, in the Texas hill country, where he and the rest of his gigantic family had raised various vegetables and sold them at farmers' markets and from various roadside stands throughout July and August and well into September.

Good-natured people, who spoke so little English that they always communicated with Casey through Lupe or Juan, the Garcias had taken Casey into the fold, treated her like one of their own, right down to the hoeing, weeding and harvesting.

She'd been proud to sell squash and tomatoes, lettuce and cabbage, cobs of corn still in their green husks, watermelons and asparagus and all the rest. If her grandparents, who traveled widely and chose to leave their sometimes unruly granddaughter in the care of the help, had known she was on the farm, wearing borrowed overalls and getting the knees grubby, digging potatoes and weighing produce and making change for passing strangers, they'd have had a fit.

They **hadn't** known, of course, until one day when Casey was twelve—not quite Shane's age now—and they'd returned unexpectedly from a European cruise, after an outbreak of food poisoning struck down half the ship's passengers, who had to be hospitalized in Barcelona. Her grandparents, whom no mere stomach bug would have dared afflict, had cut the trip short and flown back to the States more than a week early.

Naturally, they'd expected their granddaughter—she of the incessant **singing**—to be in the mansion, eagerly awaiting their return.

Instead, she'd been manning one of the roadside stands with Lupe, and when one of the housemaids called to say they were home, demanding to know where Casey was, Lupe and Juan had rushed her back to Dallas in their old rattletrap of a car.

Her grandmother, who would not hear any explanation, had fired Lupe and Juan on the spot, and never mind their years of dedicated service. They were traitors, never to be forgiven.

Soon after that incident, Casey had been sent away to a New England boarding school, where she was completely miserable, sustained only by encouraging letters from Lupe. When Casey's grandmother died suddenly a few months later, her grandfather had sent for her, intending to send her straight back to those hallowed halls of learning directly after the funeral.

But she'd cried and cajoled and, finally, her grandfather had agreed to let her stay and return to her old school, which, though stuffy and intolerant of red-haired girls who wanted to be country singers, was better than living among strangers far away.

That Christmas, she received her first

guitar. But Lupe and Juan were still gone, and Casey was still lonely, so she threw her whole heart and soul into her music. Using a Dummies book, she taught herself to read notes, and she practiced chords on that guitar until her fingertips were raw, then, mercifully, calloused.

She sang along with her radio, alone in her room, copying the old-timers— Patsy Cline and Loretta Lynn, then Reba McEntire and Faith Hill and LeAnn Rimes and anyone else she admired, which added up to a lot of people. Then she started singing on the street, to her grandfather's mortification, collecting quarters and crumpled dollar bills—and a whole lot of pennies—in her open guitar case resting at her feet on the sidewalk.

From there, she'd gotten bookings in grange halls and old folks' homes and high school gymnasiums, and she'd known even then, with her grandfather nurturing an ever-greater disapproval, that she had something special, that she was going to **make it.**

And she had. The breaks had finally

started coming, barely noticeable at first. She'd played rodeos and, having lied about her age so many times that she believed herself, bars and night-clubs.

Her grandfather had finally stopped speaking to her entirely, though she still heard from Lupe and Juan, even now.

"Mom?" Shane snapped his fingers in front of her face. "Hello? Mom?"

Casey chuckled. "Sorry," she said. "I guess I was drifting."

"How come you're not eating?" Clare wanted to know. She could be bossy at times, that child.

"Because I'm not hungry," Casey answered patiently. By the time this day ended, she thought, these children would know she'd deceived them, and they might never be together, in exactly this way, again.

Tears burned behind her eyes, but she held them back. Even smiled, which took some grit. "We're going out to Timber Creek today," she said. "All three of us."

Shane looked thrilled. "Can we take the dogs?"

"Not this time," Casey told her son with gentle regret.

Clare, not only older than Shane but female, and therefore more perceptive, studied her mother with frank concern. "What's going on?" she asked.

Casey had to swallow several times before she could answer. "You'll know soon enough," she said. "For now, let's leave it at that."

"Mom," Clare demanded, "are you sick? Are you going to tell us that you're dying of some horrible disease?"

"No," Casey was quick to reply. "It's nothing like that."

"Then, what?" Shane wanted to know. "We're moving? You're going back on the road?"

Casey almost told them the whole story then, but words failed her. She didn't like admitting that she needed anybody, but she needed Walker beside her for this one—that was for sure.

She shook her head. "We're not moving and I'm not going back on the road," she assured Shane, who was visibly relieved. "I'm calling the crew together, after Labor Day, to record some songs and block out a new video, but that's the extent of it."

She hadn't heard from Mitch by phone or email since he'd stormed off after she'd turned down his proposal, nor had she received his letter of resignation.

Hopefully, **that** mess, at least, would blow over. She liked Mitch, and he was a good manager. Besides, the thought of starting from scratch with somebody new, after all these years, was overwhelming.

Mercifully, the kids stopped asking questions after that.

Casey retreated to her room and stepped into her ridiculously large—and full—closet. She would have known what to wear if she was going to sing for a president or any level of royalty, but how did one dress to tell her children that she'd been deceiving them since birth? No harmless fib, this. Instead, it was a lie so big that it had become a lifestyle, and Casey had lived it so long and so thoroughly that she didn't know who she—or any of them—would be without it.

Black seemed too funereal and white

too innocent, so she finally chose a green voile sundress that brought out the color of her eyes and complemented her red hair. Forswearing pantyhose— there was a limit to the suffering she was willing to endure, even in this situation—she slipped sandals onto her bare feet, squirted a little perfume at the hollow of her throat and called it good.

Studying her reflection in the mirrors above her vanity, Casey made a simple, motivational speech.

"Buck up, cowgirl," she said.

CHAPTER EIGHT

The kitchen of the house at Timber Creek Ranch was probably a quarter the size of her own, if that, Casey observed, sitting numbly at the large round table, with Clare seated to her left, Shane to her right and Walker straight across. Under any other circumstances, she would have enjoyed the cozy normality of the room, the pretty cotton curtains at the old-fashioned windows, the natural-rock fireplace where cheerful blazes surely snapped and crackled on winter mornings, the rustic plank floor dotted here and there with colorful handmade rugs. At the moment, though, she was so focused on what she had to say—what she was **afraid** to say—that her surroundings barely registered.

Walker's gaze connected with hers, held. The impact reminded her of railroad cars coupling with a jolt.

The inside of Casey's head buzzed, as though her brain were a wasps' nest, and her stomach bounced continually between her pelvis and her esophagus.

"Would somebody **please** tell us what's going on?" Clare burst out, glancing from Casey to Walker and back again, speaking for her brother as well as herself, it would seem. As the older of the two, and a natural take-charge type, she often did that.

Shane remained silent, his gawky, youthful body stiff with tension. One day, Casey thought, those now-thin shoulders of his would be broad and strong, like Walker's, but, for now, they were narrow and a little stooped, making the boy look all too vulnerable.

Casey opened her mouth to reply to her daughter's question, but no sound came out. Not even a croak, though she felt a scraping sensation, as though she were trying to swallow a rusty hasp of the sort used to file horses' hooves.

Walker's grin was slight, but encouraging. "It'll be okay," he said, his voice gruff and gentle, both at once.

Casey swallowed, her hands knotted together in her lap, and nodded, but she still couldn't get her vocal cords to work.

"Mom," Clare insisted, arms folded across her beginning-to-blossom chest, eyes troubled. **"What?"**

Casey looked at her daughter, her son and then Walker.

"This is hard," she finally managed. Tears blurred her vision for a moment, and she blinked them away.

"Go on," Walker urged quietly.

Casey knew he would speak up if she couldn't, or wouldn't, but it was **her** responsibility to tell her children the truth, because she'd been the one to start that first lie rolling. And then sustain it, with many, many **other** lies.

Clare and Shane seemed on the verge of panic, though, and there was no more time left, Casey realized with a painful start. The sand had all run through the hourglass.

So she blurted it out, starkly and far too abruptly. "Walker is your father," she said.

A thunderous silence fell, filling the room, pushing the walls outward. Casey waited for the roof to cave in, though, of course, it didn't.

She could feel her own heartbeat, pounding in the hollow of her still-sore throat, and she forced herself to look squarely at her children, each in turn. Shane was not only unfazed, he was grinning, his eyes alight with wonder.

"For real?" he asked.

"For real," Casey replied softly, shifting her gaze to Clare.

The girl's reaction was the polar opposite of Shane's—the red in her hair seemed to leach into her face, making vivid pink circles on her cheeks, and her eyes were narrowed almost to slits. Her chin wobbled, and she immediately shoved back her chair, ready to bolt.

Walker stopped her by taking hold of her hand. "Easy now, sweetheart," he told his daughter, the words thick with affection and regret. "Give your mom a chance to explain."

Clare remained seated, but her whole countenance exuded defiance. "You **lied,**" she accused, glaring at Casey. "You **knew** how much we wanted a dad, Shane and me, and you let us believe we were **freaks,** conceived in some **laboratory**—"

"Clare," Casey said miserably. "Listen to me, please—"

"I **hate** you!" Clare erupted, and this time, when she started to rise, Walker made no move to keep her at the table. She swept both parents up in a scathing sweep of a glance. "I hate you **both**—"

"No." Casey fairly whimpered the word. This was what she'd feared would happen. On some level, she'd known Shane would take the news well, but Clare would feel wounded and betrayed—by the person she'd trusted most.

Clare whirled, headed for the outside door, nearly tripping over a startled Doolittle in her hurry to escape her mother's company and, by extension, Walker's.

She slammed the screen door hard and stomped across the porch, footsteps reverberating.

Casey started to rise, every instinct compelling her to go after her daughter, find a way to comfort the girl, make everything all right, but Walker put up one hand, like a traffic cop.

"Let her go," he said. "She needs a few minutes for this to sink in."

Casey, knowing Walker was right, slumped bleakly back into her chair.

Shane, still staring at Walker as though he'd just emerged from Aladdin's lamp, genie-style, remained awestruck, oblivious, evidently, to his sister's angry departure. "You're **really** our dad?" he half whispered.

"I'm really your dad," Walker confirmed.

They heard a rig come up the driveway then, a motor shutting off, ticking and clicking as it went still. A car door closed, a dog barked.

Brylee, Casey thought. The poor woman couldn't possibly know what she was walking in on.

Walker caught her eye. "I can ask her

to leave for a while," he offered. "Come back later—"

But Casey shook her head. "No," she answered. "Brylee's family, and she has a right to know what's going on."

Walker gave a slight nod.

Brylee and her dog could be heard coming up the porch steps. Her voice came gently through the screen in the door; she'd spotted Clare, probably huddled in the big wooden swing.

"Hey," Brylee said softly. "What's the trouble, honey?"

Clare's response was an angry sob, and the chains supporting the swing creaked as she started it in motion, probably with a hard kick at the floorboards.

"You can tell me," Brylee said.

"Ask **them!**" Clare cried in response. "Ask the liars!"

Casey closed her eyes for a moment, against the pain she'd caused her daughter, boomeranging back to bruise her, as well. Her stomach felt as though someone had just slammed a fist into it, hard.

Some murmuring followed, and Clare

continued to cry, fury giving way to heartbreak. Neither Casey nor Walker moved or spoke, though Shane, by then out of his chair and stroking Doolittle's head and gleaming back, seemed to be lost in a happy world of his own.

He snapped out of it long enough to make a comment, though.

"I don't get it," Shane said, amazed. "We find out we're not lab experiments— that we have Walker for a dad—and Clare's bawling her eyes out like it's the end of the world or something."

Walker, leaning from his chair, laid a hand on his son's shoulder and, though he'd done that many times before, it was different this time. Casey saw pride in the way Walker touched Shane, knew he was claiming the boy, that no matter what happened after this, they would always be father and son—the bond, finally established, was unbreakable.

"Clare will be all right," Walker told Shane. Then his gaze caught Casey's again, and he leaned back in his chair. "We all will."

The screen door opened with a slight squeal of hinges in need of oiling, and

Brylee came in, the dog right behind her.

"What's going on here?" she asked bluntly, her eyes big and her cheeks pale with concern. "Did something happen—?"

Walker was still looking at Casey, and there was a question in his eyes, as clear as if he'd asked it aloud. **Should I tell her?**

Casey merely nodded.

Walker broke the news to his sister and he was a lot more diplomatic than Casey had been just minutes before. Briefly but thoroughly he outlined the circumstances that had brought them all to this moment and this place.

A slow smile spread across Brylee's wide mouth as she listened, moved up into her eyes, shining there.

"Wow," she said when Walker finished. "That's **great.**"

Great, Casey thought dismally. Except that Clare was still out there on the porch, crying her heart out, feeling cheated and furious and sold out—by her own mother, no less.

"Can I live here now, with you?" Shane

asked Walker. "Can I have a horse? Does this mean my last name is really **Parrish,** instead of **Elder?**"

Walker smiled at the boy. "Whoa," he said. "You belong with your mom. As for the horse and the last name, we'll discuss all that later, after the dust settles and everybody's on the same page."

Casey tossed an appreciative glance in Walker's direction; he was letting her know he didn't plan on trying to take her children away from her, and she hadn't realized, until that moment, how afraid she'd been that he would do exactly that.

At least, she **hoped** that was his meaning.

She stood, unable to wait any longer, her knees wobbly and her head spinning a little, and moved past a sympathetic Brylee to open the screen door and step out onto the porch.

Just as she'd pictured her, Clare was crumpled up in a corner of the big swing, looking more like the little girl she had been, just a few short seasons ago, than the young woman she was so rapidly turning into.

Casey walked over and sat down beside her daughter on the plump, faded cushion padding the seat of the swing. She didn't touch Clare and she didn't speak, either. She just wanted to **be** there.

Clare, resting both forearms on the arm of the swing, shoulders shaking, eventually lifted her head. She didn't look at Casey, though. Instead, she stared off into something well beyond the rails of the porch, the nearby barn, even the distant horizon.

"Why?" she asked, after a long, long time. She sounded broken, as well as outraged.

Casey weighed the obvious answers. **It seemed like a good idea at the time,** though true, would sound flippant. **I thought it would be the best thing for all of us,** then? No, that wouldn't do, either, because while she'd wanted to believe that from the beginning, she knew now that it was just another lie. She'd wanted her career, too, and, dammit, she wasn't ashamed of that, for all her other regrets.

"No excuses," she said. "I should have

told you the truth, right from the start, and I'm really sorry I didn't, honey."

Clare turned puffy, accusing eyes on her then. **"Why?"** she repeated fiercely. "Tell me **why.**"

Casey sighed. "I'm not sure I know," she admitted, at some length. "Not the whole reason, anyhow. I was young, my career was just getting started and I wasn't expecting to get pregnant."

"So you chose your **music** over Shane and me and Walker?" The words pierced Casey's heart like a spray of porcupine quills.

"I wanted to keep singing," she said after deliberating for a while. "But it wasn't about choosing **anything**—or **anybody**—over you and your brother." Mitch, members of the band and other close friends had advised her to put her baby girl up for adoption, and she'd flatly refused, but she didn't think it would do any good to mention that just now. In fact, it might even make things worse.

"And you let it happen **twice,**" Clare marveled angrily, as though Casey hadn't spoken at all. "I'm sorry, but that's just **weird.**"

Casey smiled sadly, remembering the scared, pregnant girl with fame and fortune at her fingertips. By then, her grandparents were both dead, and when it came to kinfolks, she was alone in the world. "Maybe," she confessed presently, her voice small and soft. "But I can't imagine my life without both you and Shane."

Clare didn't answer right away, and she'd averted her eyes again, too. "What about Walker? Did he want us?"

"He didn't know," Casey replied, after biting the figurative bullet. It would have been so easy to blame Walker, make him out to be one of those men who make babies and then skip out, fancy-free.

But she couldn't do that—it would be the worst lie of all.

"What do you mean, 'He didn't know'?" Clare shot back. "He knows **now,** so you must have clued him in at some point—**unlike Shane and me.**"

"When I found out I was expecting you," Casey said, thinking that telling the truth was overrated, "I led Walker to believe there was another man in my life. A year later, when Shane was on his way, I knew I had to tell Walker, because he was sure to guess everything if I didn't. He was madder than a bee-stung mule at first, but not because I'd gotten pregnant again—he wanted to us to be a family then, the four of us, but I wasn't ready for that."

"You weren't **ready,**" Clare echoed, scornful again. Inside the house, Walker, Brylee and Shane talked in quiet, peaceful voices, and it seemed to Casey that they were apart from her and from Clare, in some other, unreachable dimension. "You still had to win all those Grammies and CMA awards, didn't you? Make all that money?" A shuddery pause followed. "Did you even think about **us,** Mom? Did it cross your mind that maybe Shane and I would have liked to grow up in a real house, instead of airplanes and tour buses and hotels, with a mother and a father and a **regular** life?" She gestured, taking in everything around them. "We could have lived right here, gone trick-or-treating at Halloween, ridden the bus to school in town, had friends we'd known since kindergarten, put up the Christmas tree in the same part of the same room every year. We could have been **regular people**—but, no. We had to have a mother so famous she couldn't even take us to Disneyland without being mobbed!"

Where did all that come from? Casey didn't dare ask. Not yet, anyhow. All these years, she'd thought her confident, capable children were happy living unconventional lives, at least most of the time. Obviously, that had only been partially true. Her head began to ache.

"If I could go back," she said, "I'd do things differently."

"Easy to say," Clare retorted. She'd put her stubborn face on, and she meant to wear it for a while. Maybe forever.

"I love you and Shane with all my heart," Casey said. "I always have."

Clare made a contemptuous, huffy sound, barely audible. "Whatever," she replied in bitter dismissal.

After that, an invisible wall came down between the two of them, and Casey knew there would be no reaching the girl, that the time for talking was over, for now anyway.

She stood up and went back into the house, leaving Clare in the porch swing and feeling as though she'd aged twenty years in the past hour. Worse, she was literally beside herself, a step removed from her body, oddly detached, like an observer following close on her own heels.

Brylee crossed to Casey when she entered the kitchen, gave her a wordless hug.

Casey was profoundly grateful for the other woman's support, though she had no idea how long it would last, and hugged her back.

Shane remained remarkably unshaken—it was as if he'd been told he'd won the lottery, and maybe he had. The prize was a father—just what he'd always wanted.

It hurt to know, with such certainty, that she, Casey, for all her love, for all her devotion and hands-on parenting, wasn't enough.

"I want to be Shane **Parrish** from now on," the boy announced.

Casey merely nodded, unable to look at her son or at Walker, keeping her eyes cast downward as she stood there in the middle of that plank floor, stricken all over again.

"So," Brylee said, suddenly, expansively and with a little too much enthusiasm, "suppose I take my niece and nephew out for a nice, long horseback ride? Followed by supper in town?"

"Yes!" Shane said.

"Might be a good idea," Walker agreed, standing now. Casey wondered when he'd moved, gotten up from his chair at the table. That peculiar feeling of being separated from herself remained, and the headache was getting worse, too.

"I'm not sure Clare will want to—" Casey began, but she lost momentum before she could finish the sentence. She didn't know what Clare would do next, or what she would say.

To Casey's surprise, though, Brylee easily convinced Clare to join her and Shane on an impromptu adventure, and Casey watched through the window above the sink as the three of them headed for the barn, accompanied by Brylee's dog.

Walker moved to stand behind Casey, slipping his arms loosely around her waist, giving her plenty of room, even inside his embrace. He'd always had a way about him, an ability to comfort her without making her feel cornered. "The worst part is over," he told her, his voice husky, resting his chin on the crown of her head.

The dam broke then, the one Casey had erected years ago, before she had Clare and Shane, even before she'd known Walker. A virtual torrent of emotion flooded through the barrier that had held for so long—sorrow and loss, shame and regret, loneliness and exhaustion. Casey, disoriented before, landed back in her own skin with a crash, and a cry of pain escaped her.

Walker turned her around, held her. And she sobbed into his chest, clung to his shoulders with both hands, convinced she'd collapse if she let go.

She knew that, like most men, Walker was uncomfortable with tears, but he didn't shush her, didn't tell her not to

cry, didn't prattle on about how everything would turn out just fine. He merely
stood there, as solid as the trunk of a
venerable Ponderosa pine, holding her.
It felt so right, the heat and the substance of him, the strength.

That was the trouble, of course, because it **wasn't** right. When she allowed
Walker to take care of her this way, when
she allowed **herself** to be a mortal
woman with needs and feelings instead
of a powerhouse, a star, a **success,**
things happened. **Babies** happened.

For all that, she couldn't pull away
from Walker.

Curving his hand under her chin, he
lifted her face, kissed away her tears.
"Casey," he ground out, holding her
tightly.

Their lips came together naturally—
inevitably—seeking at first, tentative,
then demanding, fusing them together
on some deeper level, where nameless
forces surged and swelled, as powerful
as a rain-swollen river on a downhill
course.

They remained where they were for a

long time, kissing, pausing to catch quick, desperate breaths, kissing again.

Vaguely, at the far periphery of her awareness, Casey heard voices— Brylee, Clare, Shane—heard the clomp of horses' hooves out in the yard, the jingle of bridle fittings, and Brylee's dog, barking with excitement.

They might have been in another world, all of them, quite apart from the one she and Walker and—somewhere nearby, Doolittle—occupied.

Her common sense, normally her north star, her personal compass, deserted her, and that wasn't even the worst part. No, the worst part was, she didn't care about practicality, about consequences, about old lessons learned the hard way and the scars they left behind.

All she wanted was to lose herself in Walker for a little while.

Need crackled between them, almost tangible.

"Are you sure?" Walker asked, reading her with perfect accuracy, the way he'd always done, at least when they were intimate.

"Yes," she said, because she'd been hungry for so long, lonely for so long, **brave** for so long. She didn't want to be her usual strong, independent self—no, instead, she yearned to give in, to let Walker's strength be enough for both of them, if only for a little while.

He lifted her easily into his arms, carried her out of the kitchen, along a corridor.

She knew she ought to stop him, right this instant, before things went any further, but she couldn't. Make that, **wouldn't.** Alarm bells should have sounded in her head—history was about to repeat itself—but they didn't. She wanted this, wanted to be swept away, wanted **Walker.**

Soon, they were in his bedroom.

Momentarily, sanity returned. What if Brylee and the kids came back?

Casey didn't realize she'd asked the question out loud until Walker answered it, his breath warm against her ear, making her skin tingle even as he eased her down onto the bed.

"They'll be gone a while," he promised hoarsely. "Bless her, Brylee will see to that."

He was already undressing Casey, even as he spoke—or was she undressing herself? Or him? Either way, their clothes seemed to evaporate, his as well as hers, like morning dew under the light of a summer sun.

Casey murmured Walker's name, feeling the steely length of him against her side as they lay together, a breeze blowing through, cooling their flesh, if not their ardor.

His mouth fell to hers then, consuming, igniting flames within flames within flames. There was no stopping this, Casey knew—they were already lost, both of them.

Walker nibbled at her earlobe, traced the length of her neck with his warm mouth, found her breast, took her nipple with a greedy tenderness that sent hot, sweet pleasure skewering through her.

It's been so long, her body whispered—or was it the wordless language of her soul that spoke so eloquently? **Walker—Walker—it's been so long.**

Casey couldn't get close enough to him; her hands roamed up and down the muscular length of his back, urging, urging.

With a low groan, Walker parted her legs, found her most sensitive place and began plying her with his fingers. He knew just how to touch her, lightly but not **too** lightly, increasing the turmoil inside her with every skillful motion of his hand.

Casey arched her back, biting down hard on her lower lip to hold back a cry of raw, primitive surrender. "Now," she pleaded, nearly strangling on her own voice. "Please, Walker—**now**—"

But Walker would not be rushed; even in the state she was in, she should have remembered that. No, he'd take his time with her, enjoy both her breasts at his leisure, kiss her senseless, and then he would—

The memory of all those other times when they'd made love electrified her, made her gasp again in anticipation, and Walker, understanding, chuckled low in his throat.

"Hang on, cowgirl," he murmured, his

lips moving against the quivering flesh of her belly now and headed slowly, inexorably south. "We're just getting started."

"I don't think—I can wait—" Casey whimpered, already wet, already expanding to receive him, take him inside her, hold him there.

"That's all right, too," Walker replied. And then he was **there,** burrowing through with his tongue, teasing her, finally taking her into his mouth.

Her entire body buckled in a spasm of frantic welcome as he shifted to his knees, slid his hands under her backside, raised her high off the sheets and went right on partaking of her, now gently, now hungrily, as though she were a honeycomb, ripe and juicy and sweet.

She buried her fingers in his hair, holding him to her even as she thought she'd surely explode into flaming fragments at any moment, like a dying star, dissolving into darkness. The pleasure was all-consuming and yet not nearly enough, a mere promise of what was still to come.

Casey rasped Walker's name, fevered, desolate, triumphant.

Walker went easy on her for a few moments, then grew more demanding again, more insistent.

Her first climax erupted like a geyser, propelling her skyward in dizzying spirals of splintered light, the force of it stopping her breath behind her throat, even as her body flexed in glorious abandon, and flexed again. Then again.

When it was over, Walker lowered her back to the mattress and Casey, though saturated with satisfaction, every muscle and bone melted, craved more. She wanted, **needed,** to feel Walker deep inside her, part of her, needed to be driven mad all over again by the friction as they moved together, in that most private, most sacred dance of all.

She could only mutter his name, though, because she'd given him all her strength, shamelessly thrown everything she had, everything she was, into that shattering, seemingly endless orgasm. For all its power, she knew it was only the first of many, each one wilder than the last, each one hurling her outside herself, outside the ordinary, everyday world, into realms of mystery and magic.

Walker shifted, and the thought flitted through Casey's mind that he was putting on a condom, and she wanted to laugh for sheer joy, though she knew she didn't have the breath for even that much effort. He'd been wearing a condom when they conceived Clare. Shane, too.

Did he remember that?

Dazed, Casey shook her head from side to side in answer to her own unspoken question. Walker was a man—was he ever—and using protection was probably a matter of habit with him. Just another responsibility.

He wasn't thinking about making babies.

"You're sure?" he rasped, poised above her now, careful not to crush her beneath his weight.

He'd always asked her that, no matter how heated the moment, and he cared about her answer. If she'd asked him to stop, he would have.

"I'm sure," she said instead.

In one powerful, earth-shattering thrust, Walker claimed her, made her his own, and she immediately climaxed again, softly, though each motion of their joined bodies aroused her more, drove her ever upward, toward another, greater release, and then still another.

Walker maintained control, even as she flailed beneath him, gave herself up to him completely, over and over again, repeated his name like a ragged litany.

Finally, though, he let go, driving deep, his whole body seizing like a single muscle as, with a long, low groan—her name—he spilled himself inside her.

Afterward, they lay in silence, too spent to talk, arms and legs entwined, skin slick with perspiration. The breeze was like a cool caress, soothing and soft. Somewhere nearby, a clock ticked, the old-fashioned kind with actual works inside, steady as a heartbeat.

Casey, flung heavenward with the last, most ferocious release, drifted slowly back to reality, floating like a feather or a snowflake. And the instant she came in for a landing, soul and body colliding with a wallop, she sat bolt upright and said, "Oh, my God, Walker—what have we done?"

He chuckled, still languid. "If I remember correctly," he murmured, "we had sex."

"Ha, ha, very funny," Casey said scathingly, though it was herself she was angry with, not Walker. After all, it wasn't as if she'd done anything to discourage him—she'd been as unstoppable as a tigress in mating season.

Now, though, she broke free of his embrace, scrambled out of bed and began snatching her discarded clothes from the floor. "I can't **believe** we let this happen!"

Walker eased himself up onto his elbows, maddeningly unperturbed, bare to the waist. Mercifully, the sheets covered him. "Simmer down," he advised, his eyes twinkling. "We're both grown-ups here."

Casey wouldn't look at him. She was struggling awkwardly into her underwear, nearly hog-tying herself in the process. "Which means we ought to know better," she sputtered.

With a chuckle, Walker got out of bed, magnificently naked, and retreated into the adjoining bathroom. Moments later, he was back, bending to retrieve his jeans from the floor, slipping them on without a hint of self-consciousness.

By then, Casey was back in her clothes and facing the mirror above Walker's antique bureau, trying to do something with her love-tangled hair. Not only had it come loose from its ponytail, it looked as though she'd been swinging upside down from a trapeze. **Bedhead** didn't begin to describe the phenomenon.

Walker sat down on the foot of the bed, the sheets and covers so tangled that a tornado might have just passed through, and watched her, feet and chest bare, hair still mussed from her fingers delving through it. His expression was calm, amused—and a little on the smug side.

And why **wouldn't** he be smug? He'd just turned her inside out—again—and she'd let him know it, too, carrying on like that.

If she'd been the violent type, she'd have thrown something at Walker Parrish's handsome head just then.

"Don't you grin at me!" she commanded, shaking an index finger for emphasis.

"Still the same old red-hot, complicated Casey," Walker drawled, undaunted, grin firmly in place. "A she-wolf in bed, a spinster schoolmarm out of it."

"What if we did it again, Walker?" she demanded, agonized by the prospect and, at the same time, hopeful. "What if we made another baby? How would we explain **that** to Clare and Shane?"

"I used a condom," he reminded her.

"Yes," she agreed tersely. "Just as you did when we conceived Clare, and then Shane."

He looked thoughtful for a few moments, then immediately brightened. "You've got a point there," he admitted, willing, for once, to concede that she was right about something. Another pause followed, while he pondered the matter in an annoyingly unhurried way. "If you're having my baby," he finally concluded, "you're going to have me to deal with, from here on, because this time, we're doing it right."

"What does that mean?" Casey all but whispered the words.

"It means, Casey Jones, that married or not, if you're having my child, **this time,** we're going to raise him or her together, as a team—not with you in one place and me in another."

And that, considering the note of finality in Walker's tone, was that.

CHAPTER NINE

Walker might have looked calm on the outside, but on the **inside,** a whole passel of contradictory emotions churned like the contents of a blender on high speed. Sorting all those feelings out was going to take some time, and he couldn't just sit there on the end of his bed until things fell neatly into place, now, could he, because if he did, he'd be there till his beard grew in white.

So, suppressing a sigh that would have revealed too much, he stood up, cutting a wide swath around a still-rattled Casey, made his way over to the closet, found himself a clean shirt and shrugged into it. He got the buttoning wrong on the first try and had to start over. Finally, he sat down again, to put on fresh socks and haul his boots back onto his feet.

This probably wasn't the time, he reasoned, in the privacy of his sex-addled head, to tell Casey that the condom hadn't held. She was on the verge of a meltdown as it was.

She looked a sight, though, and a fine one, as she ran a brush through her coppery hair and wrestled it back into a ponytail, as it was before they'd decided to take a roll in the hay.

Walker didn't regret what they'd done—no sane man would have, especially after a lengthy dry spell like the one he'd just been through—but he knew Casey had enough regrets for both of them. And if he was honest, the knowledge hurt a little.

"Do you want to wait for Brylee to bring the kids back here or go home?" he asked, figuring Casey might not say another word to him, ever, if he didn't make the first move.

She turned to face him, an act of pure bravado, he reckoned, placing her hands on her hips and straightening her spine until she reached her full and patently unremarkable height.

"I want to go home," she said. Not much ambiguity there.

"Okay," Walker agreed, standing up again. A part of him—a **big** part of him—wanted to lure Casey Elder right back into bed and make love to her all over again, but success seemed about as likely as a two-way conversation with his horse, so he tried to let go of the idea. For the time being, anyhow.

"That's all?" Casey sniped. "Just, 'okay'?"

"What do you **want** me to say, Casey? That we can pretend this didn't happen?"

She marched past him, out of the bedroom, along the length of the hallway, past a couple of other rooms and, finally, into the kitchen. Only then, snatching up her shoulder bag from a countertop and shoving one arm through the strap, did she deign to answer, drawing in a deep breath and then, in the next instant, deflating again.

"I'm doing it again, aren't I?" she asked, looking away from him and then, with visible determination, looking back. "Trying to pick a fight, so I can put some distance between us, give myself time to think."

Walker nodded, though he was a little surprised by the admission. Casey was good at fooling herself, and even better at fooling other people, and she'd been living the lie for so long that he'd begun to wonder if she could no longer recognize the truth.

"Take all the time you want," he said, at some length. "But it isn't going to be business as usual, at least as far as Clare and Shane are concerned. I'm through playing the good ole dependable family friend, Case. Insofar as they'll let me, at this late date, I want to be a **father** to them both."

"Good luck with Clare," Casey said, and while she might have sounded flippant, Walker knew by the tears glinting briefly in her green eyes and the wobble of her chin that she'd meant those words,

hadn't simply tossed them off in an effort to get under his skin or make him
back off a step or two.

Walker wanted to put his arms around
Casey then, but he didn't dare. She so
rarely allowed him to comfort her that,
when she did, they both lost control.

"Clare will come around, Case," he
said gently, because he knew she was
afraid the girl would never forgive her.
And it was true enough that long-term
family feuds sometimes started over a
lot less, so he reckoned she had cause
for concern, all right. "You're her mother,
and she loves you. Plus, she's a smart
kid—in time, she'll realize that everybody makes mistakes, often with the
best of intentions."

Casey averted her eyes from Walker,
shy all of a sudden, changeable as sunlight dancing on the surface of a creek.
For just a moment, he caught a glimpse
of the little girl inside her, the one who
had lost her folks as a baby, grown up
with stodgy if well-meaning grandparents, wealthy and past the time when
child rearing might have been a realistic
possibility, and probably at more of a

loss, with every passing day, than pride would have allowed them to admit. He supposed they'd loved Casey, in their way, tried to make the best of a difficult situation, but she was still, for all her accomplishments, a bird with a broken wing.

"I hope you're right," she finally replied.

After that, he and Doolittle squired the lady home in the truck, and not much was said along the way.

"Do me a favor?" Walker said, when he'd seen Casey safely to the front door, waiting while she fumbled through her handbag for the keys.

"What kind of favor?" she asked, looking up at him, her expression just a touch on the wary side.

"Don't go beating yourself up over all this," he answered, his voice going husky again. "You've done what you could to make things right, and that took guts, and you don't have to fight the whole battle alone anymore. I'll help as much as I can, and I know Brylee will, too, so let's try to take things as they come." He smiled. "Play it by ear, so to speak."

Casey gave a wan little grin at the awkward pun, stuck the key in the lock and turned it. Pausing on the threshold, she looked up at him again, and broke his heart into two jagged pieces with her bravery.

"I'm going to need some time, Walker," she reminded him. "And some space. I won't stop you from seeing Clare and Shane, but—"

He touched her mouth with one finger, unable to bear hearing the rest of that sentence. "One day at a time," he said.

She nodded again, stepped inside, closed the door.

Walker waited until he heard the lock engage, then turned to walk away, even though leaving Casey behind was about the last thing he wanted to do just then.

A welcoming committee composed of three eager dogs, barely more than puppies, and two more-reserved cats awaited Casey in the cathedral-like entryway to that too-big, too-fancy house.

The place was more like one huge and soulless showcase than a home, it seemed to her, especially in comparison to Walker's spacious but functional quarters. **His** house had a history—she could picture generations of Parrishes living and loving within those solid walls, imagine simple, wholesome meals being made and shared. People had surely laughed and cried there, celebrated and mourned. In good times, they would have rejoiced, in that quiet and modest way country folks did, and when times were hard, they would have made do, and rarely, if ever, complained.

By contrast, this mansion she lived in, beautiful as it was, had an air of impermanence, of anonymity, like a grand hotel. In those reflective moments, she was more grateful than usual for the rough-and-tumble attentions of the dogs, if only because they were genuinely glad to see her.

Resolving to snap out of it, Casey stopped playing the comparison game, since the score was always zero-to-zero and nobody ever came out a winner, and wondered if she and the pets were alone in the house.

It was at moments like this that she

missed the guys in the band, missed their boisterous goodwill and their willingness to make music at any hour of the day or night.

Doris, the housekeeper, was probably around somewhere, but Casey didn't go looking for her, mainly because she didn't want to answer any perceptive questions. Doris was a longtime employee and a true friend, but this fix Casey found herself in wasn't the sort of thing she could be expected to understand, being of another generation. The older woman would know at a glance, though, that something big had happened, age difference notwithstanding, and, always kindhearted, she'd try to open a dialogue—which was the last thing Casey wanted to deal with while she felt so jangled.

So she climbed the Gone-with-the-Wind staircase, secretly glad when none of the pets followed, and took lonely refuge in her room.

After a quick shower, Casey put on fresh jeans, a blue silk shirt, low-heeled shoes and makeup. When Clare and Shane came home, she'd be there to greet them, on top of things, equal to any challenge, even if she had to pretend. Angry or not, Clare needed a **mother,** strong and competent and ready to engage, not some caricature of a mad housewife, disheveled and distracted.

And never mind that she felt a lot more like the latter than the former at the moment. If she'd dressed to match her present emotions, she'd have worn an old chenille bathrobe, ratty scuff slippers and a head full of foam curlers. There probably would have been a martini in her hand, too.

Alas, weakness was a luxury she couldn't afford. As soon as the kids came through the door, it would be showtime.

Having come to terms with the situation, Casey went downstairs to the kitchen, in need of a cup of tea and mindful of the fact that it was time to feed the pets. Taking care of the menagerie was normally Shane and Clare's job, but since they weren't around to do it at the moment, she'd have to step up.

For all that, Casey might have gone

right on hiding out in her room if she'd known Doris was already in the kitchen, standing in front of the eight-burner stove, stirring something in a kettle. When the other woman looked back over a shoulder and saw Casey, she started a little.

"Oh," she said, putting a hand to her heart.

"I'm sorry," Casey said quickly. "I didn't mean to scare you."

Doris tried to smile, but there was a strange, distracted glint in her eyes, and her lips moved constantly, even when she wasn't talking.

"Is everything all right?" Casey asked, forgetting her tea for a moment. Doris wasn't herself, and that alarmed her, because Doris was **always** herself.

The housekeeper looked baffled by the question, and didn't reply right away.

The dogs and cats, knowing supper was in the offing, converged on the kitchen en masse, and for the next few minutes, Casey busied herself pouring kibble rations and rinsing and refilling water bowls while she waited—for what seemed like an eternity—for Doris to say something.

"No, dear," she finally answered, shoulders drooping, unaware that whatever she'd been stirring was now dripping from the end of her wooden spoon onto the gleaming floor. "Actually—no. Everything **isn't** all right."

Casey left the pets to their meals and approached, touching Doris's arm lightly before removing the spoon from the woman's grasp and setting it aside on the stove top. "What is it? Are you ill?"

She had to resist the motherly urge to touch the housekeeper's forehead, testing for fever.

"No, I'm— I'm not sick." But Doris's nose reddened at the tip, and her eyes grew moist. "It's my sister, Evelyn," she went on. "She's fallen and broken her hip, and she's all alone over there in Seattle, with nobody to keep her company or take charge of things."

Casey took both her housekeeper's hands in her own and looked directly into her worried eyes. "Then you've got to go to her," she said softly. "Right away."

"But what will you do without me?" Doris all but wailed. "Who will cook and clean and look after the children when you're working?"

"Don't worry about us," Casey answered, biting back an automatic **We'll be fine** because it might have hurt Doris's feelings, made her think she and the kids didn't need her. She'd spoiled them all completely, over the years, but now they'd just have to buck up and do things for themselves. "Right now, Evelyn matters most. She needs you. And you need to be with her, for your own peace of mind."

"She's so scared, lying there in a hospital bed like that," Doris confirmed fitfully, nodding her head again and again, as if in answer to some other voice that Casey couldn't hear. "She's hurting something terrible, too—Evelyn never had a very high threshold for pain, you know—and she told me earlier, when she called, that the doctors and nurses aren't listening to a word she says."

"Pack your bags," Casey said firmly. "I'll charter a plane, and you'll be in Seattle, holding Evelyn's hand before you know it." Not so long ago, Casey had owned a private jet and kept a flight crew on call 24/7, but now that she wasn't doing concert tours, she wouldn't have used it enough to justify the staggering expense, so she'd sold the aircraft and canceled the service providing pilots and other staff.

Doris blinked. She was a woman with her feet firmly planted on the ground, literally and figuratively, and, unlike Shane and Clare, who'd loved flying, she'd rarely traveled with Casey and the entourage. "Are you sure I ought to go? There's so much to do around here, and Clare and Shane don't eat enough vegetables if I don't keep an eye on them, and—"

Casey chuckled, silenced her friend with a big hug. "I'll force-feed those kids spinach and broccoli, if I have to," she teased. "Go pack your bags while I make a few phone calls."

Just over an hour later, a sleek jet came in for a landing at what passed for an airport, a strip of asphalt that served both Parable and Three Trees. Casey, who had driven Doris and her suitcases there, virtually shooed the woman aboard. Doris had barely disappeared into the cabin when the copilot descended the folding stairs to stow the bags in the cargo hold and make a final flight check.

Casey was about to get back behind the wheel of her SUV, planning to head home immediately after takeoff, but at the copilot's approach, she paused. Grinning, he tipped his hat and said genially, "Hello, there, Ms. Elder. Remember me?"

As many people as she'd met, Casey had a good memory for names and faces. "Joe Parker," she said, extending a hand and smiling. Back when she still owned a jet, one with her name and face splashed across the side, no less, Joe had occasionally joined the crew, which tended to rotate. "How are Shelley and the kids?"

Joe shook her hand, beaming with pride. He wasn't a player like some people who traveled more than they stayed home, and Casey had always respected him for that. "Just fine," he replied. "You and yours?"

"We're doing great," Casey lied. No point in burdening an acquaintance with a lot of unsettling and very private truths. "Clare and Shane are growing up too fast, but that's normal, I guess."

Joe nodded. "I know what you mean," he answered. "Our oldest starts college in the fall, and he's determined to go to an out-of-state school."

Casey felt a pang at that statement, reminded that it wouldn't be very long before Clare was leaving home, or Shane, either, for that matter. Clare was a gifted singer and played several instruments, but she'd made it clear from an early age that she wanted no part of the music business. **All I'd ever be, talent or no talent,** the child had decreed, with uncanny wisdom, for a ten-year-old, **is Casey Elder's daughter. I want to be a veterinarian.**

And Clare's ambition had never wavered since.

"You take good care of Doris for me," Casey said, and Joe nodded, executed a little salute and returned to the plane.

Once he was inside, the metal steps whirred their way back into the underbelly of the craft, and the door closed, sealing itself with a familiar hermetic sound, like a lid fusing itself to one of Lupe's jars of canned peaches.

Standing there on the tarmac, hands in the pockets of her lightweight jacket, even though it wasn't cold, Casey waited, smiling and waving when she saw Doris's face at one of the portholes.

After the plane lifted off, she drove home, and seeing that every light in the whole place was on, she knew Brylee must have dropped Clare and Shane off after the horseback ride and the restaurant meal.

Casey parked in the driveway—she only used the garage in bad weather—and steeled herself to go inside and face her children.

Shane was in the backyard, with the dogs, when she came around the side of the house on her way to the sunporch entrance.

Casey paused, gazing at him, trying to memorize the way he was right then, at that moment, poignantly aware that her son would be different tomorrow, and the day after that, and the day after that.

Look away from the boy, look back at the man. Her throat thickened.

"Hey, Mom," he said, as though it had been an ordinary day, with no mind-boggling revelations. Would there be a backlash at some point? Probably, Casey thought. She'd look into family counseling in the morning, though she knew both children would resist the idea.

"Hey," Casey answered when she could trust her voice.

"Where've you been?" Shane inquired. She detected a vaguely wheedling note in the question, knew he was about to make some kind of pitch—resuming the campaign to change his last name to match Walker's, most likely, or announcing that he wanted to live with his father.

"Doris's sister is in the hospital up in Seattle," she answered, sounding normal, even if she didn't feel that way. "I drove her to the plane."

"Oh," Shane said, absorbing that. At his age, Casey figured he was still largely preoccupied with the items on his own agenda, but Doris was practically a member of the family, and he was concerned. "Will her sister be okay?"

Casey was facing him by then, and her smile, though wobbly, was genuine. "I think so," she said. "Doris says Evelyn broke her hip, though, and that can be serious for an older person."

Shane nodded thoughtfully, ignoring the trio of dogs competing like silly jesters for his attention. "Yeah," he said.

"How about you?" Casey asked carefully after waiting out a few heartbeats. "Will **you** be okay, Shane?"

He sighed, and his expression remained pensive, even solemn. "I guess," he said. Then, "Do you think Walker wants me to have his last name, Mom?"

Casey's heart ached, but she'd had a lot of practice when it came to putting on an act, whether professionally or personally, and her facade didn't waver. "I'm sure he does," she said, very quietly. "Is that what you want, Shane?"

Rhetorical question. Of course it was—he'd already made that clear.

Shane searched her face, and, as so often happened these days, she caught a glimpse of the man he was turning into. "Will you feel bad if I do, Mom?" he asked earnestly. "I mean, **Elder** is a good name, too, and it's not like I'm ashamed of it or anything."

Casey wanted to hug her son just then, fiercely, the way she'd done when he was little and still receptive to mom moves, but she restrained herself, knowing that the moment was fragile, and the boy might be, too. "I won't feel bad," she told him. "I promise."

Shane looked relieved, but not completely satisfied. Night sounds were all around them, and somewhere nearby, an owl hooted, waking up after a long day's sleep in some hidden place. "When I asked if I could go and stay with Walker—Dad—for a while, it probably sounded like I didn't want to be with you anymore—"

He fell silent, shook his head once.

Casey stepped into the breach, the way she always did. In a one-parent household, a person had to be ready be **both** father and mother at a moment's notice.

"You want to get to know your dad.

That's natural, Shane." She paused, glanced up at the lighted windows lining the back of the gigantic house. Weary wistfulness overtook her for a second there, but she was quick to shake it off, because she had to be strong. "How's your sister doing?"

Shane sighed, shoved his hand through his hair in a way that was so like Walker that Casey's breath snagged in her throat. "She was okay while we were with Brylee, riding horses and eating supper at the burger place and stuff, but now she's all revved up in another major snit." He paused. "Why isn't Clare happy about this, Mom?" he asked, plaintive in his confusion. "We've always wanted a dad, and a kid couldn't have a better one than Walker, so why is Clare acting like somebody just detonated a nuclear bomb?"

Casey laid a hand on his shoulder, squeezed lightly. Maintaining her smile took more of an effort than before but, then, everything did. "I think she's confused, and maybe feeling cheated, too." That was a hard thing to get out, opening the door as it did to similar things that Shane might be feeling.

"I agree that you should have told us the truth, Mom," Shane said manfully. "But I know you must have had your reasons."

Casey stood on tiptoe and kissed her son's smooth cheek, blinking back tears. "I did have reasons, honey," she told him. "Lots of them. But I was still wrong, and I'm so sorry."

"It's okay, Mom," Shane said, awkwardly gracious. "Everybody does things they wish they hadn't."

"You know what?" Casey asked, mock-punching him in one shoulder, the way she did when she was proud of him, which was often. "You're sounding pretty grown-up, all of a sudden."

He beamed. Like most kids, few things pleased him more than being told that he was behaving like an adult. Why was that? Why were children so anxious to stop **being** children?

"Thanks, Mom," he said.

They went inside together, mother, son and dogs.

Clare wasn't in the kitchen, of course.

That would have been too easy, made her too accessible to her worried mother.

"Get some rest," Casey said to her son as she locked up and set the alarm. "This has been a big day."

Shane grinned indulgently and went up the back stairway, surrounded by dogs.

Casey waited awhile before heading upstairs herself, debating whether she ought to make another attempt to talk to Clare tonight or wait until morning.

Either way, she supposed, the girl would still be furious with her, and not without reason. This wasn't a brat fit, or teenage angst, after all—Clare had a legitimate gripe.

Five minutes later, Casey rapped lightly at her daughter's bedroom door.

"Go away," Clare called immediately—and predictably.

"Sorry," Casey chimed in reply. "No can do."

She waited, by no means certain that she wouldn't have to barge in.

After a few moments and a lot of bustling around, Clare opened the door a crack and peered out, none too pleased at the interruption. "I'm serious, Mom," she said. "I have nothing to say to you."

"Well," Casey replied evenly, "it just so happens that **I** have a few things to say to **you,** Clare Elder."

"That's Clare **Parrish,** if you don't mind," Clare snapped. She wasn't giving an inch, but she didn't shut the door in Casey's face, either.

"I don't mind, actually," Casey said. "That's up to you and Walk—your father."

"**Elder** is just a made-up name anyhow," Clare pointed out, staunchly petulant even in the face of peacekeeping forces. "A **show business** name."

The girl made the phrase **show business** sound like something to be ashamed of, which nettled Casey a little, but she wasn't about to take the bait. Besides, the part about their surname was true enough; the one she'd been born with was **Eldenberry,** which was not only a mouthful, but apparently an ample reason for the other girls at boarding school to make fun of her. In retrospect, it was hard to believe such a silly thing had ever mattered to her in the first place.

But it had.

She'd been lonely and homesick back then, admittedly for Lupe and Juan rather than for her grandparents, and even one friend would have made a huge difference in her life.

"Okay," Casey responded, agreeing to nothing, easing her way forward so that Clare had to either body-slam her or step out of the way and let her pass.

Fortunately, Clare wasn't the type to get physical.

"There's nothing you can say to make this better," Clare warned. Her TV was on, though the sound was muted, and both cats lay curled in the middle of her glass-and-chrome bed, peering warily over the folds in the comforter in case they had to make a fast exit.

Casey drew back the chair at Clare's desk, sat down. "I know," she said when she was darned good and ready. "But we can't stop talking to each other, either."

Clare plunked herself on her bed, careful not to sit on the cats, and folded her legs, yogi-style. She looked like an angry goddess about to rain lightning bolts over all the earth until it burned to a cinder and, though she didn't come right out and argue with Casey's statement, her message was crystal clear: **maybe** you **can't stop talking, but** I **can.**

Casey pulled in a deep breath and ratcheted up her smile, the way she did with snarky "reporters" stringing for the tabloids, or condescending interviewers with an obvious prejudice against country music and those who sang it.

"Maybe we could look at this from the bright side," she suggested. "You've always wanted a father, Clare. Now you have one. A very good one, as it happens."

"You lied to me," Clare reminded her stubbornly. "And as for Walker, I wanted a father who wanted **me,** not somebody who couldn't be bothered to mention that—**oh, yes**—I just happen to be his daughter."

"Walker had nothing to do with this, Clare. It was all **my** idea."

"'Nothing to do with it,' Mom? Get

real. I might be fourteen, but I know how babies happen." She blushed, her brows still lowered, her lower lip protruding slightly. "Other than when some chemist starts them in test tubes, that is."

"Clare, don't be mean. Lots of very good people can only have children by turning to modern medicine for help, and those children are as precious as any other human being."

Clare seemed to pull in her horns a little then—she wasn't a hard-hearted person—but it was obvious that Casey wasn't off the hook, and wouldn't be anytime soon. "I used to wonder what my donor dad was like," she said. "You know, if he was smart, if his eyes were the same color as mine, if my laugh was just like his mother's, or his sister's—"

Casey kept her chin up, but she couldn't hide her tears, or say a single word.

"And you know what?" Clare went on, remote and withdrawn again, speaking into a space just over Casey's right shoulder. "People would say I was being silly, because anybody could see that I got my brains from you, that my eyes are like yours, and my laugh is like yours, we have the same hair and even the same **voice.** No offense, Mom, but it was almost like they thought I didn't even **need** a father, because you'd conceived me all by yourself. And that, of course, is ultraweird unless you're Jesus."

Casey laughed, sniffled, snatched a tissue from the box on Clare's desk and dabbed at her eyes. So much for that last application of mascara, she thought. And how was a completely human and therefore imperfect mother supposed to react to a statement like the one her daughter had just made? With a sermon on the Virgin Birth?

Casey didn't have a clue, but she wanted to keep the conversation going because she sensed that if they stopped now, a door would close between them.

"Besides being angry with me," she persisted, "what are you feeling, Clare?"

Clare considered the question. "Hard to say," she replied eventually. "Mostly, I feel sad, I guess, and ripped off—like somebody gave a big party and didn't invite me."

She was taking a chance, she knew that, but Casey stood up then, walked over to Clare's bed, sat down beside her and slipped an arm around the girl's shoulders.

Clare stiffened slightly, but she didn't squirm away.

"I love you," Casey said very quietly.

"I know," Clare answered, just as quietly. "But I think I'm going to be mad for a while longer."

Casey smiled, kissed her daughter's temple. "That's okay," she said, choking up again. "We'll work through all this together, no matter how long it takes."

Clare nodded and swallowed hard, but she didn't say anything.

And that was Casey's cue to exit.

CHAPTER TEN

"Well, big brother," Brylee said peevishly the next morning as she set a coffee cup down on the table in front of Walker with so much force that some of the brew spilled over and burned his fingers, "you sure can keep a secret—I'll give you that."

Walker tried to smile, fell a little short of full wattage. "Why is it," he countered, "that you only wait on me when you're pissed off?"

Brylee dropped into the chair directly across from his. Decked out in her usual jeans, long-sleeved T-shirt and sneakers, with her hair twisted into a no-nonsense bun at the back of her head, she was dressed for the warehouse rather than the office, since that was where she spent most of her time. Not for her the high heels and custom-made power suits other lady CEOs probably favored.

Not that there were a whole lot of those running around Parable County, Montana, to provide him with a frame of reference.

"I wasn't 'waiting on' you," she pointed out crisply. "If you must know, my first and strongest inclination was to empty the cup over your head." The flush in her cheeks indicated that she was gathering steam. "All these years," she went on, "I've had a niece and a nephew, and you never bothered to tell me?"

Walker took a thoughtful sip of his coffee, grateful that he wasn't wearing it instead of drinking it. "Casey didn't want anybody else to know," he said reasonably. "And, anyway, I figured you'd guessed it on your own."

Brylee didn't touch her own coffee, nor was there any sign of breakfast, not that he'd expected her to cook for him or anything. Most mornings, though, she whipped up scrambled eggs or pancakes for herself, and shared them with him.

"I didn't have a clue," she said frankly, simmering down a little.

He hoped.

Walker said nothing, since excuses were all he had to offer, and he was having enough trouble with his conscience as it was.

"Why would Casey want to keep a secret like that?" Brylee asked, clearly not ready to let the subject drop, whether her brother had anything worthwhile to say or not.

A man of few words, Walker groped around inside himself for a viable reply. "She was just starting to make it as a singer at the time," he said finally. "I guess she thought I'd drag her to the altar, bring her back here to the ranch and keep her barefoot and pregnant for the rest of her life."

Brylee crooked a smile at that, but it was brief. In that getup, with no makeup on her face, she looked more like a teenager than the head of a company worth millions. "Don't try to put all the blame on Casey, Walker Parrish. You had a say in this, too. You could have spoken up at any time, with or without her blessing." She paused, and her throat worked visibly as she struggled with some private emotion. "Your daughter is devastated," she eventually went on. "And once Shane gets past the whoopee-I've-got-a-father-after-all stage, he's going to wonder why you didn't see fit to claim him and Clare a long time ago."

"I told you," Walker said, "Casey—"

But Brylee held up both palms like a referee, and blew the proverbial whistle. "Bull," she said flatly. "Since when have you ever danced to **anybody's** tune, including Casey Elder's? Nobody calls your shots but you, Walker, and **that** means that, on some level, you preferred to leave well enough alone instead of taking a stand."

"It isn't that simple," Walker said, but the words sounded lame, even to him.

Brylee didn't let up. "Isn't it?" she countered. "Face it, Walker. If you couldn't have things your own way—you and Casey married, living on this ranch, raising those kids according to some sitcom image of what a family ought to be rattling around in that hard head of yours—you were going to stand back with your arms folded and your back molars clamped together."

"That was colorful," Walker observed—once he'd unclamped his back molars so his tongue could function.

"What happens now?" Brylee demanded, cheeks pink with righteous indignation.

"Damned if I know," Walker admitted glumly.

"Well, you'd better **figure something out,** don't you think?"

Walker frowned. "Why are you all fired up about this? Aren't you even a little bit pleased to find out there's more to this family than you, me and our now-you-see-her-now-you-don't mother?"

"I'm **delighted,**" Brylee snarled, pushing back her chair and standing up so suddenly that she startled her ever-present sidekick, Snidely, in the process, sending him into a brief, skittering retreat. "But my feelings are **beside** the point right now, frankly, and so are yours and Casey's. Dammit, Walker, this is about **Clare and Shane!**"

"I never said it wasn't about them," Walker pointed out, getting to his own feet because, by God, when people yelled at him, his only sister included, he didn't take it sitting down. Not even when they were 99 percent right. "What the **hell** do you want me to do, Bry?"

Tears filled her eyes. "Give your kids a home," she said. "Give them a real family."

With that, Brylee grabbed up her purse, snatched her cell phone off the charger over by the coffeemaker and stormed out of the house. Snidely followed, pausing once to look back, sadly, at Walker and Doolittle.

Give your kids a home. Give them a real family.

Walker sank back into his chair. Did Brylee think he wanted to do anything else **but** that? He loved his children, always had, even before he found out that Clare, like Shane, was his own. Not a day had gone by without his thinking of them, and Casey, too.

But when you got down to brass tacks, he had to admit that Brylee had a point. He might not have been able to persuade Casey to marry him back then, in the thick of things, but he could have asked for—and **fought for,** if necessary—some kind of joint custody arrangement. He could have played a greater part in Clare's and Shane's lives—a much greater part.

He could have told them about their ancestors, shown them pictures in the photo albums, such as they were, let his children see parts of themselves—a smile, a set of the shoulders—in the images of those who had gone before.

He could have given his son and daughter that gift, if nothing else—the sense of continuity, of belonging, of being links in a chain that went way back.

Most of all, he could have **loved them,** openly, not in secret.

Maybe, Walker thought glumly, as all this came home to him and finally got through his thick skull, he wasn't so different from his always distant, hands-off mother. Maybe, deep down, he simply hadn't wanted to be bothered.

Or was it a matter of plain old run-of-the-mill cowardice? A subconscious fear that Clare and Shane, used to private jets and the best of everything, wouldn't have wanted what he had to offer—the country life, with chores and regular school and the kind of clothes ranch kids wore?

Hell, he thought. He was never going to figure **this** one out, especially if he stood there in his kitchen stewing about it.

He had to **do** something.

Walker summoned Doolittle, grabbed his hat from its peg and plunked it down hard on his head as he strode toward the door, still not knowing what that something was.

"Hey, Mom!" Shane yelled from the entryway. "Mrs. Dennison is here!"

Standing at the top of the front stairway, holding an armload of towels in need of washing—to her chagrin Casey hadn't been able to locate her own laundry chute, though she knew there was one, somewhere—she puzzled over the announcement for a moment, before her preoccupied brain translated **Mrs. Dennison** to **Opal.**

Being careful not to stumble, since she couldn't see her feet for the heap of towels, Casey hurried down the steps, dropped her burden nearby and stepped into the echoing foyer.

Opal stood there, grinning from ear to ear, a ratty old suitcase at her feet. She didn't seem to mind that all three dogs were sniffing at her luggage.

"I guess you must be wondering what I'm doing here, with half my worldly belongings," Opal said before Casey could manage more than a hello. The woman looked as pleased as a game show host about to award the big prize. "And the answer is, word got back to me that your Doris was called away on a family emergency, so I'm taking over for her."

In Parable, Opal Dennison was something of a legend. Wherever she went, tangled situations got **un**tangled in short order, and then there were the weddings.

Three of them, so far—that Casey knew of.

Yikes.

"Great," Shane interjected enthusiastically. "Does this mean we don't have
to eat Mom's cooking?"

Opal laughed, a deep, rich sound, full
of joy. "Now, I'm sure your mother is a
fine cook, young man," she scolded affably, "but she's probably got better
things to do than stand at the stove all
day."

"What about Joslyn and Slade?"
Casey managed to ask. After all, Opal
worked for them. "Don't they need you—
especially with another baby on the
way?" That morning, in an email exchange with Joslyn, she'd mentioned
that Doris had left town to look after her
injured sister, but she certainly hadn't
expected the Barlows to fork over their
housekeeper. She'd been venting, that
was all.

"They'll manage fine. They've got a
nanny these days, and they'll have to
learn to get by without me anyhow, since
I'm fixing to marry the Reverend Mr.
Beaumont next month." Opal slipped
out of her colorful spring jacket, hung it
neatly from one of the hooks on the

massive coat tree opposite the grandfather clock. "Not that I'm planning to lounge around watching soap operas after the wedding," she added briskly. "Being a preacher's wife is a full-time job in itself. Now, where should I put my things?"

Casey found her voice again. Nodded to Shane to handle the suitcase. "The downstairs guest room," she said, pointing toward the opposite side of the house. The little apartment off the kitchen had once been Opal's, she knew, but now it was Doris's domain, even though she was away for the time being.

Of course, Opal was aware of the guest room in question, having worked in the mansion for years as the employee of the first owners, the Rossiters, and she marched off toward it, Shane following with the suitcase, the dogs trailing behind like members of a circus parade.

As soon as they were out of sight, Casey rushed back, gathered up the pile of towels she'd dropped at the foot of the stairs and carried them into the laundry room, stuffing half of them into the washer, then stopping, peering at the knobs and switches, momentarily baffled.

In the end, it was a matter of common sense, of course, and she got the machine going. What she needed now was a cup of tea, to settle her down a little.

Just as Opal and Shane returned to the kitchen, Clare appeared, still clad in cotton pajamas and yawning behind one hand. Tendrils of her hair stuck out around her head like a coppery halo, making her resemble an angel in a Renaissance painting.

As if.

"It's about time you got up," Shane remarked, always ready with a jibe whenever he encountered his sister.

Clare made a face at him, and then turned a sunny smile on Opal, fit to bring a field full of wildflowers into bloom. For all the notice the girl paid Casey, however, she might as well have been part of the woodwork.

Opal proceeded to open a drawer, pull out an apron and tie it around her waist. "Looks like somebody ought to haul off and make some breakfast," she said, beaming, "before wholesale starvation sets in."

"Mom tried," Shane explained tolerantly, "but the oatmeal blew up in the microwave, and even the dogs won't eat it."

Casey gave her son a look, but it bounced off him like a bullet off the big **S** on Superman's chest.

Clare, still ignoring her mother, meandered over, peered into the microwave and said, "Yuck."

The word, one of her daughter's favorites, wasn't a cheery "Hi, Mom!" nor was it directed specifically to her, but Casey figured something was better than nothing.

"I was just about to clean up the mess—" Casey faltered, embarrassed. A domestic goddess she wasn't—she'd never had to be. Growing up at her grandparents' place, Lupe and her nieces had done all the household tasks, and as soon as she'd had two nickels to rub together, Casey had hired Doris.

Opal waved her away. "I don't mind doing it," she said. "Why don't you just relax for a few minutes, go on outside and admire all those beautiful flowers in the yard? I'll give a shout when the food's ready."

Clare was rooting around in the refrigerator, looking for a carton of yogurt. "Don't make anything for me," she said brightly, still refusing to acknowledge Casey's existence. "I'm on a diet."

"Diet," Opal scoffed. "Pish-posh. You'll have a decent meal, girl, and that's the end of it."

Remarkably, Clare straightened, shut the refrigerator door and stood there empty-handed, the yogurt evidently forgotten.

"Okay," she said meekly.

Casey stared for a moment. Who was this changeling, posing as her daughter? More to the point, what magic was Opal working? Was there an instruction book?

Instead of asking, she poured a cup of coffee, carried it out through the sunporch and onto the steps and did as she'd been told. She just sat there, admiring the flower beds, where roses bloomed, fat and velvety and wildly colorful, like a convention of aging madams, clad in their best outfits and meeting to compare notes and plan better brothels. The peonies—white and red, pink and candy-striped—were at the height of their brief but spectacular glory, enjoying one last hurrah before June gave way to July, while their lilac colleagues were already gone. The Gerbera daisies and the dinner-plate dahlias and the irises and the hearty zinnias flourished, though, belonging more to summer than to spring.

The beauty and the delicious blend of fragrances all but took Casey's breath away. Up until this moment, she realized with quiet chagrin, she'd barely even **noticed** the exquisite riot of color in her own backyard. She'd been too busy, but doing what?

She heard dog feet crossing the sunporch behind her, nails clicking on the tiles and the faint squeak of Shane's sneakers.

The Labs went by, one by one, brushing against Casey's shoulder as they passed. Then Shane sat down beside her on the step, watching fondly as the critters played tag and chased butterflies and rolled in the lush green grass.

Reveling in the fact that they were alive.

In that moment, Casey knew she could have walked away from her career, if not her music, even given up this mansion and her stock portfolio, fancy equipment, buses and glittering stage clothes, and still been perfectly happy, as long as she had her children, her dogs and cats, and plenty of flowers.

She thought of Walker, of the way he'd held her and made her body sing a song all its own, wordless and fierce, the day before.

Well, okay, **almost** perfectly happy, then.

She and Walker were like a pair of dancers, both determined to lead, constantly stumbling over their own and each other's feet, always a little out of step with the tune.

Nobody had everything, did they?

Shane broke the silence, and the

mood, with a chipper, "Would it be all right if I called Walk—Dad?" How long had he been working up his courage to ask her that?

"Now?" Casey stalled. Behind them, through the open door on the other side of the sunporch, Opal's and Clare's voices rose and fell, circled and finally interwove, like ribbons floating in midair, guided by a magician's wand.

"I have his cell number," Shane said, sounding mildly defensive.

Casey slipped an arm around Shane, but loosely, and was relieved when he didn't shrug her off, the way he sometimes did when there were other people around, especially kids his own age. "Go ahead and call your dad," she said with gentle humor. "You don't have to ask my permission to do that."

"I do if I want to ask him to let me go along next time he hauls stock to a rodeo," Shane said, not looking at her, but straight ahead, past the dogs and the flower gardens and the high wall at the back of the property. He was gazing, she surmised sadly, into a whole new world just opening its doors to him.

Casey set her coffee cup down beside her foot, moving with careful deliberation so she wouldn't spill the stuff. She didn't know a whole lot about what Walker actually did when he was on the road, besides hauling broncos and bulls from place to place, but she was clear on one aspect of it: he was usually gone for days at a time.

"Has he said anything about taking you with him, Shane?"

Shane shook his head. "Not recently," he admitted. "Back when Clare and I used to visit the ranch for a couple of weeks every summer, we talked about it once in a while. Walker said I'd have to wait until I was a little older." He paused, gave her a sheepish grin and spread his hands. "Well, now I'm older," he finished.

A twinge squeezed Casey's heart, and, much as she wanted to reach out and smooth Shane's sleep-rumpled hair with a motherly hand, she refrained. If Walker refused Shane's request to follow the rodeo, the boy would be crushed.

If he said yes, on the other hand, **she** would be crushed. She'd miss her son every minute of every day, and worry about him, too, and his departure, however brief the journey, would be the beginning of letting him go for good.

Her throat constricted.

"So, what's the word, Mom?" Shane asked, blithely oblivious to the fact that she was falling apart. Which, of course, was a good thing. "If Dad lets me go on the road with him, will you be cool with that?"

Hell, **no,** she wouldn't be cool with it, Casey thought. Walker worked with dangerous bucking horses and bulls bred to hurl cowboys skyward and then try to stomp them to a bloody pulp when they landed in the dirt. There was all that loading and unloading, and all those long and lonely roads.

Shane, eager to help his dad, and to prove himself, could so easily get hurt— **badly** hurt.

On the other hand, the rodeo business was as much a part of Shane's heritage as country music, wasn't it? She and Walker were like two very separate rivers, merging, and Clare and Shane were a blend of both. She'd been able to pretend for a long time that they were hers alone, but that was over.

Somehow, she had to accept that they were Walker's, too.

"Mom?" Shane prompted, determined to get an answer.

"If Walker says you can go, and he promises to make sure you stay safe," Casey forced herself to say, "then I'll deal with it. I can't say I'll be 'cool' with it, as you put it, but I'll deal." **Some-how.**

Shane grinned. "Fair enough," he said. Then he stood up, beanstalk gangly, and sprinted over to wrestle with the dogs, using up some of their spare energy and, hopefully, some of his own, as well.

If only he'd get too tired to fall in love with rodeo, Casey thought wryly.

No such luck. He was Walker Parrish's son, and that meant the cowboy life was in his blood.

Casey sat, her coffee forgotten, and instead of Shane roughhousing with the dogs, instead of her flower gardens, she saw a dusty arena surrounded by bleachers packed with rodeo fans.

She heard the auctioneer-like drone of the announcer's voice, saw a chute gate swing open and a bull explode through the gap, with a cowboy on its back, spurring hard while the animal spun and bucked.

The rider looked like Walker, but he wasn't. He was younger and leaner, with most of the hard spills still ahead of him.

He was her Shane, but Walker's, too.

Opal yanked Casey out of the vision with a hearty "Breakfast's on the table. Come and get it!"

The next few minutes were chaotic, what with all the bounding around of one boy and three dogs, Opal fussing cheerfully that she was going to trip over one of those critters and break her neck if they kept getting underfoot like that, Clare fully dressed, with her hair brushed and caught up in a clip on top of her head, her expression civil, if not exactly mom-friendly.

Once the meal was over, and the kids had cleared the table and loaded the dishwasher, Casey and Opal sat alone, in the blissful quiet, collecting their thoughts.

"See what you've gotten yourself into?" Casey asked her friend after a few moments, grinning as she lifted her coffee cup to her lips.

Opal chuckled. "Once it's just the reverend and me," she observed, "without kids and dogs and some sort of ruckus going on all the time, I'm not sure I'll know how to act."

"You'll figure it out," Casey said, confident of that much at least. "Did you say the wedding is scheduled for next month?"

"We just set the date," Opal answered with a nod. She paused to admire the respectable engagement ring gleaming on her left hand. When she looked up again, there was a hopeful expression in her eyes. "It'll be July 15—that's a Saturday—and we were wondering if you'd sing, the reverend and me. I know it's a lot to ask, you being famous and all, but, well, we thought—"

"Opal," Casey interrupted firmly. "**Of course** I'll sing. In fact, my feelings would have been hurt if you hadn't asked."

The beaming smile was back. "Thank you, Casey Elder," Opal said. A beat passed, and then the smile faded. "Now," she said, suddenly serious, "I'm just going to go right ahead and butt in where I've got no business sticking my nose. What's the holdup with you and Walker getting together?"

Casey couldn't answer for a few moments, she was so taken aback, though she knew she shouldn't have been surprised. Opal was famous—make that **infamous**—for her matchmaking, after all.

This time, though, she was definitely barking up the wrong tree.

"We're friends, that's all," Casey hedged. **Friends,** mimicked a voice in her head, as every cell in her body remembered the fevered intensity of their lovemaking, **with benefits.**

"How long do you think you're going to be able to keep **that** story rolling, once word gets around that you and Walker had two kids together?" Opal challenged, firmly but not unkindly.

Casey put one hand to the base of her throat. "Where did you hear—?"

"Your Clare told me just this morning," Opal replied matter-of-factly, "while I was making breakfast. Evidently, the news came as quite a shock to the child, though I'm sure she'll manage to wrap her mind around it soon enough, smart as she is. But right now, she's mighty rattled, and I guess I'm easy to talk to, because she poured out her heart to me."

Casey propped both elbows on the table's edge and buried her face in her hands with a weary groan.

"I hope you and Walker don't think those children are going to keep this to themselves," Opal went on, "because I might be the first person one of them told, but you can bet all those gold and platinum records you've rounded up that I won't be the last."

Opal was right, of course.

And it wasn't that Casey had expected Clare and Shane to pretend nothing had changed. She'd just been in so much emotional turmoil that she hadn't thought that far ahead, hadn't even considered that the community would inevitably find out and, after that, the media. Dear God, the media.

They'd have a field day, especially the tabloids, and Clare and Shane would be at the center of the scandal—through no fault of their own. And she'd been the one to bring it down on their innocent heads.

It was going to be awful, no two ways about it, and she might as well try to plug an erupting volcano with a wine cork as attempt to avert the red-hot lava of public scrutiny.

She needed to talk to Walker—come up with some kind of plan, though damage control was all they could hope for—and it had to happen **now.**

Casey scooted back her chair and made a beeline for the wall phone, only to find that Shane was already on one of the extensions. With Walker.

She broke right into the conversation, with all the subtlety of a stunt person somersaulting through a saloon window in an old Western movie. "Walker," she said. "We have to talk. **Right now.**"

* * *

We have to talk. Right now.

After issuing her grand summons, Casey hadn't waited for an answer, she'd simply hung up the phone, hard.

Shane had been the first to recover from the shock. "This is bogus," he'd said angrily. "Mom **just told me** I could go to the next rodeo with you if it was okay with you, and now she's already going back on her word!"

"I don't think she was referring to the rodeo," Walker had told his son with grim resignation. "You tell her to hold on—I'll be there as soon as I can."

"Do I still get to go rodeoing with you?"

Walker had given a dry chuckle at that. The boy had plenty of stick-with-it going for him, that was for sure. "My answer is still yes," he'd replied. "But your mother has a say, too."

After that, they'd said their goodbyes and ended the call.

Walker, who'd been tagging calves' ears all morning with some of the ranch hands, was wearing at least one layer of good Montana dirt, so, once he'd snapped his cell phone shut, he took the time to shower and change before he hoisted Doolittle into the truck and started for Parable.

Casey was pacing the driveway when he pulled in, better than half an hour later, and she looked four parts pissed off and one part scared out of her wits. If Clare and Shane were around, there was no sign of them, and the dog brigade wasn't in evidence, either.

Walker left Doolittle in the truck, got out and shut the door hard behind him.

"Where are the kids?" he asked, straight out, because, whatever Brylee or anybody else might think to the contrary, they were his first concern.

"Opal took them to the community center to swim in the pool," Casey answered, biting off the words. From her attitude, an objective observer might have gotten the impression that this powwow had been **his** idea, and she'd rather be doing something else.

Walker swept off his hat, swatted it against his right thigh and jammed it right back onto his head. "There's no need to get testy!" he growled, making an effort to keep his voice down.

Casey folded her arms. "You took the words right out of my mouth," she said acidly.

Walker leaned in until their noses were almost touching, and damn any neighbors who might be watching, fixing to carry the tale to every corner of the county. "What the **hell** is going on here?" he demanded. "If I hadn't been talking to Shane when you came on the line, I'd have thought something had happened to him or Clare!"

The green fire blazing in Casey's eyes cooled off a little. "We have to get married," she said.

Walker narrowed his eyes, thinking he must have heard wrong. **"What did you say?"**

She turned on one heel and hauled butt for the house, forcing him to follow.

"Dammit, Casey," he sputtered, furious because he had to tag after her like some schoolboy with his tongue hanging out. **"Talk to me."**

She waited until they'd reached the kitchen, then whirled on him, arms folded, feet so firmly planted that her heels might just leave dents in the floor.

"We have to get married," Casey repeated with elaborate enunciation, as though he was either deaf or didn't speak the language.

"I'll be damned," Walker muttered, taking off his hat and then, not knowing what to do with it, putting it on again. "You're pregnant? How can you know for sure, when it was only yesterday that the condom broke?"

Casey went white, then red again. **"The condom broke?"**

Walker sighed, and some of the fury seeped out of him. "I've got to change brands," he said.

That was when Casey laughed, though her eyes were still shooting green sparks and he knew he wasn't out of the figurative woods. Before he'd registered that she was amused, she turned again. "You weren't going to tell me?" she demanded.

He didn't have an answer.

And Casey didn't wait for one. "It'll be a marriage in name only, of course," she mused. "Just on paper."

Walker gaped for a moment, then rasped, **"What?"**

"We have to do this, Walker," Casey said, serious as a foreclosure notice now. "For Clare and Shane."

CHAPTER ELEVEN

Strange, Casey thought wearily, how everything could change without anything really being **different.** Sitting alone in the same wooden swing where Clare had taken refuge, barely a week before, on the porch of the house at Timber Creek Ranch, she went over it all in her mind—again.

Walker had been understandably shocked by her proposal of marriage, but once she'd explained her reasoning, he'd grudgingly agreed. When the story broke, it would reach far beyond the borders of Parable County, and Clare and Shane would take the brunt of it, become the objects of tabloid head-lines, the fodder for snide hosts on gossip TV, the prey of intrusive photographers and creeps who billed themselves as journalists.

A wedding wouldn't prevent that, of course, but both Casey and Walker were old-fashioned enough to believe that living under the same roof, as a family, would shelter their children from at least **some** of the fallout, and they couldn't live together without being legally married. Which was where the old-fashioned part came in.

So they'd quietly—**very** quietly—filed for a marriage license, not in Parable, the county seat, but in Missoula. Now the brief waiting period was over, and Opal's fiancé, the good Reverend Beaumont, had agreed to perform a simple ceremony in the ranch house living room, with Brylee, the kids and Opal in attendance. The hands and their families would be there, of course, along with very close friends.

It wouldn't be the wedding every girl dreams of, Casey reflected philosophically, sitting there in her simple blue sheath and sandals, but white lace and organ music and a fancy cake hadn't been in the cards for her and Walker anyway. Too much water under the bridge, as the old saying went, trite only because it had been true for so long. Besides, this wasn't exactly a love match—they both loved their **children,** no doubt about it, but the sad fact was, she and Walker didn't get along anywhere but in bed.

And that, by tacit agreement, was a place they'd been steering clear of since the last time.

The screen door opened just then, and Clare came out of the kitchen, looking pretty in a green sundress, with her hair tumbling around her shoulders in lovely spirals. She hadn't forgiven Casey for the deception yet, or Walker, either, for that matter, but she'd stopped pouting, slamming doors and hiding out in her room, anyway.

Sitting on the opposite end of the swing from Casey, Clare smoothed her skirt, bit her lower lip and said her piece, probably after much rehearsal.

"I know you don't really want to marry Walker, Mom. This whole thing is a sham—it's damage control."

Unlike her brother, who was thrilled about the marriage and already called Walker "Dad," Clare had shown a definite lack of enthusiasm from the first, and when she spoke to her father, which wasn't often, she still addressed him by his first name.

"We're doing what we think is best," Casey said calmly.

Clare had the good grace not to throw the big lie in her face, and Casey dared to hope she and her daughter would find common ground again soon. "What if it doesn't work?" she asked. "I mean, you'll probably throw the media off the trail, mostly anyway, but suppose you and Walker find out you can't live together and end up getting divorced? What do you think that would do to Shane?"

Casey had asked herself all the same questions. It was true enough that the scandal, just now starting to break online and in a few of the tabloids, would flare up, marriage or no marriage. And, thank heaven, it would fade into oblivion when a juicier story came along.

The deeper scars would remain, though. After the media circus moved on and set up their tents somewhere else, Clare and Shane would still be wondering what their friends thought, what it all meant. Their confidence in Casey, always rock solid before, might never be the same again.

"Whatever happens in the future," she replied carefully, "it's right now that's important. You and Shane will be legitimate, whether Walker and I stay married or not."

"'Legitimate'?" Clare echoed. She wasn't scoffing, but there was a jaded note in her voice just the same. "Please, Mom. That's so Victorian. This is the twenty-first century, and **lots** of kids' mothers aren't married to their dads."

Casey bristled a little. "Maybe so," she replied, "but that doesn't make it an ideal situation, not by any stretch. Two-parent families might not be as common as they used to be, and God knows, they're not perfect, but they're worth having, Clare. They're worth holding on to, worth fighting for."

"Why now?" Clare persisted, sounding honestly puzzled. "After all this time, I mean? In a few years, Shane and I will be grown up and away at college. What will it matter then if you and Walker are married?"

"It matters," Casey insisted quietly. "Someday, I hope you'll understand why."

And I hope I'll understand, too. Parts of the decision were still a mystery to her, and she suspected it was the same for Walker.

A short silence fell. In the near distance, horses whinnied and bulls snorted, pawing the ground and kicking up dust in their sturdy pens. There was a certain peace in the rustic ordinariness of it all, and Casey clung to that, like a blind person clutching a fragile thread that might just lead her into the light, if she could just hold on.

Clare's next remark was a humdinger.

She stood up, sighed a worldly sigh and said, without a hint of sarcasm, "I'll bet the **real** reason you and Walker are getting married is because you have to. Are you going to have a baby, Mom?"

Casey stiffened as though her daughter had just flung a bucket of cold water on her, and not just because the question caught her off guard. She might well be pregnant, given her and Walker's track record—and the broken condom. Neither of which she intended to discuss with her fourteen-year-old daughter, thank you very much, either now or in the foreseeable future.

"Your mother," Casey told the girl evenly, "is marrying your father. For now, that's all you need to know."

Clare spread her hands in a gesture of helpless resignation.

A string of cars and pickup trucks slowed down on the county road, the first of them turning in at the main gate. The wedding guests were arriving. There weren't many of them, only their closest friends.

"If there **is** a baby," Clare said, very softly, and with a note of wistfulness that bruised Casey's heart, "he or she is one lucky kid to be born with both a mom **and** a dad, and grow up here, on this ranch." With that, Clare vanished into the house.

Casey stood, but only after a few moments had passed and she was sure she could trust her wobbly knees to hold her up. At any other time, she would have caught up with Clare, tried to reach the girl with words or hugs—or something.

But, like it or not, that conversation would have to wait. There was a wedding in the offing, and the guests were here.

The various vehicles reached the top of the driveway, one by one, and people in dress clothes got out—Opal and the Reverend Walter Beaumont were the first, soon followed by Joslyn and Slade Barlow, Boone and Tara Taylor and Hutch and Kendra Carmody. Patsy McCullough brought up the rear, at the wheel of a specially equipped van, her son Dawson riding with her.

Only Hutch looked uncomfortable, and that wasn't surprising, considering that Timber Creek Ranch was Brylee's home as well as Walker's. Hutch and Brylee had come within an I-do of getting married themselves, a couple of years before, and accounts of the inter-rupted ceremony still surfaced occa-sionally, when there was a lack of fresh gossip.

Brylee was inside somewhere, prob-ably as nervous as Hutch, but this was one wedding she wouldn't dodge, since the groom was her brother.

Casey welcomed everyone with a smile and a hug, especially Joslyn and Tara and Kendra, her closest friends, while Slade and Hutch stayed behind to help Patsy with Dawson and his wheel-chair.

"When's that baby coming?" Casey asked Joslyn in a whisper after the crowd had come inside the house and moved on toward the living room, where the ceremony was to be held. Kendra lingered with them, smiling.

Joslyn sighed happily, resting her hands on her enormous belly. **"Babies,"** she corrected, sotto voce. "We're hav-ing twins. Both boys."

Casey hugged her again. "That's great!"

Joslyn nodded, beaming.

"Are you ready to get married?" Kendra asked Casey, looking as pleased as if this wedding were the real deal, instead of a public-relations move and a too-little, too-late attempt to set a few things right.

"About as ready as I'm ever going to be, I guess," Casey responded. Very few people knew the truth, but Joslyn, Kendra and Tara were among them, and not one of them had tried to talk her out of it. In fact, they actually seemed **happy** for her and Walker.

They were so certain things would work out. Casey herself, not so much. All she could do was try her hardest, dig in her heels and refuse to give up.

"What about a honeymoon?" Joslyn asked.

Casey kept her expression bland, because there were some things she wasn't ready to reveal, even to her best friends. Such as, there wasn't going to be a **wedding night,** let alone a honeymoon. "That's a secret," she said mysteriously.

Joslyn and Kendra exchanged glances, then proceeded into the living room, to seat themselves on rented folding chairs. Their husbands soon joined them.

Casey waited in the kitchen, wringing her hands a little, until Shane was beside her. Handsome in his best suit, which he was about to grow out of, he jutted out an elbow. "Showtime, Mom," he whispered, grinning. "Ready to be given away?"

A lump formed in Casey's throat. She smiled and brushed a lock of hair back from Shane's forehead, a gesture he normally wouldn't have appreciated. "Ready," she managed.

Shane escorted his mother out of the kitchen, through the formal dining area and into the wide, arched doorway leading to the living room, where they stopped.

Walker and Reverend Beaumont stood in front of the flower-festooned fireplace, Walker looking dazed, the minister all smiles.

The folding chairs were filled, and Opal had taken her place at the piano, her fingers poised to play the customary processional.

A hush fell over the gathering, and Joslyn, Kendra and Tara all turned in their seats simultaneously and gave Casey a perfectly synchronized thumbs-up.

Brylee, the only bridesmaid, stood up front, a little to the minster's right, smiling encouragement at Casey and Shane.

Careful not to look too closely at Walker—no getting around it, he was one handsome hunk of cowboy—Casey swept one last glance around the room, her heart pounding a little, looking for Clare, praying her daughter hadn't decided to hide out somewhere until the "sham" was over.

But Clare was made of better stuff than that. Whatever her misgivings, she walked, head high, into the living room through another archway, and stood next to Opal, by the baby grand piano. Tears stung the backs of Casey's eyes as she realized the implications of that.

Clare, who never sang in public, was going to sing today. It was her gift to Casey and to Walker.

Opal began to play.

Casey froze, and Shane had to give her a little tug to get her moving, between the rows of folding chairs and up to Walker's side.

Walker looked down at Casey, his eyes shining, and the smallest smile crooked the corner of his mouth.

The piano went still, then started right up again.

Casey and Walker both turned to watch as Clare began her solo, a song Casey had written long ago, as a sort of lullaby for her children. Though it was about the forever kind of love, and not about sleeping, she'd sung those words to Clare and Shane a thousand times, on buses and airplanes and in backstage dressing rooms, always at bedtime.

Now, listening to Clare's beautiful voice, Casey thought she might just burst with love and pride, and she knew, after a sidelong glance his way, that Walker was feeling pretty much the same.

When the song ended, Clare took her place up front, next to Brylee, and Brylee wrapped an arm around her niece, gave her a squeeze and whispered something to her.

Casey felt an achy surge of love for both of them.

Everything after that seemed to happen in slow motion, in the midst of a silvery haze.

Reverend Beaumont made a little speech laced with Bible references but otherwise a blur, as far as Casey was concerned.

The usual questions were asked.

The usual vows were exchanged.

It never crossed Casey's mind to say anything but the expected "I wills" and "I dos," and Walker didn't hesitate, either. They slid matching gold bands onto each other's ring fingers when prompted.

And then the minister pronounced them man and wife, and Walker, eyes twinkling, pulled Casey close and kissed her soundly—so soundly that, if he hadn't been holding her firmly by the waist, her knees might have buckled.

The guests cheered, and Shane, in a momentary lapse of preteen dignity, jumped high in the air, jamming one fist toward the ceiling, and yelled, "Yes!"

That made everybody laugh, including Casey, though she still felt like an actress, playing a part in a made-for-TV movie. Nothing seemed real—except for the echo of Walker's kiss, that is. Her mouth tingled at the recollection, and for a very long time afterward, even as the time-honored rituals continued.

Casey and Walker posed for photographs, endlessly, it seemed to her.

They cut the impressive cake Brylee had stayed up half the night to bake and decorate, and congratulations came from all sides. There was a group phone call from the guys in the band, all of them talking at once and finally coming together to sing a rowdy song that made Casey laugh and cry at the same time.

Even Mitch, who hadn't been in contact since he'd left Casey's place in a huff after she'd turned down his proposal, sent a short video, via Shane's cell, wishing the newlyweds well.

Casey was both pleased and touched, knowing Mitch's pride would have made the gesture difficult for him, to say the least. In a few days, she'd call her manager back and try to smooth things over. They'd been over bumpy ground before—Mitch periodically threatened to resign and then changed his mind later—and Casey genuinely hoped this time would be no different from the others.

After the refreshments, the hugs and handshakes and digital photos, guests began to leave, a few at a time.

Dawson McCullough, dressed up in a suit, wheeled over to Casey and Walker and, with a big smile, congratulated them. Patsy, hovering behind his chair, said nothing, but added a shy nod of agreement. Walker and Shane followed them out, to help Dawson into the van and stow the wheelchair in back.

Glancing around, still trying to come to terms with the incomprehensible fact that she and Walker were really and truly **married,** Casey spotted Hutch and Brylee standing near the piano, talking earnestly.

Kendra appeared at Casey's side, watching the exchange with quiet approval.

"What's that about?" Casey asked, worried. When it came to Hutch Carmody, her otherwise amenable sister-in-law was notoriously stubborn and prone to making scenes.

Kendra took a sip of punch from the crystal glass she held in her right hand. Swallowed. "Some fence mending, I hope," she replied. "Hutch never wanted to hurt Brylee, and we've all been worried about her." A pause, during which Kendra's perfect eyebrows drew closer together for a moment in apparent consternation. "Plus, it's awkward. You and Joslyn and Tara and I are all friends, and now you're married to Walker, which means we'll all be running into each other even more often than before. Unless we all want to walk on eggshells forever, somebody had to do something."

"You know what?" Casey said, touching her friend's arm. "You're amazing. A lot of women in your place wouldn't be so open-minded. Some of them might even be jealous."

Kendra smiled, serene as a Christmas-card Madonna. "There are a lot of uncertainties in this world," she responded, "but there's one thing I'm definitely sure of. Hutch Carmody loves me as much as I love him, and that isn't going to change."

Casey swallowed as, once again, the backs of her eyes stung with tears she wasn't about to shed. What would it be like, she wondered, to love a man like that, and be loved the same way in return? Kendra knew. So did Tara and Joslyn. Would it ever be that way for her?

Presently, Hutch left Brylee's side and came to collect Kendra. He kissed Casey's cheek, congratulated her one more time, and they left.

Casey waited a few beats, then made her way through the dwindling crowd to Brylee's side.

She was standing with her back to the room by then, gazing out the picture window toward the green hills, and Casey, looking at her sister-in-law in profile, saw a single tear slip down Brylee's cheek.

"I'm here," Casey said gently. Sometimes, that was all one person could offer another, just their presence.

"Thank you," Brylee answered with a sniffle. "I've been such a fool," she added softly, a few moments later.

"What do you mean?" Casey asked, frowning a little. Love was love, and even when it didn't end with happily-ever-after, it was nothing to be ashamed of.

Brylee surprised her then, turning her head to bestow a wide, watery smile. She seemed illuminated from the inside. "Hutch always said I was in love with love, not with him, and, finally, I believe him."

"He must have said something pretty special just now," Casey speculated.

Brylee laughed. "Not really," she replied happily. "He told me to grow up, stop feeling sorry for myself and get a life."

Casey's mouth fell open, just briefly. "And you didn't slap his face?"

Brylee was actually glowing. "No," she said. "Because I realized he was right on all counts. I also realized that, while he might be **Kendra's** Prince Charming, he's all wrong for me. Not exactly a frog, since there's no denying the man's easy on the eyes, but we'd have gone bust sooner or later, for sure, and we'd both have had a few warts and wounds to show for it."

Casey didn't know what to say, but she was stricken with admiration, and she supposed it showed, because Brylee gave her a quick hug and laughed again.

"Time to round up the kids and head for town," she said. "That menagerie of yours will be waiting at the ole mansion."

Brylee had offered to spend a few days at Casey's house, looking after Clare and Shane and the dogs and cats, so the bride and groom could be alone together, in lieu of a honeymoon.

Since the marriage was a matter of convenience, rather than mad, passionate love, a part of Casey dreaded the moment when she and Walker were the last men standing—so to speak—but another part of her was intrigued, even eager.

"Give me a second with Clare first," she told Brylee, who nodded and went off to speak with the last of the departing guests.

Casey found her daughter sitting on the piano bench, idly plunking out the bare-bones version of "Heart and Soul" with one index finger. Considering that she could play Chopin without sheet music, not to mention a rendition of

"Great Balls of Fire" that would have impressed Jerry Lee Lewis himself, Clare was playing for herself, not for anyone's entertainment.

Casey slid onto the bench beside her daughter and played the other half of the time-honored duet.

Clare glanced at her, smiled shyly and showed what she could do.

When the song ended, Walker, Brylee and Shane, standing in a semicircle behind Clare and Casey, applauded.

Casey leaned over, rested her forehead against Clare's and whispered, "No matter what, sweetheart, you'll always be my baby girl. Please don't forget that."

Clare's eyes filled with tears, and her smile dazzled. "I'm still pretty mad at you," she responded softly. "Will you still love me when I finally get over it?"

Casey kissed the girl's cheek with the kind of smack only a mom can get away with. "You can take it to the bank," she promised. "I will love you forever and ever."

Clare chuckled. "Amen," she said.

After that, Casey hugged Shane goodbye and reminded him to behave himself, and then Brylee herded her niece and nephew out of the house and into her SUV.

Only Casey and Walker remained once the door closed behind those three.

And, of course, Doolittle, who seemed relieved that things might be returning to normal.

With an audible sigh, the dog curled up in front of the cold fireplace, settled his bones and drifted off to sleep.

Walker chuckled, took Casey's hand and led her through the house to the kitchen, where she collapsed into a chair and kicked off her dress shoes.

"We did it," she said with a sigh comparable to Doolittle's.

Walker grinned, arched one eyebrow and undid his tie, then the top buttons of his dress shirt. "Champagne, Mrs. Parrish?" he asked, lifting one of the half-filled bottles off the counter and holding it up for her inspection.

"Don't mind if I do, Mr. Parrish," Casey answered. She was accustomed to wearing either sneakers or boots, and those shoes had been pinching like crazy ever since she'd put them on.

He filled champagne flutes—plastic ones, from the supermarket—for both of them, carried them to the table.

After setting the glasses down, Walker sat, lifted one of Casey's feet onto his lap and began to massage away the ache.

Casey groaned with pleasure. If the man was trying to seduce her, he was on the right track.

Walker chuckled, enjoying her reaction. "So what do we do now?" he asked lightly. "Play checkers? Watch TV? Build on a couple of bedrooms for the kids?"

Casey moaned again, but the sound was part laugh. Dear God, Walker's fingers were magic, and not just in bed. She'd forgotten how he could melt her simply by rubbing her feet. "For now," she replied in a near croon, eyes closed, "let's just keep doing this."

"I'm doing all the work," Walker complained with a smile in his voice. "You're just sitting there, shamelessly enjoying my husbandly attentions."

"Mmm," Casey agreed, almost floating.

After Walker had turned that foot into a quivering heap of jelly, he started in on the other one.

"Our daughter has quite a singing voice," he said. "Is she planning to follow in your illustrious footsteps?"

Casey chortled without opening her eyes, even as she felt a mild pang of sadness. Clare was Walker's child, as much as her own, and there was so much he didn't know about her, or Shane, for that matter.

"No way," she answered. "Clare wants to be a veterinarian. She's had all the show business she wants for one lifetime."

"How about you?" Walker asked, with a deceptive note of nonchalance. "Where do you stand on the issue of show business, Casey Jones?"

Casey opened her eyes, studied him. She might be tired of the road, tired of waking up in one city and going to sleep in another, never quite sure which town was which, but she knew she'd never completely retire. Music was in her blood, and there were times when she needed to be onstage, needed to engage with an audience.

"Is it a deal breaker?" she asked. Her lifestyle, after all, was night-and-day different from Walker's. He liked ranch life, with the occasional rodeo thrown in for spice. And she liked singing, sometimes in church, sometimes in the shower and sometimes onstage in a sold-out arena.

"I'm not trying to close any doors in your face, Casey," Walker assured her quietly. "I'm just wondering how we're going to proceed from here, that's all. We haven't talked about that much."

"No," Casey agreed. "There's a lot we haven't talked about."

One corner of Walker's very inviting mouth quirked upward. "We're a pretty unconventional pair, I'll say that for us."

Casey nodded. "We are indeed," she agreed. "Any regrets, cowboy?"

"Only that we didn't do this sooner," he answered. He sighed. "Get married, I mean. Shane's all right with having an instant dad, at least on the surface, but Clare isn't planning on letting bygones be bygones anytime soon, as far as I can make out."

"You're right about that," Casey answered.

He raised an eyebrow, his expression wry. "Wait a minute," he joked. "Did I just hear you say I'm **right** about something?"

She laughed, which was ironic, since she was close to tears. "What if some woman comes along," she began, unable, for some reason, to keep from poking at her own sore places, "and you fall head-over-bootheels for her, and here you are, tied down with me?"

Walker's expression turned solemn, but a sparkle soon leaped into his eyes. "I don't foresee that happening," he drawled.

Casey's heart picked up a little speed. It wasn't an "I love you," but she was reassured anyway. Mustn't get too comfortable, though.

"We're not having sex," she said.

Walker chuckled, shook his head. "Hell, woman," he said, "we're married, aren't we? Shouldn't some part of this crazy situation be fun?"

She pulled her foot from his lap, reached for her champagne flute and downed the lukewarm contents in a couple of gulps. Suddenly, she was all too conscious of the fact that they were alone in the house, and Walker was hot, and they were wearing each other's wedding bands.

Not to mention that his bed was just a few rooms away.

"**Now** what's gotten under your hide?" Walker asked, frowning.

"It's still light out," Casey said, ignoring his question. "If it's fun you want, let's saddle up a couple of horses and ride."

Maybe on horseback, she could behave herself. Outrun the temptation she was feeling now.

Why not just go to bed with Walker?

Because when Walker made love to her, she lost complete control, and that terrified her. She was all about living up to the image of Casey Elder she held in her mind, about standing strong, marching to her own drumbeat, setting goals and meeting them, making decisions and abiding by them. When she was in

Walker's arms, she became another person entirely, a stranger, willing to bare her soul, show her deepest needs and emotions.

And that scared her half to death.

She waited for Walker's answer, knew that if he held her, or kissed her, or even started rubbing her feet again, for pity's sake, she'd be lost.

Finally, he sighed, shoved back his chair and stood.

"All right," he said, with more resignation than enthusiasm. "Let's change clothes and go saddle ourselves some horses."

The few things Casey had brought along were in a nearby guest room, still packed away in a small suitcase.

She went off to swap her wedding dress and pantyhose for jeans and a long-sleeved T-shirt, and when she got back to the kitchen, Walker was already back from his own room, clad in regular clothes. He'd even had time to brew a cup of coffee, and he smiled over the rim before setting it aside on the counter.

His gaze glided over her, leaving fire in its wake.

"You sure do fill out a pair of jeans just right, Mrs. Parrish," he said.

Casey made a face, though she was secretly pleased by the compliment, as casual and offhand as it had been.

Leaving Doolittle behind to recover from the festivities, they left the house together, heading for the barn.

No one was around—even the ranch hands were elsewhere, though they'd been present for the wedding—and yet there was a feeling in the air that made Casey uneasy. Stopping in the yard, she turned in a full circle, very slowly, looking for the source of her discomfort.

Sunlight flashed off something in one of the nearby oak trees, a silvery glint, and that was when Casey spotted the reporter, lurking in the high branches. She muttered a very unladylike word and headed in that direction, fists clenched.

Rapid clicks sounded as the sneak took pictures.

Walker, keeping pace, tilted his head

back, adjusted his hat and grinned. "I'll be damned," he said.

This kind of intrusion was new to him, but Casey was anything but amused. "Get down from there before you break your darn fool neck!" she ordered, looking around again as the branches rustled and shook overhead. Where there was one photographer, in her experience, there were a dozen.

Worse, that particular tree was situated close enough to the house to provide a clear view of the living room, where the ceremony had taken place.

"This is a free country," the tree man argued, sounding braver than he probably was. "There's the First Amendment—and freedom of speech—"

"Don't you lecture me on the Bill of Rights, you jackass," Casey shot back. "It just so happens that I have a few rights of my own!"

Walker chuckled again. He was loving this, which only made Casey more furious.

"You carrying a gun, cowboy?" the spy asked warily. A round, bespectacled face peered down at Walker through the foliage.

"No," Walker answered affably, "but I could lay my hands on one in short order, if I were so inclined." He paused. "If I were you, buddy, I'd get the hell out of here before this redhead decides to climb right up there after you and smash that camera of yours over your head."

More branches shifted and creaked, and the photographer, a portly sort who had, in Casey's view, defied gravity as well as good manners by hauling himself up into that tree in the first place, made his way down.

Backing away quickly, he huffed, "Don't let her get me!"

And then he turned and ran for his life.

CHAPTER TWELVE

Walker was practically doubled over laughing as he watched the pudgy, tree-climbing. reporter making an awkward dash for the tall timbers, but Casey was **not** amused. While she understood that tabloid stringers and photographers had a right to earn a living like everybody else, she'd had so many private moments interrupted or flat-out ruined over the course of her career that she'd run out of patience a long time ago.

It only made matters worse that, since settling in Parable, she and the kids had enjoyed a certain slackening of media attention, though they'd never been entirely free of it, and now, as she'd expected and feared, the semihiatus was obviously at an end. Game on.

Time to shift emotional gears from neutral to overdrive. **Again.**

Folding her arms, Casey sighed and watched balefully as the reporter finally disappeared into a stand of brush down by the main road. Moments later, a car engine started up with a roar, soon followed by the screech of tires as he tore out of there.

Walker, quiet now, slipped an arm around Casey's shoulders—which, she realized with a stab of annoyance, were trembling. She'd better buck the heck up, she thought, because the die was cast and, by God, **her children** weren't going to come out on the losing end.

"Case," her new husband said, very quietly and with a gentleness that was very nearly her undoing, "it's **all right.** He's gone."

"For now," Casey conceded grudgingly. She did let Walker hold her close against his side, though, and it felt good not to be alone, not to have to be strong, if only for a few moments. **Too good.**

"Let's go for that ride," Walker said, steering her toward the barn.

Casey looked around, but she knew they were by themselves, at least in terms of sneaky reporters. It was small comfort, because there **had** been others, of course. They'd simply been faster than Tarzan of the Oak Tree—by now, they were probably in Three Trees, behind the doors of their cheap motel rooms, swilling beer and congratulating themselves, anticipating the fat checks they'd soon be banking. Thanks to modern technology, they'd probably already zipped very personal photos and wildly speculative stories about Casey, Walker, the children and the wedding itself off to waiting editors.

"What if we're followed?" Casey fretted. Secretly, she'd entertained a fantasy that she and Walker might consummate their marriage after all, somewhere out there under the big sky, sheltered by venerable trees and high grass, with their horses grazing peacefully nearby.

Now, of course, sex in the tall grass

was out of the question. The thought of their being seen making love, let alone **photographed,** chilled her blood.

"Don't be paranoid, Casey Jones," Walker counseled with an easy grin. His arm was still around her shoulders, strong and sure, and they had almost reached the barn door. "If that guy was an example of his breed, they won't be following us on horseback, and we'd hear anything with a motor from a long way off."

Casey nodded, biting her lower lip, but she was still thinking that such things were easy enough for **Walker** to say, because he'd never been stalked, never had to console disappointed children after an innocent and entirely ordinary outing—a birthday party, an afternoon movie, a visit to a zoo or a theme park— had been spoiled, cut short by obnoxious photographers and pseudojournalists.

He'd probably never had to watch Fourth of July fireworks or the New Year's Eve countdown on a hotel TV, instead of celebrating in person, or attend weddings and christenings and even fu-

nerals in the company of several bodyguards, because there had been a rash
of death threats.

While she pondered these recollec-
tions, Walker saddled a gelding named
Smokey for her and then Mack, the
buckskin, for himself.

Back outside, in the afternoon sunshine, he gave Casey a leg up into the
saddle. She'd been too preoccupied to
prove that she could damn well mount a
horse on her own, whatever he thought
of her riding skills.

Walker swung onto Mack's sturdy
back and they were on their way, passing between the horse pasture and the
bull pens and on into an open field, rippling with sweet-scented grass. The sun
was warm on their backs, and the stur-
diness of horse flesh and the creak of
leather began to calm Casey's nerves,
degree by degree.

"Tell me what life's been like for you,"
Walker said quietly, resettling his hat as
he spoke, and reining Mack in a little to
keep pace with the more sedate Smokey.
"Not the visits to the White House, or
being named Entertainer of the Year all

those times, stuff like that—but the nitty-gritty, day-to-day things."

The response that leaped to Casey's mind was "lonely," interestingly enough, but she didn't say it. For one thing, she was too proud, too attached to her independence and the strength she made it a point to project, even when she didn't feel it.

For another, she knew Walker was still thinking about the reporters and photographers, not the good ones, the courteous professionals, of whom there were many, but the intrusive, obnoxious types who apparently lived to invade her privacy and that of her children. **Those** people, mostly men, though there were a few women in the mix, could put a scurrilous spin on something as simple as a picnic in the park or a routine stint in the hospital.

Outdoor meals with the band members and their families became cult meetings, and a bad case of strep throat, complicated by exhaustion brought on by weeks on the road and requiring IVs and medical observation, could be twisted into a secret abortion. Casey could handle being the target of that kind of gossip, but it wasn't always directed at her alone—sometimes Clare was dragged into it, and even Shane had been credited with a serious drug problem.

Casey told Walker those stories, and a few others, as they rode, and difficult though some of it was, she felt relieved just to vent to this quiet, nonjudgmental man, listening attentively to every word she said.

That was a new experience, mostly. She'd discussed such things with Mitch, and with the guys in the band, but only because they'd usually witnessed the incidents for themselves, so there was no hiding it from them. The bodyguards and members of law enforcement encountered in the course of her travels were **paid** to care what happened to Casey Elder and her children, though they were unlikely to have any real emotional investment in possible outcomes.

Joslyn, Kendra and Tara, new friends and yet among the best she'd ever had, would have sympathized, of course, but burdening them with problems brought on by her own public persona seemed unfair. After all, prying eyes and wagging tongues were part of the deal—by choosing fame, riding tall in the figurative saddle, she'd made herself a lightning rod.

All of which meant that Casey had always carried most of the load herself, and tried not to complain about the effort, even in the sanctuary of her stubborn soul.

By the time she'd finished the tale, she and Walker had reached the tumbled-down cabin in the hills, the site of his forebears' nineteenth-century homestead, via a different route than before.

Only then, when he'd dismounted and reached up to help Casey down off Smokey's wide back, did Walker offer a comment on the long and complicated diatribe.

"Things are going to be different now," he said, facing her, the reins still in their hands, their bodies not quite touching as they stood there in all that quietness, surrounded by the singular gifts of a big sky summer—the cloudless, overarching canopy of watercolor blue in a shade so tender it bruised the heart to look up at it; warm, soft breezes, caressing the flesh like the touch of an angel's fingertips; the faint, perfect fragrances of wildflowers and old-fashioned peonies; the occasional chirp of an unseen bird, guarding its nest in one of the trees.

Casey must have looked a little skeptical at Walker's words, because, seeing her expression, he gave a low chuckle and planted a light, swift kiss on her forehead.

"Things are going to be different," he reiterated without a trace of male arrogance, "because I'll be around. I figure if one of those guys gets out of line, all I have to do is make an example of him, and the others will get the message."

Casey opened her eyes wide. "You don't mean you'd **punch** one of them or something like that?"

"I mean," Walker clarified, in all sincerity, "that I'll do whatever is necessary to keep my wife and my children safe."

"Oh," Casey said. While she didn't believe that violence, the bare-fisted cowboy kind or any other, was an acceptable solution, a part of her definitely

liked the idea that anybody who meant her or the kids harm would have to get by Walker Parrish first.

Only a fool would even make the attempt.

But, then, fools had never been in short supply, now, had they?

"There's something else I've made up my mind about, Case," Walker added, cupping her chin in his hand. The spark remained in his eyes, but it was one of passion now, of quiet but unshakable conviction, not amusement. "We got married for Clare and Shane's sakes—I understand that. But if you're sleeping in one room and I'm in another, well, that sort of defeats the whole purpose, mostly because of the message it sends—that we're together but separate. We might as well have skipped the whole process of getting hitched, if that's how it's going to be."

Casey's heart picked up speed until it was racing. She knew Walker was right, but sharing his bed every night was a huge risk in itself—she'd be vulnerable, and not just sexually, because her mind and soul would be laid bare to him, as well as her body.

The spirit might be willing, but the flesh was weak. Hell, the flesh—**her** flesh—wasn't just weak, it was flagrantly **wanton.** Given a voice, every part of her would have been shouting a hallelujah chorus of "Bring it on, cowboy!"

"Sex wasn't part of the deal," she reminded him, somewhat lamely.

He kissed her, not in the way he did when he fully intended to seduce her, on the spot, but with reassuring affection. "True enough," he said. Then, after an agreeable pause, he asked, "When was the last time I forced myself on you, Casey Jones?"

She straightened her spine, set her hands on her hips. She knew a full-court press when she was the object of one. "That's just the trouble," she retorted. "You don't **have** to drag me off into your cave by the hair. All **you** ever have to do, Walker Parrish, is **touch** me in the right places—and, dammit, you know just where those places are!"

He laughed, pushed his hat to the

back of his head and countered, "Doesn't that tell you something?"

"It tells me," Casey answered, going on pure bravado, "that when you turn on the charm, my clothes tend to fall off. It's all bliss—until I come to my senses again."

"That," Walker responded affably, "sounds like a personal problem."

"How do you figure that?" Casey snapped. More bravado. Things were melting inside her, expanding, getting ready.

"I'm your husband," he reminded her, not in a demanding way, but as a person stating a simple fact. "Therefore, it's my prerogative to 'turn on the charm,' as you put it, but all it would take to put the brakes on is a simple **no** from you, and you know it. I might be about as cordial as a wounded bear for a while, but I'm not going to barge in—so to speak—where I'm not wanted."

Casey merely stared at him, at a loss for words, furious because every single thing he'd said was true. Saying **no** was **her** responsibility, when push came to shove, not his.

And she was no damn good at saying **no** to Walker Parrish. She had two children, a skittish heart and a twitch in the pit of her stomach to prove it.

"I'll sleep with you," she finally said. "But you have to promise not to touch me."

"Sorry, lady," Walker answered, clearly enjoying her discomfort, "but that's a promise I can't make."

"Whatever happened to win-win negotiations?" Casey demanded, flustered, thinking she'd faint if her heartbeat didn't slow down soon.

Walker smiled, but his eyes and the set of his jaw remained serious. "I've done things your way for a long time," he told her after mulling the words over silently for a few moments. "But the way I see it, marriage is a partnership, and that means you're going to have to do some things **my** way, Mrs. Parrish. And sharing my bed is one of them."

"What about my right to say **no?**"

"You can refuse," Walker said easily, "but you'll have to pack up your stuff and move back to the mansion if you do. Either we're husband and wife or we're not. Make a choice."

Casey felt her face flush with heat. She was in that storied place—between a rock and a hard place. And she was stuck.

"Is this an ultimatum?" she challenged, though she felt anything but tough-minded at the moment.

Walker considered the question for longer than she would have liked. Then he adjusted his hat, crooked a grin at her and said, "Not exactly. I'm definitely hoping you'll decide to stay right here on the ranch with me, but if you insist on celibacy, well, then, I guess we've got a standoff."

She huffed out a breath, folded her arms again, glared up at her hardheaded husband. She wouldn't have chosen to marry Walker, since they didn't get along most of the time, now being a case in point, but she couldn't begin to imagine being anybody **else's** wife, either. Never had imagined it, actually, for all that she'd longed for a real home and an old-fashioned family setup.

And that was a big part of her problem, the main reason she had a string of go-nowhere flirtations behind her, but not much else. As far as she was concerned, there might as well have been only one man in the world: this one.

When it came to Walker, she was damned if she did, and damned if she didn't.

Forget win-win.

So she finally caved. "All right," she said. "You win." A pause. "This once."

At that, Walker threw back his head and gave a shout of laughter. Then he lifted Casey by the waist, spun her around until she was dizzy and, finally, set her back on her wobbly feet and kissed her senseless.

When it was finally time to turn in for the night—as in, when Casey ran out of stall tactics like folding the rented chairs, taking down wedding decorations, wrapping and freezing what was left of the cake and, in the end, whipping up a supper that proved inedible—Walker breathed a silent sigh of relief.

While he collected Casey's suitcase from the guest quarters and carried it to their room, she locked herself in the master bath and took what must have been the longest shower on record. When she finally came out, looking shy as a novice nun recently released from her vows and sent home from the convent, she was swaddled in his ancient flannel bathrobe—more like **lost** in it, since it all but went around her twice.

Walker rarely used the robe, preferring, except in the dead of winter, to simply let himself air-dry after a shower, since, for all intents and purposes, he'd lived alone for most of his adult life. Plus, it saved on towels.

How things had changed, he thought now, with an inner grin. He was already in bed, with the covers resting roughly at his waistline and a couple of pillows fluffed up behind his back, and hoped he didn't seem half as eager for Casey to join him as he was.

If this had been a real wedding night, of course, she'd have on some sexy wisp of lingerie instead of his ugly bathrobe, he mused, but there was always an upside. Since she'd been in the shower when he brought up her suitcase, she was probably bare-ass naked under all that faded flannel.

He smiled and, catching him at it, Casey planted her feet and folded her arms, waxing stubborn. Not that that was any big stretch, when you considered how wide her streak of cussedness probably was.

"What?" she demanded. She was flushed, either from the heat of the shower or from embarrassment, and her red hair had steamed itself into limp spirals.

"I was just thinking about wedding nights in general and ours in particular," Walker drawled, cupping his hands behind his head and settling in for whatever fate had in store for the two of them.

"I'm here under duress," Casey protested. "In this room, I mean."

Walker chuckled and shook his head. If he hadn't been enjoying this so much, he'd have been riled, he supposed. She seemed to be forgetting, conveniently, that this marriage had been **her** idea.

"No," he argued, amused, "you're

here because you chose to stay instead of going back to town."

"Semantics," she said dismissively, marching over to the mirror above his bureau and studying her reflection closely, as though she'd expected to see somebody else's face looking back at her. Maybe she **was** wondering who that woman in the bathrobe was, and what she'd done with the indomitable Casey Elder.

"Are you planning on wearing that robe to bed?" Walker asked mildly.

"You just never mind what I'm wearing to bed," she told him peevishly. Then she marched herself over to the bench next to the fireplace, where he'd placed her suitcase, opened the lid and rummaged through the contents until she came up with plaid flannel boxer shorts and a T-shirt that had seen better days, if not better decades.

"You're not serious," he said, referring to her choice of nightwear. He'd have preferred the robe, by a country mile.

She gave him a look calculated to quell any stirring that might be going on under the sheets, retreated into the bathroom again and came out five minutes later, looking young enough to be jailbait.

The shorts had a placket in front, and the T-shirt was downright disreputable, with a hole under one arm and a sprinkling of bleach stains across the front.

Casey whirled slowly for his benefit, like a runway model showing off the latest fashion, fairly exuding irony.

Walker frowned. "Whose shorts are those?" he asked.

Suddenly, Casey's green eyes twinkled and, though she was still careful to keep her distance, she actually smiled. "Jealous?" she retorted.

"Hardly," Walker replied, still frowning. Whoever had owned them was a scrawny dude, obviously.

"They used to be Shane's," Casey generously informed him, all in her own good time. "He decided they were geeky and gave them a toss."

Relieved to learn that the boxers hadn't been left behind by some lover of Casey's, scrawny or not, and willing to die before he'd let on that he'd been the least bit worried, Walker smirked a little. "I'm with Shane," he said. "They're definitely geeky."

"Get used to it," Casey replied, saucy as all get-out. "I have half a dozen other pairs and I always sleep in one of them."

Walker locked his gaze with hers and tossed back the covers on her side of the bed with a smooth motion of one arm. "There are some things a man can't be expected to get used to," he answered, grinning now. "And sleeping with somebody in boxers definitely falls into that category."

Casey hesitated, then hotfooted it over to the bed and jumped in beside him. Most likely, Walker thought, she was afraid somebody was hiding outside in the shrubbery with a camera, ready to record her wedding-night attire for posterity.

Fortunately, none of the windows lined up with the bed—he'd made double-sure of that earlier. Besides, the blinds were all pulled.

She huddled on her side of the mattress, sheets and lightweight blankets drawn up almost to her chin. Her eyes were huge.

Walker became exasperated. "Will you please stop acting like a scared virgin?" he asked, tossing aside one of the two pillows he'd been propped up on and lying down flat. "It's only been about a week, in case you've forgotten, since the last time you were in this bed, clawing at my back with your fingernails and begging for more."

Color washed up from her neck to her cheekbones to her forehead. Her temper was rising, which, as far as Walker was concerned, was a good sign. He'd been starting to think she really **was** afraid of him.

"I hope you bought better-quality condoms since then," she said. Then, after a regretful pause, "Not that we're going to need any of those."

Walker rolled onto his side, propped his head on one elbow and regarded her steadily. "You're right about one thing, Mrs. Parrish," he said, in a low rumble. "We're not going to need condoms."

Again, her eyes widened. "What do you mean by that?" she asked.

As if she didn't know.

"I mean," Walker murmured, his mouth very close to hers now, "that that particular horse is not only already out of the barn, but halfway across the county by now. And you and I have never had much luck with condoms anyway, have we?"

She blinked. "You're not planning on kissing me, are you?" she asked.

"I'm planning on doing one hell of a lot more than that," Walker replied. "But if you want me to stop at any time, all you have to do is say so."

Her mouth opened, and her throat worked, but no sound came out.

Walker chuckled, covered her mouth with his and, at the same time, hauled those boxer shorts down over her knees and then her ankles.

With a groan, the kiss having turned into a sparring match between their two tongues by then, Casey kicked free of the boxers and wrapped her arms around Walker's neck.

He dealt with the T-shirt next, pushing it up until not only her silky belly but her luscious breasts were bared to him, felt a soaring triumph when she broke the kiss just long enough to pull the garment off over her head and hurl it away. An instant later, she was burying her fingers in his hair, initiating the next kiss herself, her perfect body already inviting him into her depths.

There was no foreplay that first time, because neither one of them could wait that long. Their bodies, in full mutiny, remembered the glorious fire of their last encounter viscerally, at the cellular level, and would not be denied the fusing they craved so fiercely.

Casey spread her legs wide, and Walker positioned himself between them, found the velvety entrance to all the heaven he needed at the moment and took her in a single thrust of his hips.

She crooned and arched her back as she received him, and she gasped his name. Again, their mouths sought and found each other, and their tongues did sweet battle, and Walker deliberately slowed his pace.

It wasn't easy, especially with Casey doing everything she could to drive him over the edge, but Walker called on every ounce of self-control he possessed, determined to make this ecstasy last.

Casey's hips flew, and she was warm and soft, everywhere, inside and out. Her palms roamed over his back, his shoulders, his buttocks, urging, taunting, claiming.

Walker nearly lost his mind, but he didn't surrender.

Slowly—very slowly—he moved, sheathing and unsheathing himself in Casey, breathing her name, pausing now and then to nibble at an earlobe or suckle one of her hard and waiting nipples.

She grew more and more desperate, whimpering and writhing, gasping out his name in ragged bursts.

When at last she began to climax, he knew it by her cries and the way she tightened around him, seized him, held him captive inside her. With one last thrust and a low, raspy shout of nearly unbearable pleasure, Walker let go.

It seemed like forever before their mutual releases finally subsided and they collapsed onto the mattress, landing hard, like a pair of skydivers whose parachutes had failed to open.

Because bolting out of bed on a surge of moral regret was Casey's usual M.O., Walker was ready for it. He pinned her beneath him, gently clasping her wrists and pressing them into the pillow on either side of her head.

"Say it," he challenged, getting hard again, letting her feel him pressing against her thigh. "Say **no.**"

Casey made a sighing sound instead, closing her eyes.

I love you, Casey Elder, Walker thought with soul-sundering clarity, but he knew better than to say those words out loud. She'd either throw them back in his face or pretend she hadn't heard, and there was no telling which of those reactions would have hurt more.

They remained as they were for long moments, skin on skin, breath on breath, heartbeat on heartbeat, savoring those things, neither of them moving a muscle.

Walker, having admitted the truth, if only to himself, might have seemed still, but inside he was busy grappling with wild surges of emotion. He'd probably loved Casey from the instant he laid eyes on her, but the realization had taken a long time to surface, like a seed planted too deep in the ground.

Presently, she opened her eyes again, and they shone like molten emeralds, casting the kind of spell that lasts forever.

Did she know what she was doing to him?

Walker doubted it. There was a certain confounding innocence, a sort of reckless naïveté, about the woman— fame, fortune and two children born out of wedlock notwithstanding. She was part firebrand and part angel, and he liked her that way.

Casey might be infuriating at times, but she was never dull. There was too much rip-roaring, pepper-and-vinegar, go-for-broke **life** in her.

They searched each other's eyes, and Walker finally ground out a rusty "Well?"

She smiled a little, nodded, welcomed him inside her.

*   *   *

Walker slept soundly, like the thoroughly satisfied man he was, and Casey, sitting up in bed, watched him, loving the way a lock of his hair fell across his forehead, loving the sweep of his unfairly thick eyelashes, the rise and fall of his muscular chest. She rested her palm over his heart, lightly, so she wouldn't wake him, and delighted in the smattering of silken furriness.

I love you, Walker Parrish, she vowed silently.

When had she fallen for him, exactly?

Hard to tell. Maybe it was that first night, when they met in a run-down cowboy bar after a rodeo held on the back acre of nowhere, and slow-danced to the jukebox. The next day, with her heart wedged into her throat and her eyes scalding with inexplicable tears, she watched him ride a bull named Say Your Prayers.

Watched him win.

When the weekend was over, they'd parted ways—Casey had some bookings coming up, and he was headed back to Montana—but running into each other became something of a habit in the months to come.

They'd taken their time becoming lovers—Casey, while not a virgin, was inexperienced, and Walker—well, suffice it to say, he'd had a reputation for knowing his way around a woman's body—but when it finally happened, in a motel room in Cheyenne, Wyoming, the skies split open and the angels sang. At least, that's how it was for Casey.

She'd been astounded by the things Walker made her feel, taking her outside herself the way he did, curling her toes with a simple kiss, causing her heart to take wing and soar, like some great bird glorying in its wildness.

And she'd been terrified. Friends warned her that Walker Parrish was the love-'em-and-leave-'em type, and she could believe it. Women swarmed around him, in bars, behind the chutes at the rodeo, even in parking lots.

Still, their paths continued to cross—Casey couldn't deny that she'd booked herself and the band at as many rodeos as possible—and each time they made love, she became more determined to guard her heart. And each time, that was harder to do.

Then Clare was conceived. Casey's career was just starting to take off by then—she was opening for some of the biggest acts in country music, and she'd just signed a recording contract. To say that pregnancy was inconvenient would have been the understatement of the modern era, and Casey knew the advice she was receiving—put the baby up for adoption—made sense, from a practical standpoint.

But her heart wouldn't hear of it.

Word had gotten back to Walker, and he'd shown up at the stage door one night, determined and bristly.

And she'd lied to him, having convinced herself that she couldn't have done otherwise, swearing that another man had fathered her child.

Walker hadn't believed her at first, but she'd kept on insisting, and, finally, she'd seen something fracture behind his eyes.

Watching him walk away was one of the hardest things she'd ever had to do, and she'd had to fight to keep herself from calling him back, telling him the truth, letting fate take over from there.

Now, she thought, with a bittersweet pang crowding her throat, things had come full circle. She was married to Walker, for better or for worse. They didn't get along any better than they ever had, except when they were having sex, and what were they supposed to do the **other** twenty-some hours of the day?

On top of that, she'd bet her first guitar that she was pregnant—for the third time. Which only went to show that some people never learned their lesson.

CHAPTER THIRTEEN

Casey sat at the kitchen table, her feet tucked behind the rung of her wooden chair, studying a dog-eared cookbook she'd found in a drawer, its margins crowded with handwritten comments from way back, judging by the faded ink and formal penmanship. There were also sticky notes jutting out from many of the pages, different, more recent observations, written in a loopy scrawl and plentiful as the feathers in a bird's wing.

The finer points of food preparation still eluded her. What did it mean, for instance, to "braise" a cut of beef? What happened when a batch of fudge "sug-ared"?

She eyed her smartphone, the source of easy answers—run a quick search and the mysteries of braising and sug-aring would be revealed, she figured.

Too bad about the **hard** answers, though, replies to questions like **How do I love Walker Parrish without los-ing myself in him completely?** and **Besides Casey Elder, superstar, who am I? Is there more to me than my singing voice?**

The landline rang then, startling her out of her musings.

Since Walker was outside, conferring with his foreman, Al Pickens, Casey got up, crossed to the nearby counter and picked up the cordless receiver. Still dis-tracted, she practically croaked, "Hello?"

"Good," a female voice said on a sigh. "It's you."

"Who is this?" Casey asked, frown-ing, back to the cookbook again, riffling through it, determined to find a recipe she could conceivably follow well enough to make something Walker might actu-ally **eat.**

Unlike last night's effort at spaghetti, which wound up as one big clump of half-done noodle-substance and would have had to be cut into slices, if served in the first place, instead of spooned out in lovely, steaming dollops.

"It's Brylee," came the answer, patient but a little breathless. "Your sister-in-law?"

"Oh," Casey said, closing the cookbook, which was roughly the size of a classroom dictionary. Now that she was tracking the conversation, her first question was, as always, "Are the kids okay?"

"So far," Brylee said, causing a little trapdoor to swing open in the pit of Casey's stomach, one she might just fall through if she didn't hold on. "We're at the supermarket in Parable, and we're **surrounded.**"

"By what?" Casey asked, nerves jangling like a pocket full of small change.

"By reporters," Brylee answered, almost in a whisper. "There are all these— these **people** out in the parking lot, with cameras and microphones. Even vans with satellite dishes on top. Evidently, they've been keeping out of sight, waiting for us to come out of your house, so they could follow us. They keep calling out Clare and Shane's names, and the manager locked the doors, but he's worried about keeping customers out, too. And **in,** of course. It's like being under siege."

Casey paced, too agitated to sit or even stand still in one place. She strode over to the back door, opened it and yelled, "Walker!"

"Oww," Brylee complained, probably wincing and holding her cell away from her ear.

"Sorry," Casey threw out.

Walker immediately broke off the discussion he'd been having with Al and several of the ranch hands, looking worried, and hurried in her direction.

"Stay put," Casey said to Brylee. "Tell the manager not to open those doors until Walker and I get there—"

"Wait," Brylee broke in, calmer now. "The manager just called the sheriff's office—Boone Taylor is on his way over here right now, with a couple of deputies for backup. He'll get us to the ranch okay, so there's nothing to fret about."

Nothing to fret about. Casey fought down a swell of exasperation; this was no time to lecture Brylee on mob psychology.

Walker burst in from the porch just then, almost tearing the screen door off its hinges in the process. His face was stony with concern, his eyes narrowed. "What is it?" he demanded, shuffling to one side so he wouldn't step on Doolittle, squeezing past him through the slim gap.

"Put Clare on for a moment, will you, Brylee?" Casey asked, and mouthed **Stay calm** at Walker while she waited to hear her daughter's voice.

"Mom," Clare said, moments later, a note of panic in her voice. "The tabloids came out early—special editions, evidently—and we're **all over** them, you and Walker and Shane and me. The headlines—they're all about us being your guilty secrets, and they're calling you a liar—"

"Clare," Casey broke in, "never mind the headlines for now. We can talk about all of that later, when you and Shane are back here, with us, where you belong."

Walker was glowering by then. He looked like an old-time gunslinger facing a showdown and more than ready to draw and fire. "I don't read lips," he informed Casey in a scratchy whisper.

Casey waved her hand, tried to ignore him. Not easy, since he seemed to fill that kitchen from wall to wall and ceiling to floor, he was so—**present.**

"Do we, Mom?" Clare's voice was small, shaky. She was used to living in the limelight, but this latest development was clearly getting to her. "Do we belong anyplace, Shane and me? What's real and what isn't?"

Those questions pierced Casey like the tip of a poisoned spear. "Listen to me, sweetheart. Boone—Sheriff Taylor—will be there any minute. He'll bring you home and we'll deal with the situation then, when we're all together."

"Okay," Clare whispered uncertainly.

Once, she'd believed Casey would keep her and her brother safe, no matter what. Now, her faith had been shaken, maybe toppled, and little wonder. She'd been lied to, by her own mother, repeatedly.

Casey felt sick, pressed her free hand to her stomach.

Brylee came back on the phone. "Boone's here," she said with obvious relief. "We'll be on our way shortly."

Casey nodded, opened her mouth to answer, but the dial tone was already buzzing in her ear.

Numbly, she turned to Walker, explained that the press had effectively cornered Brylee, Clare and Shane inside a supermarket.

Walker shoved a hand through his hair as he listened, his jawline so tight that a white pallor pulsed under his tan. He'd caught the reference to Boone, though, or he might have been even more upset than he was.

Casey finished the account as it had been relayed to her, and then swallowed hard, willing herself not to cry. She'd had run-ins with the tabloid press before, of course, but never like this, with her children trapped inside a public building, and never in Parable or Three Trees. She felt violated, helpless and scalded all over with fury, all at once.

Walker took her firmly by the shoulders, probably afraid her knees would give out and she'd crumple to the floor if he didn't hold her up. The rage in his eyes softened to a kind of bleak comprehension.

Casey knew he was realizing what it could really mean, being married to someone like her, and in another moment or two, he'd be wishing he'd never **heard** of Casey Elder, let alone fathered two of her children, brought them all here to Timber Creek and effectively blown the lid off his otherwise ideal life.

"I'm sorry," she whispered.

Walker drew Casey close, just when she would have expected him to push her away, cupped the back of her head in one hand, squashing her ponytail. "Don't apologize," he said hoarsely. "This isn't your fault."

She tilted her head back, looked up at him, astonished. "Of **course** it is, Walker," she argued. "And I wouldn't mind if I was the only one who might get hurt in all this, but I'm not. Shane and Clare are directly in the line of fire, and so are you."

He kissed her forehead, gave her ponytail a light, teasing tug. "The kids are safe, Casey," he reminded her. "Brylee, too. Right now, that's what matters. And you saw this coming, remember?" His mouth twitched at one corner. "It's the main reason you got down on one knee and asked for my hand in marriage, as I recall."

Casey gave a raw little rasp of laughter, in spite of herself, and thumped Walker's chest with the side of her right fist. "I **didn't** get down on one knee," she said. "Let's get that straight."

The twitch became a full-fledged grin. "But you **did** propose," he insisted.

"I **suggested.**" Even as she spoke, Casey wondered what was wrong with her. Why was her first response to Walker always an urge to argue?

Just then, a rap sounded, rattling the screen door, and Al Pickens stuck his head partway inside. "Boss? Is there a problem?"

Walker turned to look at his most faithful employee and longtime friend, and smiled. "It might be time to circle the wagons, all right," he said.

Briefly, Walker explained the situation.

Casey frowned, puzzled. **Do what?**

Al clearly understood, which was more than she could have claimed. He nodded and said, "I'll put a couple of men at the main gate, and the rest can beat the brush for any of them sneaky reporters, make sure they don't get close to the house again."

Walker nodded. "No rough stuff," he specified mildly.

"Darn." Al grinned, showing a few missing teeth, and tugged once at the brim of his battered hat. His face was round and weather-worn, his eyes small and twinkly. "I was kinda looking forward to going all John Wayne on at least one of those yahoos."

Walker chuckled, waved Al off with a motion of one hand and focused his attention on Casey again.

She felt as though the floor had turned to rubber under her feet, and she thought she might throw up.

Walker eased her back into the chair she'd been sitting on before the phone rang, lost in the arcane realm of home cooking, and related what Brylee had told her about the supermarket siege.

He walked over to one of the cupboards, got out a glass, moved to the sink, filled it to the brim with cold water and brought it to Casey.

She took the glass in both hands, sipped slowly, in hopes that the stuff would stay down.

Walker took the chair nearest hers and waited with her, lightly massaging her nape, where the muscles had clenched up tight, like a knot in a length of steel cable.

Slowly, Casey began to feel a little better, though she knew she wouldn't relax completely until Shane and Clare got there, until she could see both her children with her own eyes and touch them and know for sure that they hadn't been hurt.

"Has this happened before?" Walker asked gently, after she'd stopped trembling and begun rolling her head from side to side in response to the massage. The release of tension was almost sexual.

"I've tangled with the so-called press a few times in the past," Casey responded, "and they've made up some pretty nasty stories about Clare and Shane along the way, too. Especially Shane. They claimed he was on drugs and I sued them for that one, but this is the most aggressive they've ever gotten." She remembered what her daughter had said about the early editions of the weekly tabloids, headlines and photos blazing with manufactured scandals. **Extra! Extra! Read all about it!**

Thoughtfully, Walker sorted through her answer in his head. Then he pushed back his chair, crossed to the desktop computer on a counter against the far wall and logged on.

Even before she saw his back stiffen, Casey knew it was bad. Maybe worse than bad.

Walker swore under his breath, clicking from one site to another.

When he turned around to face her again, his face was like a storm cloud. He looked as though he might be about to go find Al and the other cowboys and form a posse, vigilante-style, forgetting the "No rough stuff" decree he'd issued earlier.

Casey went to him, slipped her arms

around his waist. This time, **she** was the voice of reason. "This will pass, Walker," she said gently. "It always does."

He looked grim, even harried. Again, he raked his fingers through his hair. "Greaseball reporters are one thing," he ground out, "and the crazies who take everything they write as gospel are **another,** dammit. Suppose some freak job hears voices telling him to kidnap Clare and Shane and actually follows through? Have you ever thought of that?"

She touched his cheek, felt the stubble of a new beard bristling against her palm, even though she'd watched him shave less than two hours before. "Only about a million times," she answered softly. "Walker, I'm truly sorry for dragging you into this—"

Walker's nostrils flared, and his eyes flashed, bull angry. "'Dragging me into this'?" he retorted through his teeth. "These are my **children** we're talking about here, Casey. I should have been in the loop a long time ago, don't you think? I'm Clare and Shane's **father,** remember? What if something had happened to them because I wasn't around to protect them?"

Casey had never seen Walker, or anybody else, so furious. "Nothing **did** happen, though," she said, very carefully and very quietly. "I was never, **ever** careless about their safety, Walker. When I thought there was a need for extra security, I notified the police, in whatever city we happened to be in, or I hired bodyguards—"

His nose was practically touching hers, and his eyes continued to shoot fire. She was half expecting him to paw at the ground with one foot, sprout horns and lower his head to charge. **"I'm their father,"** he said. "You kept me from them, all this time." A pause, one of those dangerous moments when everything can change. "How am I supposed to forgive you?"

There it was, the elephant in the room, the thing they hadn't really talked about.

If Walker couldn't forgive her, Casey reasoned dizzily, he certainly couldn't **love** her, either. The honeymoon, such as it had been, was definitely and permanently over, and last night's lovemaking, as powerful, as transformative, as **sacred** as it had seemed, hadn't been **love**making at all. It had been garden-variety sex, the cheap, meaningless kind that belonged in the backseats of cars or in trashy rooms rented by the hour.

If Walker had drawn back his fist and punched Casey in the stomach, he couldn't have hurt her any more deeply. She reeled away from him, shrugged him off when he tried to lay his hands on her shoulders, stared blindly out one of the windows until she saw Boone's squad car turn in the gate, lights whirling.

Two other official cars followed close behind the sheriff's, while news vans and less impressive rigs of all sorts trailed behind, at a cautious distance, but advancing just the same.

Casey got to the door before Walker did, even though he was closer, elbowed her way past him and dashed across the porch, down the steps, out into the yard.

Boone brought his cruiser to a stop nearby, and, through the windshield and the blinding blue-and-white swirl of light,

Casey spotted Brylee's face on the passenger side, pale moon rising. Clare and Shane rode in back, behind the grill, and as soon as Boone put on the brakes, they spilled out on either side of the vehicle, dashing toward her.

Casey wrapped one arm around each of them.

Clare cried, while Shane, almost gleeful, seemed to see the experience as an adventure.

Walker stood at a little distance, painfully separate, while Brylee rounded the car from the other side, heading toward her brother, and Boone climbed from behind the wheel, his expression sober.

"It was so awesome, Mom!" Shane crowed. "Like one of those action-adventure movies, where Bruce Willis goes after the bad guys, even when he has to walk barefoot over broken glass—"

Casey winced at the image, but it was Clare who spoke.

"Oh, shut up!" she broke in tearfully, glaring at her brother. "It **wasn't** awesome! It was **terrible!** And this **isn't** one of your stupid **Die Hard** movies!"

Shane rolled his eyes, looking disgusted by this display of emotion. "Whatever," he said in a dismissive drawl. Then, under his breath, he added, "Hormones."

Casey gave her son a warning look and he shrugged and ambled off toward Walker.

She took Clare's face between her hands. "Honey," she said, "I know this was scary, but those guys wouldn't have hurt you—they just wanted a story."

Clare pulled free, glared at her. "Oh, yeah?" she challenged furiously. "Then how come the **sheriff** had to bring us home in a **police** car, with a bunch of deputies to run interference?"

How could Casey answer that? Maybe the **reporters** presented no physical danger, they were just pesky, but Walker had been right—the "freak jobs" who obsessed over every aspect of a celebrity's life definitely did pose a threat. And they tended to follow the newshounds wherever they went, getting some kind of sick satisfaction out of hanging around on the fringes, watching and hoping to get involved in some way.

Clare, evidently tired of waiting for an

answer her mother didn't have to offer, pulled away and hurried into the house, slamming the screen door hard behind her.

Casey, feeling that odd sense of dissociation again, as though she'd split into two people, one concerned, one impassive, walked over to Boone, who tried to smile and failed.

"Thank you," Casey told him, putting out her hand.

Boone took it, gave her fingers a squeeze, nodded ever so slightly. "I can post a couple of deputies at your gate if you'd like," he said, inclining his head in that direction, "but it looks like the ranch hands have things under control, for the moment, anyhow."

Casey swallowed, nodded back. "We'll be all right," she assured the sheriff. "Once the excitement dies down a little, anyway."

We'll be all right.

She and the children? They'd be fine, because a **new** story would come along any minute, and the stringers would be off chasing some other celebrity, climbing the trees in their yard, harassing

their children, peeking through their windows and generally complicating every other aspect of their lives. No matter how juicy the current scandal, there was always another, better, one, waiting in the wings.

But would she and **Walker** be all right? As a couple?

Not likely. Walker was a regular person, those spectacular looks aside, and things like this didn't **happen** to people like him. Try though he might to understand, intelligent as he was, he had no frame of reference for the downside of fame. How could he?

To him, fame meant bright lights, glamorous photo shoots, designer clothes, star-studded parties, limos and private jets and packed arenas all over the world. Thousands of unseen hands holding up their lighters, creating a flickering backdrop of flame.

To Casey and, by extension, to her children, it meant those things, all right, but there was a whole heck of a lot more to the celebrity lifestyle. It meant taking extreme security precautions, even in places where normal people felt safe. It meant keeping her eyes wide-open, no matter how tired she was, staying alert, even when there were bodyguards on all sides. It meant avoiding malls, popular restaurants and movie theaters, never personally answering a knock at a hotel room door, even when room service was expected. It meant flinching when someone raised a camera or shoved a pen at her, when all they wanted was a snapshot or an autograph.

Usually, that was all it was. And then there were the other times.

Had John Lennon expected to be shot dead by a fan, right out in front of his own apartment building? Of course not—the possibility probably hadn't even crossed his mind. Why should it? He'd been going about his business, that was all. Living his life. Meeting someone for drinks or dinner, expecting to be home before bedtime.

Except that none of that happened.

Stop it, Casey told herself. **Get a grip.**

Shane and Clare were already inside the house by then, and Brylee was close behind. Casey followed, while Walker remained where he was, talking solemnly with Boone and the deputies.

In the kitchen, Brylee tossed a fistful of undersize "newspapers" onto the table, while Clare fled to her appointed bedroom and Shane crouched to greet a waggy-tailed Doolittle with an ear-ruffling and a tummy rub.

"If we had a parrot, we could use these," Brylee said of the tabloids, "to line the cage."

Casey reached for a copy, her hand trembling slightly, and, though she'd thought she was prepared, the sight of Clare, photographed standing beside the piano the day before in her pretty, modest dress, singing the song that was her wedding gift to her parents, struck Casey like a freight train going downhill.

Clare was fully clad, of course, unlike certain movie stars who'd been captured for posterity sunbathing nude on the deck of some yacht, or British royalty indulging in hanky-panky beside a swimming pool, but there was something too intimate about the shot just the same. It was, Casey decided, the sense of close proximity; the picture might have been taken by someone attending the ceremony, instead of through a window.

Love child turns songbird, the caption read and, beneath that, in smaller print, **But will she fly the coop, now that her famous mama and cowboy daddy have finally tied the knot?**

"Love child," Casey murmured, shaking her head. She supposed the term was apt enough, if ridiculously outdated. She and Walker **hadn't** been married when it counted, that was true, but there had never been any doubt that Clare was loved, and Shane, too.

Brylee busied herself at the counter, brewing coffee. "Snidely's still in town," she fretted. "I thought we'd be going back to your place after we picked up the stuff to make tacos, but—"

Snidely, Casey recalled distractedly, was Brylee's faithful German shepherd, and, according to Walker, they went everywhere together.

"Dad and I will go get him for you," Shane assured her manfully, getting to his feet and heading for the refrigerator. Growing as fast as he was, he was forever taking on fuel. "Maybe we can bring our dogs out here, too. The cats will probably be okay where they are for a while—"

Brylee, moving deftly, stepped between Shane and the fridge. "Wash your hands first," she said.

"Good call," Casey agreed, distracted, still leafing through the other "special editions." There were pictures of her and Walker exchanging vows, then, later, laughing as they fed each other wedding cake, an image of Shane loading Dawson's wheelchair into the back of Patsy's van while Walker lifted Dawson himself onto the passenger seat. None of it was offensive, but **all** of it was too personal, too private.

The headlines, however, grew progressively worse.

One rag featured a picture of Walker, crouching beside Dawson's wheelchair on the ranch house porch, talking earnestly, faces solemn.

Another of the cowboy's love children? screeched the inch-high, bold-faced line beneath the photo.

Shane, meanwhile, washed his hands,

as ordered by his aunt, then rooted through the fridge in earnest, coming away with an armload of cellophane-covered refreshments left over from the wedding.

He and Brylee discussed the plan for dog retrieval in quiet voices, somewhere at the periphery of Casey's awareness.

When she thought enough time had elapsed, Casey headed for Clare's room—once Brylee's—and tapped at the door, resting her forehead against the panel while she waited.

"Go away," Clare said predictably.

"You know I'm not going to do that," Casey responded, keeping her tone light. She turned the glass knob, realized that she was locked out. Got her hackles up just a smidge. "Let me in, Clare."

"There's nothing you can say to make this better," Clare retorted.

"Let me in," Casey repeated. When it came to stubbornness, her daughter would find her a worthy opponent. Besides, Brylee could probably come up with a spare key to the room in no time.

Clare's sigh was loud enough to come

right through the thick wood of that sturdy door. There was a scraping sound as she worked the lock, and then she was peeking out, the crack so narrow that only one of her eyes was visible.

Casey eased the door the rest of the way open, careful not to push too hard and stub one of Clare's toes, which were probably bare, since, like her mom, the girl never wore shoes if she could avoid it.

The room was spacious, though not as big as its counterpart on Rodeo Road, with a window seat and built-in bookshelves and even a small Franklin stove. The closet ran the length of one wall, and the furniture was obviously antique: four-poster bed, matching bureau, chest of drawers and nightstands. A pair of delicate chairs, slipcovered in a muted pink floral fabric, faced the stove.

A few of Clare's belongings were scattered around, here and there—the tiny chiming clock she treasured, a stack of books, a framed photo of the three of them—Casey, Clare and Shane—with a remarkably authentic Santa Claus, back when the lie was still working.

Casey picked up the photograph and smiled, remembering the Nashville party where it had been taken, four or five years before. Was it really that long ago? It seemed like yesterday.

"That was quite a night," she reflected somewhat wistfully, setting the photo back on the shelf where she'd found it.

The bed creaked as Clare leaped into the middle of it and sat cross-legged, the way she liked to do, but her expression was snarky, not nostalgic. "Yes," she said. "Everybody there was either famous or **related** to somebody famous, and doesn't **every** Santa Claus wear a real velvet suit, trimmed in the best fake fur available, and pass out state-of-the-art iPads instead of candy canes?"

Casey sighed, let the gibe pass. She saw herself in Clare, recognized the trick of picking a fight in order to establish boundaries. "What, exactly," she began wearily, "do you hope to accomplish by being so difficult?"

"I'm letting you know that I'm unhappy," Clare said pertly. "We're having a dialogue."

"You've been watching too many **Oprah** reruns," Casey answered, perching on the edge of the bed, not too close, but not too far away, either.

"You might want to take in one or two episodes when you get the chance," Clare answered airily. "Oprah was always big on telling the truth."

Zing. Shot through the heart. Casey knotted her fingers together in her lap and silently counted to ten.

"What do you want, Clare?" she asked evenly when she was relatively sure she wouldn't lose it.

Clare rolled deftly onto her stomach, cupping her chin in her hands and bending her knees to swing her feet back and forth. She was wearing cut-off jeans and a skimpy top that ended a good eight inches above her waist. Casey didn't recognize the outfit, and was about to say as much when she spotted the tattoo.

It was just a tiny rosebud, nestled in the graceful curve at the base of Clare's spine—not a skull and crossbones, not a gang symbol or a four-letter word—and yet the sight of it stunned Casey.

"When did you get **that?**" she asked very quietly.

Clare looked back over one shapely shoulder, acknowledging the tattoo's presence with a nonchalant glance, and shrugged slightly. "Last year, in Vegas," she said blithely. "When you were doing that one-night charity gig at Caesar's, with Brad and Trace and everybody."

"You were **thirteen** at the time," Casey reminded her daughter. "Who signed the permission slip?" Even in Glitter Gulch, where practically anything went, minors couldn't get tattoos without the signature of a qualified adult. In short, a parent or guardian.

"You'll be mad," Clare warned.

"I'm **already** mad," Casey replied. **"Who was it?"**

"It was some reporter guy," Clare said. "I got bored hanging out in the suite while you were rehearsing, so I gave the bodyguards and Uncle Mitch the slip and went out for a walk. This man with a camera came up to me on one of the sky bridges and asked me if I was your daughter. I figured he already knew I was, or he wouldn't have asked me in the first place, and he looked nice enough, so I said yes. He told me he wrote for a real newspaper, not a tabloid, and we ended up striking a deal. He wanted an interview, and I wanted a tattoo. So we went into this shopping center, where there was one of those places where you can get body piercings and stuff—it was **nice,** Mom, and very clean, and there were **loads** of people around, so nothing was going to happen. They had these computers, and all you had to do was scroll through the different designs until you found the perfect tattoo."

Casey closed her eyes for a moment, imagining her thirteen-year-old daughter wandering around Las Vegas by herself, talking to strangers, finagling a tattoo. A shudder went through her. Not only had this **happened,** but she hadn't known a thing about it—until now.

Clare, apparently uncomfortable with the silence, launched back into the story. "Anyway, the reporter guy pretended to be my dad. I paid for the tattoo myself, of course—out of my allowance—and **it hurt like anything**—the tattoo, I mean, not forking over the cash. He asked me a couple of questions and that was that. No big deal. **Plus,** I was back in the suite before anybody even noticed I was gone."

"Excuse me," Casey said, standing up suddenly. Clare's new room came with an adjoining bath, cramped but blessedly nearby and, at the moment, it was a good thing.

"Mom?" Clare asked, sounding mildly alarmed. "Mom, what—?"

Casey hurried into the bathroom, lifted the lid of the toilet and threw up everything but her socks.

CHAPTER FOURTEEN

Walker was prying a pebble out of Mack's right front foot with a hoof pick when he heard his daughter's voice behind him. He glanced up, saw her standing in the breezeway, arms braced atop the stall gate, watching him.

"Walker?" she queried. Shane called him "Dad" these days, but Clare was holding out, unwilling to give so much as an inch of ground. It was as if she believed he and Casey could turn back the clock and set everything right, if only they weren't so all fired determined to make her life as miserable as possible.

Teenage girls. He hadn't had to deal with that particular species since Brylee was Clare's age, but now it was all coming back to him, and the prospect was discouraging. His sister hadn't even **begun** to snap out of it until she started college, which meant the snit-storms weren't likely to let up anytime soon—in fact, they were bound to get worse.

He sighed inwardly, straightened, lowered Mack's foot and turned in her direction. He couldn't blame the kid for being angry, of course—probably would have been pretty damn furious himself, in Clare's place. Fit to be tied, as his dad used to say.

"What's up, shortstop?" He opened the stall gate, and Clare stepped back so he could pass. His little girl was turning into a **big** girl and, though it would take a while, he knew it was out there, waiting, the time when she'd no longer need him, or even Casey, in any real way.

It made him feel, well, **optional.** And he had nobody to blame but himself— and Casey.

"Mom just threw up." Clare looked

genuinely worried, and somewhat guilty, too. Her color was high and her mouth was a mite wobbly, as though she wanted to cry and was doing her darnedest not to. "And it's my fault."

Walker frowned. "Your mom's had a hard day," he said, trying not to show his own concern. "Lots of stress—the media blitz, getting married, moving to the ranch." He paused, studying Clare's face. "How do you figure any of that's your fault?"

Clare swallowed, gnawed at her lower lip for a moment. A sheen of tears glistened in her eyes. "I got a tattoo," she said meekly. "It was a long time ago, but Mom just found out and—"

"And that tattoo is such an awful sight that your poor mama took one look at it and lost her lunch?" Walker asked lightly. He had his own theory as to why Casey might be feeling a little green around the gills, but it might be wishful thinking.

A third child. Wouldn't that be something?

Clare flushed, but a little grin tugged at the corners of her mouth, and she blinked away the tears. "Mom thinks I'm too young for a tattoo, and that's just plain hypocritical if you ask me, because she's got this tiny guitar on one ankle—"

"You **are** too young," Walker said after his daughter's voice trailed off into an uncertain, shaky-chinned silence. He knew about the little guitar, of course, and the butterfly, too, though that was on a less obvious part of Casey's anatomy, a place he particularly liked to kiss. "Your mother, on the other hand, is an adult, legally entitled to make her own decisions. How is that 'hypocritical'?"

Clare's expression turned stubborn, but she backed down quickly enough. She knew how to push Casey's buttons, Walker figured, but he was another matter. "Aren't you going to check on her?" she asked petulantly. "I just told you she was feeling sick, after all."

"I'm headed her way," Walker replied, resting his hands on his hips and regarding his daughter solemnly, "but I've got a few things to say to you first."

Clare's green eyes, so like her mother's, widened, and the thick lashes fluttered a couple of times. "What?"

"I realize that finding out that you're

mine must have come as a shock, and you'll need a while to sort through all of it, but, mistakes or no mistakes, your mom has had your best interests at heart all along, yours **and** your brother's. Sooner or later, you're going to have to make a decision, Clare. You can rebel and make an all-around fool of yourself, like the poor, abused children of other celebrities we could both name, or you can make her proud. You can try to get back at her, or you can **stand by** her, the way she's always stood by you. So, which is it, cowgirl? In the long run, are you going to be an asset or a liability?"

"Wow," Clare breathed after a few moments, looking amazed. "Coming from you, that was practically the Gettysburg Address. I'm used to cowboy-speak, like **yep** and **nope** and **howdy** and **so long.**"

"Get used to **dad**-speak," Walker advised, firmly but not unkindly. "You can be as mad at me as you want to. You can yell and throw things and call me by my first name until we're both old and gray. But you **will not** make life harder

for your mother, punishing her for whatever sins you think she's committed—
not on my watch. Understood?"

Clare sighed, and she didn't answer
for a long time.

"Understood," she said, conceding
that round.

Walker returned to the house then,
Clare and Doolittle following, and found
Brylee and Shane in the kitchen, playing
Parcheesi at the table.

"We need to go get the dogs, Dad,"
Shane said.

Walker gave a crisp nod. "In a little
while," he replied, his gaze sliding to
meet Brylee's. "Is Casey in our room?"

Brylee nodded.

Walker made his way past the dining
and living rooms and into the corridor.
After rapping lightly at the bedroom
door, he stepped inside.

Casey lay in the middle of the bed, almost in a fetal position, fully dressed
and shivering a little.

She looked so small and so alone that
Walker's heart turned over, a slow, bruis-
ing process. Casey Elder might be world
famous, and one of the strongest, most

courageous women he'd ever known, but she'd been fighting her own battles for so long that she'd worn herself out.

Gently, he covered her with a quilt his grandmother had made before he was even born, and sat down on the edge of the bed, wanting to touch her but not sure he ought to.

"I hear you're feeling a little under the weather," he ventured when Casey didn't say anything.

"I'll be fine," she said, her voice so small he barely heard her. "Eventually."

"You don't **sound** fine, Casey Jones," Walker pointed out. "And you don't **look** all that terrific, either."

"Gee," she murmured with flimsy irony, **"thanks."**

Walker chuckled, laid a hand lightly on her shoulder, squeezed. "Anything I can do?"

"Shoot me," Casey groaned, then gave a strangled little chortling sound that might have been part sob.

"Not an option," Walker replied. "I'm a law-abiding man."

Pulling the quilt up over her head, Casey started to cry.

Walker sighed, methodically kicked off one boot, then the other, and stretched out beside her, gathering her quilt-bundled self into his arms, careful not to hold her too tightly. The moment was fragile, and so was his wife.

"Talk to me," he said.

Her voice was muffled and croaky. "I'm pregnant."

Walker waited out a swell of pure jubilation. "Isn't it a little early to know that?" he asked gruffly. "It's only been—"

"I **know** when I'm pregnant, Walker Parrish," she said.

"And you figure this is a bad thing?" he prompted carefully. There wasn't much he was afraid of, but the thought that Casey might not want this baby scared the hell out of him.

"Of course not!" she wailed, sounding for all the world as though she was still hoping he'd shoot her. How the devil was he supposed to know how she really felt when she acted one way and talked another?

Walker uncovered her face, which was tear-streaked and puffy around the eyes, kissed her red-tipped nose. "If it's a boy," he teased in a mischievous drawl, "can I raise him to be a bull rider?"

Casey laughed and freed one hand from the quilt long enough to slug him in the arm. "No," she said with reassuring spirit. "He's going to be president."

Walker grinned. "And if this little stranger turns out to be a girl?"

"President," Casey reiterated firmly, finally snuggling up a little closer.

After that, the conversation lapsed into an easy silence.

Walker held Casey, stroked her hair and waited. He'd had a whole lot of practice at waiting for Casey Elder, he thought, and, most likely, he'd have plenty more of it in his future. He propped his chin on top of her head. No matter what the future might bring, he was in this for the duration.

He was just about to tell Casey that, straight out, when he realized she'd drifted off to sleep.

When Casey woke up, afternoon was fading into evening, and she was still wrapped up snug in that time-softened, lavender-scented quilt Walker had

spread over her earlier. When had anyone done that for her, seen to her comfort in that simple, homey way?

It had been years before, she realized, when she'd had a bad case of
stomach flu and Lupe—dear Lupe—
had looked after her. Slowly, things came
into sharper focus.

Walker was gone now, and she wondered how long he'd stayed with her,
holding her, letting her feel what she
was feeling without any apparent need
to hurry her through the crying jag. Walker's head had left an indentation in the
pillow, and his fresh-air, meadow-grass
scent lingered, too.

With a smile, Casey touched the crumpled covers next to her, where he'd lain,
and even though the warmth of Walker's
body was long gone, she got a sense of
him, a physical vibration, just the same.
She rolled onto her back, waited to see
if her stomach would rebel and, when it
didn't, she stretched out luxuriously,
peeled away the quilt and got up.

The ranch house, while not huge, was
good-sized, and she heard voices from

the distant kitchen, laughter and the intermittent, happy barking of the dogs.

Casey padded into the bathroom she now shared with Walker, brushed her teeth, splashed cool water on her face, fluffed out her hair. Her T-shirt was wrinkled, but her jeans looked okay, so she didn't bother changing clothes.

When she reached the kitchen, brightly lit and ranch-house cheery, Brylee and Clare were there, with the three chocolate Labs and Snidely keeping them company. Shane and Walker were absent, and Doolittle must have been with them.

Casey greeted her dogs with head pats and the nonsense words that meant "I love you," at least to those of the canine persuasion.

"I see the rescue mission was successful," she said with a smile.

"Went off without a hitch." Brylee grinned. "And we didn't see a single reporter, either. They must have crawled back into their holes."

Casey chuckled. "Good," she said.

Clare's expression was more subdued, a combination of sadness and stubborn pride. What was going on in that complicated adolescent brain of hers?

"The cats are here, too," she offered. "I put them in my room."

Casey smiled. Could this child possibly know how much her mother loved her? Probably not, though that would change when Clare was grown-up and married, with children of her own.

Don't go there. She's still your girl.

"They'll feel safe there," she said of the cats. "In your room, I mean."

Clare nodded slowly. For a moment, she looked as though she might say something more but, in the end, she cast a brief glance at Brylee and went back to what she'd been doing when Casey came in—which was peeling potatoes.

Amazing.

"Are you feeling better?" Brylee asked Casey. Her tone was light, nonintrusive, but her eyes betrayed quiet concern.

"I just needed to rest for a little while," Casey said with a nod. "Are Walker and Shane around?"

"They're doing chores," Brylee replied. "Walker sent the ranch hands home early, since they've been guarding gates and patrolling the property lines on horseback most of the day."

Casey winced inwardly—nothing could prepare hardworking, down-to-earth people like Walker and Brylee for the kind of onslaught they'd experienced that day, and yet Walker was out doing chores and Brylee was making supper, which was probably business as usual.

"Can I do something to help?" Casey asked, mindful of her sad lack of cooking skills but still optimistic that she could at least learn the basics, given half a chance. She'd taught herself to read music, after all, along with a number of other useful things.

Brylee started to say no, caught herself, smiled warmly and scooted aside to make room for Casey at the counter, where she was dipping plump pieces of chicken in beaten egg, then rolling them in seasoned flour. An electric frying pan stood nearby, the grease inside it hot enough to bubble.

Casey, normally a stickler for good nutrition, grinned. **Good old-fashioned**

country food, she thought apprecia-
tively. **Just what the doctor ordered.**

Pretty soon, she was taking over for
Brylee, who stood virtually at her elbow
to supervise. The chicken went into the
waiting pan, piece by piece, each time
raising a loud sizzling sound, and the
aroma was heavenly, even at that early
stage.

"Bacon grease," Brylee explained with
wicked glee. "I usually bake chicken,
and eat it without the skin, but once in
a while, a person's got to pull out all the
stops and go for broke."

"Amen." Casey laughed. "What do we
do now?" she asked when all the chicken
pieces were in the frying pan and the
noise had abated a little.

"We brown the bird on one side,"
Brylee answered, happy to be helpful,
"and then we brown it on the other. Then
we put on the lid and turn down the heat
and wait."

The side door opened then, and
Walker and Shane came in, fresh from
doing chores. Shane was walking tall,
his face flushed with pride, his eyes
shining. He washed up at the kitchen

sink, following Walker's lead, and then sniffed the air.

"Mom." He beamed. "You're **cooking.**"

Casey grinned. "With a lot of help from your aunt," she said, but she was as pleased as if her son had just given her a big compliment.

"I'm cooking, **too,** dweeb," Clare put in, glowering at Shane.

"Peeling potatoes," Shane said. "Anybody can do that."

Clare stuck her tongue out at him, but there was no venom in the response. It was, Casey figured, sibling lingo, habitual and, in an odd way, nice.

"I'll keep an eye on the chicken," Brylee told Casey, raising her eyebrows comically, widening her eyes and inclining her head toward Walker.

Casey got the message—only a lighted billboard could have conveyed it more clearly—and approached Walker, taking his outstretched hand.

He led her out onto the side porch, and the two of them sat down in the swing.

The sky was a pale shade of purple

by then, and the stars were popping out everywhere. The moon, full and brilliant, seeming almost close enough to touch, loomed over the western foothills.

Casey pictured the remains of that old homestead, where Walker's people had settled so long ago, imagined how it would look in the twilight, surrounded by tangled mobs of flowers, and felt soothed, connected, somehow. She could fall in love with Timber Creek Ranch, she thought, if she let herself.

They rocked slowly back and forth, she and Walker, content with saying nothing at all. Lights glistened on the far side of the river, and distant laughter rode over on the breeze—children playing games, dogs barking with glee, screen doors creaking on their hinges, grown-ups calling out that supper was ready.

Ordinary sounds, Casey supposed, but they brought back precious memories—not of her life in her grandparents' stately mansion, but of the times she'd spent with Lupe and Juan in the country, running free with their legions of nieces and nephews, playing softball and hide-and-seek until it was too dark to continue.

Rare and precious as those interludes had been, they were more than Clare and Shane had had when they were small, their other advantages aside.

Just be, Casey told herself. **Let now be now.**

Walker didn't release her hand, and she allowed herself to enjoy the sensation as he stroked her knuckles lightly with the calloused pad of one thumb. There was nothing sexual about his touch, but Casey knew that would change once they were alone in their bedroom later that night, and she felt a racy little thrill at the prospect.

"I guess I was a little overemotional this afternoon," she said, for his ears alone. "Thanks for riding out the storm."

Walker let go of her hand then, but only so he could slip his arm around her shoulders. She allowed herself to lean into him, rested her head against his strong upper arm. "Anytime," he finally replied.

She felt a need to warn him, like an honest person selling a used car with a few hitches in its get-along. "I'm like that when I'm—stressed out."

"It happens," Walker said easily. "You're allowed, Casey Jones."

Casey was willing to lose herself in **this** Walker, the gentleman rancher, the easygoing cowboy, the expert lover, at least for a little while, but that didn't mean she'd forgotten the **other** one, the man who wasn't sure he'd ever be able to forgive her for keeping him from his children for so long. **That** Walker was just as real as the one who'd covered her in a quilt a few hours before, held her while she cried, made her feel safer than safe and finally led her out here to sit in a porch swing and admire the moon and the stars.

"This is good," she told him.

"And it'll get better," he promised with a grin.

Sure enough, after supper was over and the dishes were cleared away, after Brylee had retreated into her apartment, taking both kids and four out of five dogs right along with her to watch the current crop of reality shows on her big-screen TV, after Walker and Casey had shared a bath in his long, deep tub, things **did** get better, and then better still.

Montana sprawled all around Walker, blessedly normal, as he and Shane rode out to look for strays, accompanied by all three of the boy's dogs.

The uproar in the media had gone on for the better part of a week, but then, after a catastrophic earthquake in South America, Casey and Walker and their "love children" became old news.

Hell of a way to escape the limelight, though. Relief agencies from all over the world had their operations up and running at the scene of the disaster, and the situation was dire.

Deliberately turning his mind back to his usual concerns, since there was nothing he could do for the earthquake victims besides making a donation, Walker readjusted his hat and shifted a little in the saddle, wondering how Casey had managed to raise Clare and Shane to be reasonably grounded human beings when practically everything she did or said seemed to be a matter for public scrutiny. Granted, this last round had been unusual, even for them, but Walker wouldn't be forgetting it anytime soon.

Beside him, riding Smokey, Shane mimicked the hat-shifting gesture the way he mimicked just about everything Walker did. The kid seemed to be trying out different mannerisms, picking the ones he liked.

Walker was both amused and touched.

"So the Parable County Rodeo is coming up," Shane said. It was an intro, of course, a preamble, an opening riff.

Walker grinned to himself. Let the kid think he was being subtle. Where was the harm in that?

"Yep," he agreed. Remembering what Clare had said about his one-word sentences, he grinned again. "It's always the weekend right before the Fourth of July."

"And we'll be providing the bucking stock?"

"Always do," Walker said. Two words now. Why, he was turning downright loquacious! He didn't ask the boy where the conversation was headed, because he already knew.

Sure enough, Shane finally came out with it. "Do you think I could enter one of the junior events?"

Walker didn't smile, but he wanted to. "You mean, like the mutton busting?" he teased. The younger kids rode sheep in that particular event, and it was a lot harder than it looked—Walker had done it himself, back when he was knee-high to the proverbial grasshopper. So had Brylee.

Shane colored up, glaring out from under the brim of the hat he'd found in the tack room a few days before and immediately appropriated. It didn't quite fit him, and he kept having to push it back off the bridge of his freckled nose, where a red welt was forming. "Riding **sheep?**" he marveled furiously. "That's for little kids!"

Walker was unruffled. He cast a side-long glance in his son's direction and drawled, "You're too easy to rile, boy. If you don't get over that, and quick, you'll get nothing else done but defending your honor."

Shane gulped and scowled into the distance, ostensibly looking for strays.

"As for the rodeo," Walker went on idly when Shane didn't reply, "you're gonna have to consult your mother on that one."

"You're my dad," Shane pointed out, still testy but leaking steam instead of spouting it, as before. "Your permission should be enough."

Walker chuckled. "That theory might have held water once upon a time," he said, "but 'once upon a time' was quite a while ago."

"So you're saying Mom is the boss and you'll do whatever she says?"

He sighed. "Watch it," he warned pleasantly. "What I'm **saying** is, your mother has raised you and Clare this far, with no help from me, and I can't see my way clear to step in now and start overriding her decisions."

Shane grumbled under his breath for a few moments, riding along beside Walker in silence, but it soon became clear that he hadn't been retreating, he'd been reloading. "You'd **never** go against anything Mom said?" he challenged.

"I didn't say that," Walker answered. "But I'd have to feel pretty strongly to raise an objection, because she's a smart woman, and it just so happens that she's right about most things."

A long, throbbing silence fell.

Then Shane asked evenly, "Do you think she was right to lie to Clare and me since we were babies?"

He'd been expecting this for a while, but it still unsettled him a little.

"No," Walker replied reasonably, "but sometimes people do the wrong thing for the right reasons. Things aren't as cut-and-dried as they seem from your perspective, son—a lot of decisions are shots in the dark, judgment calls, essentially, and it's **real** easy to make a mistake."

Shane mulled that over for a while. They spotted half a dozen strays on the other side of a thicket of brush and rounded them up, with considerable help from the dogs, heading them toward the main herd.

They bawled and kicked up dust, those cows, too stupid to know they were on their way back to good water and safety in numbers. Walker cussed them a little out of sheer habit, calling them sorry-looking, lop-eared knot-heads, much to Shane's amusement.

"You got something against cows, Dad?" the boy asked.

"Facts are facts," Walker replied with a grin. "Dogs are smart. Horses are smarter yet. But there's only one do-mestic animal dumber than these crit-ters, and that's a sheep."

The remark brought them right back around to the subject of the upcoming junior rodeo, albeit indirectly.

"I'm too old for mutton busting," Shane said.

"Tell that to your mother," Walker an-swered.

An hour later, when they got back to the barn, Shane did a creditable job of unsaddling Smokey, leading him into his stall, checking his hooves and giving him a good brushing down.

Casey came out of the house as they were approaching, looking four kinds of good in trim jeans and a white suntop with a few strategically placed ruffles. Walker drank in the sight of her, thinking they'd get through life just fine, the pair of them, if they made love every night and took care not to say more than two words to each other in the daylight.

They had their tender moments, Walker was willing to admit that much, but they still disagreed on just about every subject known to civilization.

She favored one political party, he supported the other.

She wanted to keep Clare and Shane close to home, so they wouldn't be kidnapped, develop drug habits or give interviews to scumball reporters.

Walker believed in giving kids as much freedom as they could handle. How else would they learn to stand on their own?

Casey insisted on going to church as a family, while Walker thought he was more likely to make God's acquaintance on the open range than inside some building with a belfry and pews.

It seemed to Walker that they both had one foot in the marriage, and one foot out, and either one of them might bolt at any time.

Oh, but the sex was better than good.

And Casey was all but certain she was carrying their baby.

Count your blessings, cowboy, Walker thought.

"Mom," Shane began, "I was wondering—"

"Not now," Casey broke in. She tried to smile at her son, but something was wrong and Walker knew it. "Go on inside so I can talk to your dad."

Shane jerked off his hat, slapped it against his thigh and stalked off toward the house.

Walker and Casey remained where they were—just outside the barn door, in the last blaze of afternoon sunshine.

Walker tensed, knowing something—God only knew what—was coming.

"Might as well just come right out and say it," he said, adjusting his hat.

"Mitch called," she said. "Some artists are putting together a benefit concert—for the earthquake victims."

In his mind, Walker saw instant replays of some of the news clips out of South America. Children separated, perhaps permanently, from their parents. Bad water and broken roads, houses and buildings toppled, tents serving as temporary hospitals, doctors and nurses working shifts that were measured in days, rather than hours.

"And you want to be part of it," Walker said. He understood her desire to help, and shared it, but he saw this as the beginning of a tug-of-war that might last for the rest of their lives. Work pulling against home and family, and vice versa. Eventually, the rope would break.

Casey swallowed, nodded. "Yes."

"Where?" Walker asked, turning his hat brim in his hands, in slow, thoughtful revolutions.

"L.A.," Casey answered, watching him closely. "The concert will be shown live all over the world, next Saturday night. There's some setting up to do, though, and of course I'll want to rehearse with the band—"

"Of course," Walker agreed, thinking he'd sounded snappish, when he hadn't meant to, but not ready to backpedal and make it right.

"I know that's the weekend of the rodeo over in Parable, and I was supposed to sing the national anthem, but—"

"Folks will understand," Walker put in.

"Will you?" Casey asked.

The question stung. She knew he'd seen the devastation left by that earthquake; did she think his heart was made of concrete?

"Do what you have to do, Casey," he said gruffly. "I'll look after the kids and the critters and we'll all be just fine."

She slipped her arms around him, laid her cheek against his chest. "I thought you'd try to talk me out of this," she confessed. "Because of—everything."

He curled a finger under her chin, lifted her face so he could look directly into her now-misty green eyes. "I'd rather you stayed," he said, in all honesty, "mainly because there might be a baby on the way, and for a few other reasons, too."

Casey's whole being twinkled as she gazed back at him, casting her spell. "Will you miss me?"

"You, yes. The sex, yes. The bickering—not so much."

She pretended indignation. At least, Walker **hoped** she was pretending.

"You know that old phrase **honest to a fault?**" she asked.

"I know it," Walker said.

"It describes you to perfection."

He laughed and then, because he couldn't help it, because he could already feel her slipping away into that other life, where he was a foreigner, he kissed her.

CHAPTER FIFTEEN

Casey took a commercial flight out of Missoula the next morning, changed planes in Seattle and landed in Los Angeles after several delays, to be met outside security by a smiling Mitch, the guys in her band, her technical crew and other important members of the entourage.

While they waited for her luggage near one of the baggage carousels, autograph seekers and a few representatives of the tabloid press crowded in close.

Casey had always thrived on this kind

of attention—hell, she'd **loved** it, would have felt invisible without it, even just a few months before—but something had changed. All she could think about was Walker and the kids and the peaceful grandeur of Timber Creek Ranch, with its canopy of sky and miles of open space, that sacred sense of being tucked into the heart of God.

Nothing if not professional, though, she smiled and signed her name and posed for cell-phone snapshots, even answered a few questions from the "reporters," but part of her simply wasn't present.

Mike Reynolds, her lead guitar player and longtime friend, must have seen through the act, because once they'd collected her bags, made their way to one of several waiting limos and ducked inside, he looked her straight in the eye and said, "I've seen sadder brides, but I can't remember when."

Mitch and two assistants rode with them, but, mercifully, they had their heads together, busily conferring over various schedules—rehearsals, radio and TV interviews, a few public appearances in random places like shopping malls, and photo ops with politicians and other celebrities.

Casey tried to smile at Mike, but she'd used up most of her wattage back there in the baggage area. Her comeback— "How many of those sad brides were yours?"—fell a little flat.

Mike merely grinned, used to being kidded about his overactive love life, but his eyes were solemn as he looked at her, seeing too much. "Case," he said patiently, "this is me. Mike. Next best thing to a brother. Please don't tell me things are going wrong between you and the cowboy already."

"'The cowboy,'" she reminded him gently, "has a name. It's Walker. And, no, it isn't that. I'm just a little—"

I'm just a little pregnant.

Maybe.

Please, God.

"Worn-out?" Sweet Mike, prodding for answers and then trying to throw her a conversational lifeline.

She shook her head. **I'm not sure I even want this crazy, wonderful gypsy life anymore,** she thought to herself.

And if I'm not Casey Elder, country-music hotshot, then who am I?

This was an identity crisis.

"I miss Clare and Shane, and Walker, of course," she replied. That was purest truth, but it wasn't the **whole** truth. Not that she owed an explanation to Mike or anybody else. Would have been nice to understand it **herself,** though. "It's been great, spending so much time together. Not being on the road, rushing from place to place, setting up gear and taking it down again."

As if she'd set up or taken down equipment since the earliest days of her career, but still.

Mike ducked his shaggy head slightly and looked at her even more closely than before. "Really? You really don't miss the road? Because I've been climbing the walls—itching to hit the concert circuit and soak up some bright lights and unbridled adoration."

Casey chuckled, but deep down, she felt an ache of guilt. She couldn't expect Mike or the others in the group to cool their vocational heels indefinitely, waiting for her to take up where she'd left off. They were talented musicians— some of the best in the business—and they were still in the prime of their lives, working and otherwise.

They had plans and dreams of their own, naturally, and even though money wasn't an issue for any of them, the occasional recording and video session at her house in Parable, Montana, wasn't going to be enough to satisfy their creative drive, not forever, anyhow.

"You getting restless, Mike?" she asked finally.

Beyond the tinted windows of the limo, palm trees and looping tangles of freeway zipped by. Cars were everywhere, taking people somewhere else, always somewhere else. Why wasn't it okay to just **be** in one place, even for a little while?

Mike took her hand and patted the back of it. "It's not that," he said. "I just miss the music we made together. So do the other guys."

"Me, too," she said. "Sometimes."

Mike smiled. "And other times?"

"Other times, I just want to learn to cook comfort food, ride horses and sit in the porch swing, watching that big Montana sky change. The kids are growing up so fast it makes my head spin—I can't stop thinking about the way time slips by." She paused for a deep, slow breath, knowing her talk of home and family probably sounded pretty prosaic to Mike, a man used to traveling in the fast lane, always at full throttle. "I like my life." **And I** love **Walker Parrish, even if I am scared to tell him so.**

"Okay," Mike said, musing, gazing out the car window now.

Clearly the conversation was over, for the time being at least, and if nothing had been settled, well, Casey was getting used to that. She'd always been so certain, so focused. Now, she was totally uncertain.

Clare was still angry and confused, and Shane, though he put a good face on things, surely had some issues of his own.

And then there was Walker, the man she loved. The man she'd basically cheated out of his son's and daughter's childhoods. At times, she could almost believe that Walker cared for her, cared deeply, especially when they made love. **Other** times, like now, she wondered if he'd ever be able to forgive her completely, as hard as he might try.

Battling despair, she settled deeper into the cushy seat of that limo and silently reminded herself that, problems or no problems, the Casey Elder show must go on. She knew all her lines, and why wouldn't she? She'd had years of practice, built herself a successful persona. But was there a real person behind the polished image?

Hard to say.

Brylee couldn't help with the kids while Casey was away because she had her annual "motivational retreat" scheduled for that week, and several hundred of her salespeople would be converging on the campgrounds near her company headquarters to stay in cabins, sit around campfires, receive awards and be inundated with workshops and speeches.

She was taking Snidely with her, and she'd invited Clare to go along, but it seemed to Walker that the girl had developed mildly antisocial tendencies since Casey's departure for L.A. She mostly hid out in her room, where, according to Shane Parrish, Master Spy, she kept company with her cats, changed the polish on her fingernails and toes roughly every ten minutes, read books, surfed the internet and picked out mournful ballads on an old guitar.

Once or twice, Walker got as far as her closed door, fist raised to knock companionably, but each time, something had stopped him. She'd been singing, and her voice was so like Casey's that it haunted him, as did the few lyrics he could make out. The theme was clear enough, though—loneliness, deception, betrayal.

Was this regulation teen angst, Walker wondered helplessly, or genuine sorrow?

Back in the day, when he'd been the guy who came to dinner now and then, he'd have known how to reach Clare. Ironically, now that he'd assumed the role of father, he didn't seem to have a clue.

No, what he had, apparently, was a gift for saying the wrong thing.

Relating to Shane was easier, since they had more in common, both being male for starters. They shared a love of horses and wide-open spaces and rodeo, too, and their outlooks and basic thought processes were remarkably similar. Though the boy did show flashes of resentment now and then, he also tried hard to make the best of whatever came his way.

The same could not be said of Clare, though, and it worried Walker, not just because her attitude hurt Casey, but because she seemed to be drifting away from all of them, becoming someone else, closing the book on their efforts to forge the framework of a family.

Life went on, though, and there were chores to be done, meals to be cooked and eaten, plans to be made, with the rodeo coming up so soon. Walker put one foot in front of the other, mostly, missing Casey with an ache that ground inside him 24/7.

"I forgot to ask Mom if I could enter the rodeo," Shane said on the third night Casey had been gone, after they'd eaten supper and done the dishes. The two of them were alone in the kitchen, except for the dogs; Clare had eaten a few bites and helped clear the table after the meal, but she hadn't said more than two words the whole time, and she'd retreated to her room at the first opportunity.

Walker refrained from pointing out that the boy had had plenty of chances to make his pitch, since Casey called regularly and texted even more often than she dialed the home number.

"So text her," he said.

"She's rehearsing," Shane reminded him. "And then she's having dinner with a bunch of VIPs. The vice president is going to be there."

Walker knew all that—he'd spoken often with Casey, though always briefly and in a sort of awkward, out-of-step way. "She'll read the text and answer when she gets a chance," he told his son. "As she always does."

Shane rolled his eyes. "She'll say **no,**" he said. "Without even thinking about it.

Because that's what she does when she's busy, which is all the time. She just says **no** and goes right on doing whatever she's doing."

"That being the reason you haven't asked her," Walker observed mildly.

"All I want to do is enter one stupid rodeo event," Shane persisted. "What's the big, huge, hairy deal?"

Walker, sitting at the table now, with one last cup of coffee going cold in front of him, stifled a smile. "Which 'stupid event' do you have in mind?" he asked, in his own good time.

Shane's whole face lit up. "Bareback riding," he answered. "Broncs."

Oh, hell, Walker thought. He knew what bucking horses could do, because he bred them to do it. "That's a rugged game," he said. "Even in the junior category."

"They're **all** rugged," Shane argued spiritedly. "That's the whole point. It's **rodeo.**"

"Have you ever been bucked off a horse?" Walker asked calmly.

Color flared in the boy's earnest face. Tanned and freckled from all the time he'd been spending outdoors, helping Walker and the hands with ranch work, he was beginning to look more like a real, rough-and-tumble country kid than the sheltered son of a famous singer. Casey had done a good job raising him, and his sister, too, despite the present rocky road they were all traveling, but she wasn't big on letting either one of her children take chances.

It went without saying that taking foolish ones, like hitchhiking or messing with drugs or alcohol, would never lead to anything but trouble and heartache. But calculated risks? That was another thing, an important part of growing up and learning to hold your own in a tough world.

"Did **you** enter the junior rodeo when you were a kid?" Shane wanted to know.

He'd make a damn good lawyer, Walker thought, or even a politician, though he sincerely hoped the boy wouldn't take that route. Most politicians ranked pretty low on Walker's list.

"Yes," Walker replied wearily. "But I'd ridden horses all my life, Shane, and my dad believed a few hard knocks were good for a person." **My mother, on the other hand, far from being overprotective like yours, just didn't give a damn what I did, one way or the other.**

"How am I supposed to grow up to be just like you if you won't let me **do** anything?" Shane pressed.

Walker, ridiculously pleased that the boy even **wanted** to be like him, now or at any time in the future, thought the kid had a point. Risk was part of life, and not much could be accomplished without it.

"Here's the deal," he said at some length. "I'll ask your mother if you can ride in the rodeo—do my best to talk her into it, too—but if she says **no,** then **no** it is. Agreed?"

Shane put out his hand to shake on the agreement, beaming again. "Agreed," he said.

Obviously, the boy had more faith in his dad's influence over Casey than history justified, but there was no harm in trying.

Shane took the dogs outside, Doolittle included, waited while they did what dogs do outside and then merrily retreated to his room to play video games on his computer, his feet barely touching the floor as he walked out of the kitchen, trailed by a trio of loyal canines.

Doolittle stayed behind, resting his muzzle on Walker's knee and gazing soulfully up into his eyes.

Walker laughed and patted the mutt's head. "You're a good old dog," he said.

He sat there a while, wondering if he'd be interrupting something important if he called Casey on her cell, then took the advice he'd given Shane and texted her instead. **Call me when you get a chance,** he wrote. **Nothing to worry about on this end, but I've got a question to ask.**

Five minutes later, his phone rang, and he felt a little leap of anticipation when he saw Casey's number in the caller ID panel.

"Hey," she said, sounding shy and slightly breathless.

"Hey," he said back.

"So what's the question?" she prompted after waiting a few beats.

When are you coming home? was certainly a contender, and so was **Do teenage girls speak a language all their own and, if so, can you clue me in on some of the basic vocabulary?**

Walker cleared his throat. Best stick to the point. "Shane wants to enter the rodeo."

"No way," Casey said immediately.

"Not the regular rodeo—the one for kids."

A silence.

"Are you still there?" Walker prodded.

"Riding sheep or something like that?" Casey asked. He could practically feel the wheels and gears turning in her head.

"Not exactly."

"Then, what?"

"Bronc busting," Walker said, feeling much as he had as a kid, when the river froze over and he took the first, cautious step onto the ice, hoping it would hold his weight.

"Bronc busting?" Casey echoed. "Not just no, but **hell,** no."

"Casey, this isn't bull riding at the National Finals. It's kid rodeo, in Parable,

Montana. I provide the horses myself and, trust me, the ones for the junior events are not the kind you're probably picturing right now."

"Shane is thirteen," Casey reminded him. "The only time he's done any horseback riding at all was when he visited you on the ranch. Walker, **he could get killed.**"

"Or he could just get a mouthful of dirt, feel real good because he tried and be ready the next time he faces a challenge."

"You want to let him ride," Casey accused. She might have used the same tone to say, **You told him to jump off a bridge.**

"Yes," Walker said. "He's good on a horse, Case—a natural."

He didn't need to see her face to know she was biting her lower lip, torn between the knowledge that Walker was right about Shane's abilities and the rigors of growing up and a natural desire to protect her child from unnecessary dangers.

"I'm his mother," Casey said, rhetorically, of course. "It's my job to make sure my son doesn't break his neck in some rodeo arena."

"And I'm his father," Walker pointed out quietly. "So he's **our** son."

"Is this some kind of macho thing?" Casey asked after another silence. "Is it some rite of passage?"

Walker chuckled. "Neither," he said. "Shane doesn't have to prove himself to me or anybody else, Casey, but he wants this. A lot."

"It's genetic," Casey spouted. To hear her tell it, a person would have thought Walker had passed down a penchant for robbing banks through his DNA, instead of a love for all things Western, including rodeo.

"Maybe," Walker allowed. "But this isn't about me, Casey, and it isn't about you. It's about Shane, pure and simple, and the man he'll be some day."

"If anything happens to him, Walker Parrish—"

Inwardly, Walker sighed with relief and no little amazement. **I'll be damned,** he thought, **she's caving.**

"Nothing's going to happen to Shane," he said when she left the last part of her sentence dangling. "Most likely, he'll take a spill, but that's one hell of a lot better than hanging back because he's afraid. Trying will net him some bruises for sure, but **not trying** will hurt his soul."

"I hate it when you're philosophical."

"No, you hate it when I'm right."

Another pause. "If he's afraid, why does he want to enter the rodeo?" Casey asked, sounding resigned now, but also confounded.

"Courage isn't about not being scared," Walker explained gently. "It's about being frightened out of your mind and going ahead with whatever it is you want to do, in spite of the fear." He paused for a second or two. "Kind of like stepping out onto a stage that first time, and singing for an arena packed with people who might or might not like what they hear."

"That's different," Casey said, but weakly.

"Is it? Weren't you scared the first time you opened for some big-name act, thinking you might get booed off the stage if only because you weren't the performer the audience came to see?"

"Heck," Casey answered, "I **still** get scared."

Walker smiled. That was a big admission, for one of the queens of country music. "I miss you," he said.

"Me, too," she answered. "I mean, I miss you and the kids, not that I miss myself."

"I figured that was what you meant," Walker teased. He wanted to say he loved her, right then and there, but he didn't, because there were over a thousand miles between them and things like that had to be said face-to-face, if only the first time. "Come home soon."

"Sunday morning," she said with a little sigh that raised Walker's spirits considerably. "In the meantime, it's interviews, and fancy dinners with speeches, and plenty of rehearsals and sound checks."

"Speaking of fancy dinners," Walker said, wondering if he was detaining her, keeping her from rejoining the VIPs, "Shane says you're eating with the vice president."

"Yes," Casey confirmed in a whisper, "and the man is a dweeb."

Walker laughed. "I voted for that guy's running mate," he said. "And, therefore, indirectly, for him."

"There is no accounting for taste," Casey replied succinctly. "How's Clare doing?"

"Well," Walker joked, "she hasn't been arrested or run off to join the circus or anything drastic like that."

"Gee, that's comforting," Casey responded.

"Clare's acting like what she is," Walker said, seriously now, "a fourteen-year-old girl whose life was just turned upside down, trying to figure out what the heck hit her." They were all dealing with some variation of the same theme, he supposed.

"Keep them safe, Walker," Casey said. It was a request, not a command—almost a plea.

"Count on it," Walker replied.

"See you Sunday," she said. "We'll probably talk before then, but . . ." Again, her voice trailed off.

"See you Sunday," Walker affirmed gruffly.

Sunday, it seemed to him, was a long way off.

The junior rodeo opened on Friday afternoon, and Shane strutted around with his number pinned to the back of his shirt, sporting the new hat Walker had bought him and brimming with confidence. He was eager to ride, and bone-certain he'd wind up in the money when the final scores were tallied. Stranger things had happened.

Walker hoped the boy would place, of course, but he knew most of the other kids entered in the competition, and they were good. The horses and bulls, while tamer than some, were appropriate for the sport, which meant they were flat-out ornery and guaranteed to do their best to unseat a cowboy long before the buzzer sounded.

Clare, who had come along only because Walker refused to leave her home alone, shook her head as she watched her younger brother conferring with other cowboys his age. "He's such an idiot," she said.

Walker, just back from taking a look at the day's stock, all of which belonged to him, adjusted his hat. "Harsh words," he replied easily. "If I thought you really believed that, I'd be mighty discouraged."

Clare sighed heavily. She was wearing jeans, sneakers and one of Walker's old shirts, and she carried a backpack, a fact he didn't register as unusual. Not at the time, anyhow.

"What if Shane gets hurt?" she fretted.

Walker grinned down at her. "Chances are, he won't," he said.

"Mom will **kill** you if Shane breaks a bone or gets a concussion or something," the girl warned. "He's her favorite, you know."

Walker hid his surprise. "She will indeed be four kinds of furious if anything like that happens," he agreed, "but what makes you think your mom favors either one of you over the other?"

"Parents always have a favorite," Clare said wisely, still watching her brother.

"They just won't admit it, but kids know anyway."

"Well," Walker replied slowly, "I'm a parent, it just so happens, and I love you just as much as I love Shane."

Clare made a sputtering sound with her lips, a sort of modified raspberry, adequate to convey her skepticism. "He's a **boy.** Dads always like boys better than girls."

"Not true," Walker said, wondering why important conversations like this one always seemed to start up in public places, when there was little or no time to pursue the matter. On impulse, he plopped his hat onto his daughter's head and tugged the brim down over her eyes.

Much to Walker's relief, Clare laughed. "Really?" she asked, pushing back the hat and looking up at him with the first hint of a sparkle he'd seen in her in days.

"Really," he confirmed, choked up and trying not to show it.

She took off his hat, handed it to him. That quick, the father-daughter moment was over.

"Some of my friends from school are here," she said, not bothering with a segue. "Mind if I go find them?"

Walker nodded his permission, but qualified it with "Stay on the rodeo grounds, and check in, either by cell phone or in person, every hour or so."

She sighed dramatically but Walker thought, by the look in her eyes, that she was glad he was looking out for her. Later, he'd wonder if he was any better at predicting teenage behavior than he was at saying the right words at the right time, but at the moment, he was a sucker for a pretty girl—especially when that pretty girl was his daughter.

"All right," she agreed, and disappeared into the growing crowds.

Walker immediately had second thoughts. There were a lot of spectators on hand for the big weekend, out-of-towners as well as locals. Had he done the right thing, letting Clare go off looking for her friends? Casey, given her tendency to hire bodyguards and avail herself and her children of police escorts, probably wouldn't approve.

The trouble was, it was too late to

call Clare back—she was already out of sight and, unless he missed his guess, she wouldn't answer if he called her cell.

This is Parable County, Montana, he reminded himself. **Not the mean streets of some big city.**

The opening ceremony was impressive, with flags and firecrackers and a six-jet flyover, courtesy of the United States Air Force. The kids in the high school chorus group sang "The Star-Spangled Banner," and every hat was off as men, women and children joined in.

When that part was over, Walker made his way behind the chutes, looking for Shane but trying not to be too obvious about it.

The calf roping was just starting, soon to be followed by steer wrestling—also known as bull dogging, in rodeo lingo. After that would come the barrel racing, an all-girl competition, and a show of skill on the part of both the rider and the horse that never failed to rouse Walker's admiration.

Shane appeared as quickly as his sister had vanished, standing beside Walker at the fence. He'd probably been hanging out with his buddies from school, but none of them were around at the moment.

"Does that hurt the calves?" the boy asked quietly, watching the competition over the top rail of the fence. Clearly, this wasn't a concern he wanted broadcast all over the rodeo grounds. "Being roped like that, then jerked off their feet and tied up?"

"No," Walker said. "It's not like roping a human being or a dog and throwing them down. Calves are sturdy little devils, but if they look at all fragile for any reason, we pull them before the competition gets started." He paused, watching the proceedings for a few moments. Shane hadn't said anything in reply, which might mean he had his doubts. "Roping calves is part of ranching," Walker went on. "It's usually the only way to give them their shots or treat them for disease or any kind of injury."

Shane nodded. "I guess calves don't

come when you call them, the way dogs do," he observed.

Walker laughed and slapped his son on the shoulder. "Nope," he said. "They surely don't come when you call them."

They watched another competitor and then another, in companionable silence, as did lots of other fathers and sons. Both calves evaded the rope entirely, to the discouragement of the youthful and very earnest cowboys attempting to lasso them from the back of their trained horses.

"I drew a bronc called Backflip," Shane said as the announcer chatted up the audience while another calf and mounted rider prepared to make their run.

Walker knew Backflip, of course—knew all the horses, because he owned them. This particular animal was a fair-to-middling bucker, but he didn't have the juice for the main event, so he'd wound up in the junior category. "He's a good ride," Walker said, studying the boy out of the corner of one eye. He seemed nervous, which only showed he had good sense, but wasn't out-and-out scared.

"I guess eight seconds probably seems like a long time, when you're out there trying to stay on some bronc or bull."

"It can be an eternity," Walker said, speaking from experience. He'd given up rodeo a long time ago, except for some fooling around out on the ranch, when he and Al and the hands were winnowing out the duds, broncos and bulls who weren't athletically inclined, and there were times when he missed it a lot.

What he **didn't** miss was eating dirt, hitting the ground hard and running like hell for the fence when a bull came after him instead of just trotting off across the arena, the way they usually did, proudly showing themselves to be cowboy-free.

"If you don't feel ready to tackle this, Shane," he added quietly when the boy didn't say more, "that's okay. Nobody will think any less of you for it, including me."

Shane beamed at him. "I'm gonna do

this," he said, and that was the end of that particular discussion.

Clare checked in by cell phone, as agreed, some forty-five minutes later. She was hanging out with some of her friends from school, and they were all headed for the carnival, set up right there on the fairgrounds, to try out some of the rides.

Walker, reassured, told her to have fun and call back in an hour.

By then, Shane had wandered off with a few of his pals, and Walker, thinking this fathering business wasn't as hard as folks made it out to be—folks like Casey, for instance—didn't give the matter another thought.

When the bareback event finally got underway, Walker kept some distance between himself and the chutes, knowing it would embarrass Shane if he hovered too close.

Shane was the third rider in the lineup, as it turned out, and Backflip proved himself worthy of his name by shaking the kid off at the three-second mark.

Shane landed hard, sprawled on his back, while the pickup men herded

Backflip out of the arena without incident.

"A good try for a first-timer!" the announcer boomed as Shane got his wind back, rolled to his feet and stooped to retrieve his hat. "That's Shane Parrish, ladies and gentlemen, from over in Three Trees. Let's give him a hand!"

The crowd cheered.

Using his phone, Walker snapped a quick picture of his son, dented and dust-covered as he ambled toward the fence, grinning from ear to ear. He texted the shot to Casey, so she'd know Shane was alive and well in spite of entering the rodeo, snapped the device shut and dropped it back into his shirt pocket.

Shane scrambled deftly over the fence to stand beside Walker, with that grin still splitting his face.

"I did it," he said.

"You sure did," Walker agreed, resting a hand on the boy's shoulder, his voice a mite gruff.

In the next moment, his phone rang, and Walker plucked it out of his pocket, expecting the caller to be Casey.

Instead, it was Treat McQuillan.

"One of my officers just arrested your daughter on a charge of shoplifting," the chief of police said, not even trying to hide his satisfaction over this turn of events. "We're holding her here, at the station."

CHAPTER SIXTEEN

Casey, taking a break in her dressing room between rehearsals, smiled at the snapshot Walker had sent, showing a recently thrown Shane sauntering across the rodeo arena back in Parable, covered in dust and grinning as widely as if he'd just been named All-Around Cowboy for that year.

She was about to respond with a digital thumbs-up when the second message came in. Expecting another installment in the Shane saga, Casey opened it.

This new image brought her up short,

made her breath catch in her throat and her heart lurch, then go into free fall. The picture showed a sullen Clare, hands cuffed behind her back, being placed in the back of a police car.

Fresh shock jolted through Casey before the first rush had entirely abated, swamping her whole system with adrenaline. She paced, shaking, and Mitch, who had been chatting with the hair and makeup people, noticed her distress, came over to her and silently took the phone from her hands.

She watched, helpless with panic, as her manager took in the shot of Clare, and though his color changed a little, he stayed cool. Expertly, Mitch thumbed from that screen to another, searching for the sender's name.

Casey could have told him not to bother, that he wouldn't find it. People who took pictures like that, delighting in the havoc it would wreak, normally crawled right back under their favorite rock as soon as the deed was done.

"No information," Mitch said with a sigh. "I can get in touch with your service provider, have them do some checking—"

"Forget it," Casey said. "Even if we found the sender, it wouldn't help." She drew in a breath, thought of all the good people who were depending on her and the other performers to make the benefit concert a big success. A **lifesaving** success, for some of the victims of that South American earthquake. "I've got to get back to Parable, Mitch. As soon as possible."

"Your show is tomorrow night," Mitch reminded her gently. "And it's live, Casey."

"We could record our performance—"

"Casey. Get a grip. It looks as though Clare's in some trouble, all right. But she's not injured or sick. If this turns out to be an emergency, fine, Godspeed, catch the first plane home, do whatever you need to do and I'll cover for you on this end. But we don't know that it **is** an emergency, do we?"

Knowing Mitch was right didn't do one thing to calm Casey down. Concerned raged in her like a fever. "That's my **daughter** in that picture, Mitch," Casey replied in a ragged whisper.

"And she has a father," Mitch replied reasonably. This was the old Mitch, the one she knew so well, not the one who had proposed to her, and that was reassuring. "Walker's right there, isn't he? Anyway, the situation probably isn't as bad as it looks. Kids do stupid things, Casey. It **happens.**"

All well and good, but this wasn't some nameless stranger, some statistic—this was **Clare.** Her firstborn, her baby, and she felt 100 percent responsible.

It made sense to call Walker, though. She shooed Mitch and the others out of her dressing room and speed-dialed her husband's cell number.

Walker's voice was taut when he answered, an immediate giveaway that he already knew Clare was in trouble, and he probably knew why. Instead of **hello,** he said, "Take a breath, Casey. I'll handle this."

Casey thought the crown of her head might just shoot skyward, like a dinner plate spinning atop an erupting geyser.

"You'll handle it? Walker, **what happened?** Why did I just receive a picture of my daughter in handcuffs from some—some **onlooker?**"

"I'm on my way to the police station right now," Walker replied calmly, though his voice was as rough and rocky as the bottom of a dry creek bed. "All I know is Clare's been charged with shoplifting. One of Treat McQuillan's officers arrested her, somewhere on the rodeo grounds."

Somewhere on the rodeo grounds?

He'd let Clare go wandering off, unattended? Didn't he realize how many things could have happened to her?

She didn't dare go there, not now, anyway.

"Shoplifting? Clare?" Casey stopped pacing and collapsed into the chair in front of her dressing-room mirror. Seeing herself in triplicate was hardly comforting, so she wheeled the seat around backward. "It must be a mistake."

Walker took a beat too long to answer. "We'll see," he said, measuring out his words in a sparing way that put an invisible wall between them. "Casey,

I'll call you as soon as I know exactly where things stand—I promise. In the meantime, try to be calm."

So much for good intentions. "Calm? **Calm?** I leave home for a few days— **less than a week,** Walker—and something like this happens?" While she didn't actually accuse him outright of neglecting their daughter, the implication was there just the same. **I trusted you.**

"I'll call you, Casey," Walker reiterated flatly, drawing the words out, leaving wide spaces between them.

Casey nodded, overcome, remembered Walker couldn't see her and said, "Do that, please."

The call ended there.

Since there was nothing Casey could do but wait, she practiced deep breathing until her shoulders lowered, no longer pressing against her ears, and the muscles in her neck, though still tight, began to relax a little. If she hadn't had reason to believe she was pregnant, she probably would have sent out for a drink—a double shot of whatever, on the rocks. Moonshine, maybe. Did they sell moonshine in L.A.?

It didn't matter.

Clare mattered and she, Casey, was two plane rides away.

The spiffy new Parable Municipal Police Station occupied the spot where the town's "historic" water tower had stood, until a few concerned citizens tore it down the day Dawson McCullough fell fifty feet and did permanent damage to his spine.

Walker parked his truck in one of three spots marked Visitor, shut off the engine and shoved open the door. "Wait here," he told Shane, who was sitting, pale and wide-eyed, in the passenger seat.

The station house was small, with a reception area in front, composed of a counterlike desk, a computer, a multiline phone and not much else. The chairs were plastic, and there were a few outdated magazines scattered around, in case somebody wanted to do a little light reading while they waited to see a prisoner, evidently.

There were a grand total of two cells in back, behind Treat McQuillan's cubicle-size office, giving the place a distinctly Mayberry feel. That was where the similarities ended, though, because McQuillan was nothing like the genial Sheriff Andy Taylor. No, he was a puffed-up, self-important little pit bull of a man, and he had to be enjoying **this** situation, big-time.

Walker didn't recognize the receptionist, a woman in her mid-forties who, going by the insignia on her starched blue uniform, doubled as a crossing guard or maybe a meter maid. Since the whole town of Parable only boasted a dozen parking meters and school was out for the summer, she must have worked the desk during the intervals between nothing-much and nothing-much.

"I'm here to see Clare Elder," he told the woman after giving his name.

The woman picked up a clipboard and made a production out of scanning several pages of official documents. Serious business, this. She and the Parable Police Department had a dangerous criminal on their hands, and they couldn't be too careful.

"I have a Clare **Parrish** listed," she said.

Walker unclamped his back molars. "That would be my daughter," he replied.

She gave him a look, as though she might have expected him to get the prisoner's name right in the first place, if he was Clare's father.

"I'll have to check with Chief McQuillan," the woman said after pursing her lips for a while, turning to open a door behind the counter, whisking through and shutting it with a click that struck Walker as faintly authoritarian.

Almost immediately, the chief popped out of his office, looking very pleased with himself, and when he spoke, his tone was gratingly cordial.

"Well," he said, "you certainly got here quickly."

"I want to see my daughter," Walker said evenly.

McQuillan opened the door wide and gestured grandly for Walker to precede him. The meter maid ducked out, looking smug.

Inside, Clare sat miserably at a small

round table, head lowered. She wasn't handcuffed, at least, and she wasn't wearing an orange jumpsuit with a number stenciled on it, but Walker took small consolation from those observations.

"I'm sorry," she said without looking up at Walker.

Walker scraped back a chair, sat down across from her. He glared at McQuillan in silence until the chief stepped out, leaving them alone.

"Clare," Walker began, as the girl began to cry without making a sound, "tell me what happened."

She spent a couple of moments gathering her composure, but she still wouldn't look at him. "I stole some earrings, from one of the vendors at the fairgrounds," she answered. A tear zigzagged down her right cheek, and she seemed to be folding in on herself, trying to disappear, shoulders stooped, head down, spine curved forward.

"Now, why would you do a thing like that?" Walker asked calmly. He would have expected to be angry as hell. As it turned out, he was heartbroken instead.

No need to ask where he'd gone wrong—
he knew that already.

"I don't know," Clare said, very softly.

"I think you do," Walker replied, his
tone mild.

She raised her eyes then, and he saw
shame in them, along with naked, hope-
less truth. "I was going to give the earrings back," she said, "or pay for them,
honest. I just wanted to see if I could
get away with it."

"Now you know," Walker said. "I've
heard stupider ideas in my time, but not
many of them. What were you thinking?"

Clare's shoulders rose and fell in a
semblance of a shrug, and that was answer enough. She **hadn't** been thinking—and that was the problem.

"I tried to explain when the vendor
caught me, but she was really pi—really
mad—and she called the police right
away. I guess it was technically the sheriff's jurisdiction, since the rodeo grounds
are outside the city limits, but maybe
some wires got crossed. Anyway, when
the cop got there, he must have recognized me, because he sort of sneered
and said celebrities' kids think they're

above the law, and he hoped some judge would make an example out of me." She paused, and the look on her face made Walker ache inside. She was only fourteen and, as far as he knew, she'd never been in this kind of trouble before. Throwing her mom's fame in her face seemed unfair, but that was the way of the world.

"Can we go home now?" she finished meekly.

She was young—too young to be tossed into a jail cell—but that didn't mean the situation wasn't serious. Walker wondered if his head was going soft, right along with his heart, but his instincts told him Clare was telling the truth—thus far, anyway.

He didn't answer her question right away. "So what was the purpose of the backpack?" Walker asked, having spotted the one she'd been carrying earlier on a table behind her.

Clare's chin wobbled, and tears brimmed in her Casey-green eyes. "I was going to run away," she admitted. "But then I got to thinking about how it was a dumb plan, about kidnappers and perverts and all the stuff they warn you about, and I changed my mind." She studied him closely. "Really, Walker. That's how it was."

He figured if she'd been trying to snow him, she'd have called him "Dad," not 'Walker," but there was no way to know for sure. He was going to have to trust Clare, at least for now. He'd give her a chance to prove she wasn't a bad kid; he owed her that much. He simply watched her, arms folded, saying nothing.

Clare sniffled. "Does Mom know?"

"She knows you've been arrested. We'll fill her in on the details in a little while."

Fifteen minutes later, acting as though he were turning Bonnie Parker loose on an unsuspecting society, McQuillan released Clare into Walker's custody, taking care to point out that, if the vendor followed through and pressed charges, a date would be set for her to appear in juvenile court.

Walker couldn't bring himself to thank the chief or shake his hand, either, but he made one concession. After signing the papers, he waited until he was outside to put his hat back on.

Clare, backpack slung by one strap over her right shoulder, opened the back door of the extended cab and climbed inside.

Shane, sitting in front, glanced back at her once, but a warning look from Walker stopped him from making any comments on his sister's budding criminal career.

Walker started the engine, got out his cell phone, keyed in Casey's number and handed the device back to Clare without a word.

The girl said, "Hi, Mom," and then broke into wrenching sobs. If this contrition was an act, Walker thought, it was a darn good one.

While he drove toward home, Clare sputtered out the story.

Walker stayed silent, and so did Shane.

They were almost at the turn-in at the ranch when Clare thrust the phone back at Walker, over his right shoulder. "Mom wants to talk to you," she said.

Walker drew the truck to a stop at the

gate, and Shane jumped out to swing it open. "Hello, Casey," Walker said stiffly, pressing the phone hard against his ear.

"Thanks," Casey said, and it sounded as though she wasn't in much better emotional shape than her daughter was. "Thanks for picking Clare up and taking her home, Walker."

What had she **thought** he'd do? Leave their fourteen-year-old in police custody? Suggest that Clare be remanded to some juvenile detention center to ponder the error of her ways?

Walker's voice was ice-cold when he replied. "You're welcome."

"I'll be home Saturday night—tomorrow—right after our gig is over," Casey said. "We can decide what to do then."

"We will definitely be deciding some things," Walker answered. He was madder than a scalded cat all of a sudden, but he couldn't have said if that anger was directed at himself, at Casey or at Clare. All he really knew was that some changes had to be made, and the sooner the better.

Casey drew a breath, but whatever

she'd been about to say, she held it in. "I'll see you tomorrow night."

"Good," Walker answered.

And they both hung up.

"Mom's disappointed in me," Clare said, very quietly, as they drove through the open gate. Shane shut and latched it behind them, but instead of getting back inside the truck, he rode on the running board, holding his hat in place with his free hand.

"She'll have to take a number," Walker replied.

Doolittle and the three chocolate Labs—Walker still couldn't keep their names straight, so he called them all "Dog"—were waiting at the kitchen door when he stepped over the threshold, and it cheered him up a little, their eager, uncomplicated welcome.

Clare lit out for her room right away, and Walker made no move to stop her.

While Shane fussed over the dogs and subsequently took them outside for a much-needed yard break, Walker washed his hands at the sink, as he'd done about a million times before, and opened the freezer side of the refrigerator, looking for supper possibilities.

Brylee, bless her practical and somewhat compulsive soul, cooked often, and he found a covered casserole dish, marked "Lasagna," wedged in behind a pork roast and a bag of green beans.

Lifting the lid, he noted that the food hadn't sprouted a coating of ice-fur or shrunk away from the sides of the dish, and thought, **Good enough.**

There were no instructions, but since Brylee's culinary concoctions always seemed to call for thirty minutes at 350 degrees, he turned the oven to that setting and waited for it to heat up.

Shane came back inside with the dogs, and hung his hat carefully beside Walker's on one of the pegs next to the door. After that, he rolled up his sleeves, washed his hands and face and the back of his neck at the sink, and used paper towels to dry off.

That last part, an improvisation, made Walker smile to himself.

"Clare's never been in trouble before," Shane announced very quietly.

Since the boy rarely if ever defended

his sister, Walker was struck by that
statement. He glanced over at Shane
and said, "All right."

"You believe me?"

"Why wouldn't I?'

The boy flushed with conviction and
maybe pleasure because Walker was
taking him at his word. "I think Clare did
what she did to get attention. Things
have been kind of confusing lately. I
mean, one day you're Mom's friend, a
sort of uncle, and the next, you're our
dad, and Mom's husband—"

"I know that, son," Walker said. The
timer buzzed and he opened the oven,
slid the dish of lasagna inside.

"I guess you'll probably just wash your
hands of us now," Shane went on. "Clare
and me, I mean. Because we're too
much trouble."

Walker turned slowly to face the boy.
"Son," he said, "I'm not going anywhere,
and neither are you or your sister. We're
a family now, and we're going to stick
together, the four of us, and figure things
out. It'll take gumption and elbow grease,
but we can do it."

The relief in Shane's face was so profound that Walker came as close to crying in that moment as he ever had in his adult life. Reaching out with one arm, he pulled the boy to him, gave him a quick but firm hug.

Shane clung to him for a moment, before remembering that he wasn't a little kid anymore and stepping back.

They finished throwing supper together, and Shane took a plate to Clare, along with a glass of milk and a wad of paper towels to serve as dinner napkins.

Later, Shane got out his cell phone and showed Walker a jerky video of that day's ride, taken by a friend of his.

"Not even three seconds," the boy commented, sounding unfazed.

"Three is better than nothing. I once got thrown while they were still opening the chute."

Shane looked pleased. "Really?"

"Gospel truth," Walker answered, holding up one hand to underscore the oath.

It was after midnight when Casey's chartered plane landed at the small airstrip midway between Parable and Three

Trees, and she was exhausted. Mitch had promised to have a car waiting to take her home to the ranch, but when she peered out of one of the oval-shaped windows, she saw a pickup truck instead.

Walker. Her heartbeat sped up a little, the way it always did when the two of them entered the same airspace. This proximity usually resulted in something more like a collision than an embrace, but she was glad he was there, nonetheless.

He got out of the truck as she came down the steps from the airplane, hatless in the thin moonlight, but he didn't approach. No, he just stood there, straight-spined and broad-shouldered, unsmiling.

Casey forced herself to move slowly, though she wanted nothing more than to run to Walker and leap into his arms. She stopped about three feet away from him, heart pounding.

"Clare's fine," he said at some length. "And so is Shane."

Casey swallowed hard, nodded. Behind her, the small private plane taxied for takeoff. She hadn't even brought her luggage along, she'd been in such a hurry to leave L.A.

"Do we have a chance, Walker?" she heard her own voice ask.

He frowned, and neither of them moved. "What do you mean, 'Do we have a chance?'" he asked.

"After all that's happened," Casey choked out, watching him. "Two babies, all that time apart, all the mistakes and the lies—" She couldn't go on.

Walker took her gently by the shoulders and said the words she'd thought he'd never say. "I love you, Casey. And the mistakes and lies belong to both of us, so why don't we just let them go and move on?"

"Did you just say you love me?" Casey all but whispered. Her voice was almost gone, and not just because she'd sung her heart out on live TV a few hours before.

The slightest smile lifted one corner of Walker's mouth. "That's what I said, all right. Am I in this all alone, or what?"

She gave a sob of laughter then, and threw her arms around his neck. "I love

you now, and I always have, Walker Parrish," she blurted out, clinging to him,
reveling in the hard, warm substance of
him.

"You might have said as much," he
told her gruffly, his breath warm at her
ear, his arms tight and strong around
her.

"Back at you, cowboy," Casey said,
happier than she'd ever thought she
could be. "I didn't hear 'I love you' coming from your direction, either."

He chuckled, and then he kissed her,
so deeply and so thoroughly that her
last doubts gave way.

At home, the kids and the dogs were
all asleep, which was a good thing because Casey and Walker had had a heck
of a time even getting that far before
they started making love.

Walker picked Casey up in the kitchen
and carried her to their room, his strides
long.

There was a lot to settle—the problems with Clare, for starters, and where
things would go from here—but this
time, this shining strand of moments

and minutes and hours, belonged only to the two of them.

Behind closed doors, they undressed each other, stepped into the shower stall together, kissing even as the warm spray of water drenched them both, slickening their fevered bodies, spiking their eyelashes, soothing away everything but the desperate drive to be joined, two beings melded into one.

They took things slowly, though, savoring every kiss, every caress, every whispered word. All the unsaid "I love yous," stored up for years, came rushing to the surface now, as unstoppable as lava from a volcano.

They lathered each other with soap, rinsed away the suds, and Casey marveled at the pitch of her arousal. Lovemaking wasn't new to them, but that night, it **seemed** new, a first in the history of Creation.

Presently, Walker knelt, his hands stroking Casey's thighs before he parted her, ever so gently, with a motion of his thumbs.

When he took her into his mouth, her whole body convulsed with primitive pleasure, and she bit down hard on her lower lip to keep from shouting his name in welcome, in need, in love. Not the paper roses and Valentines kind of love, but the real thing, a sacred equation of one man and one woman.

Satisfaction came quickly for Casey, consuming her like a fire. She flexed and flexed again as Walker continued to enjoy her, her hands locked behind his head to hold him there.

But once was never enough, and when the violent shudders of release had finally ceased, Walker draped her legs over his shoulders—they wouldn't hold her any longer—and nuzzled in for an encore.

The water turned lukewarm, but neither of them cared; they might have been making love under a summer rainfall, or anywhere. The place didn't matter, nothing did, beyond the simple fact that they were together. **Really** together, for the first time ever.

Somehow—Casey was in too much of a daze to recall the mechanics later—they wound up on top of their bed, still slippery-wet, hair dripping, bodies frantic, and she saw their whole future in Walker's eyes as he looked down at her, silently asking her permission, the way he always did.

She saw them raising Clare and Shane together, with all their combined love and determination.

She saw them bringing home the new baby, the one growing inside her, nurtured not only by her body, but by her soul.

She saw more children, and grandchildren, too. All of them as much a part of the ranch as the land and the creeks, the river and the sky.

Most of all, she saw love, the tough, durable kind that knows no endings, but only beginnings, only a shared freedom, and the gift to grow in all directions, like those flowers rioting around the ruins of the homestead cabin up on the hill.

She nodded, said it again. "I love you."

Walker was inside her in a single stroke, going deep, commanding, conquering, and yet with a tenderness so poignant that Casey's spirit soared, even before her body did.

Their releases were simultaneous, a

fusion of two lightning bolts into one cataclysmic flash, and achieved only after much sweet striving. They were locked in a kiss all the while, their cries echoing between them.

The descent was long, slow and delicious.

In between skirmishes, the lovers slept, arms and legs entwined, Walker's chin resting atop Casey's head. Each time they awakened, they made love again, sometimes sleepily, sometimes desperately, and when dawn finally broke, they were joined, and the sunrise became Casey's climax, blinding and beautiful, all pink and gold dazzle, a sky full of fire.

July 15

Opal stood at the front of the little church, head high and shoulders squared, beside her bridegroom, the Reverend Walter Beaumont. One of the reverend's colleagues had come to Parable especially to perform the ceremony, and every pew was packed.

Standing in the choir loft, Casey

scanned the congregation, found Walker and Clare and Shane, and she was glad she wouldn't have to sing for a few more minutes, because just then, her heart was filling her throat.

A family—**her** family, with all the attendant challenges and triumphs, all the ups and downs. How did she get so lucky?

Walker looked up at her then, as if he'd heard her thoughts. His expression was completely solemn—until he winked.

Casey smiled, blushed a little and looked away.

She spotted Joslyn and Slade Barlow, their firstborn squirming between them on the pew, as toddlers will, each of them holding a blue-wrapped bundle in loving arms. Shea, Slade's stepdaughter, was there, too, beaming proudly at one of the week-old twins, then the other.

She found Hutch and Kendra Carmody next, sitting with their shoulders touching and their gazes on the bride and groom. Their little girl, Madison, sat beside them, fussing over her baby sister, kicking and cooing in her infant seat.

Boone and Tara Taylor, with four children between them, took up most of one pew. Tara's arm was looped through Boone's, Casey noticed, and her head rested against his shoulder.

Casey brought her gaze back around to Walker and Clare and Shane, and happy tears filled her eyes, because there sat Brylee, big as life, her face glowing with joy as Opal and Walter exchanged their vows.

Walter's kiss was Casey's cue to sing, and sing she did.

The song was a special one, a collaboration between herself and Clare, about love finding its own way, in its own time, and enduring.

Clare turned to look up at Casey midsong, mouthing the words they'd written together at the piano in the ranch house living room, and Casey's heart swelled again, with love for her daughter, her good husband, her fine son, and the wings of her gratitude carried her voice to the heights.

When the song ended, there was a stirring silence, almost palpable.

Then Opal and Walter broke with tradition and turned, smiling up at Casey and clapping their hands. The rest of the congregation joined in, and Casey stepped back, out of view, and descended the stairs from the small loft.

The celebration, held at the house on Rodeo Road, which Casey used as headquarters and a place to record with the band, went on for hours. She still wasn't doing concert tours, but singing itself wasn't optional for her—she had to have music, had to **make** music— and Walker not only understood, he was proud of her.

Except for a brief flurry of media attention centered around Clare's brush with the law—the shoplifting charges had been dropped, but Walker and Casey had insisted she perform some kind of community service just the same—the tabloids and other "news" outlets had backed off. Clare helped Marti Wren out three afternoons a week at the animal shelter, and once remarked that if this was punishment, she should have gotten into trouble sooner.

Shane, a cowboy through and through, rode the range with his dad as often as possible, and did his chores without complaint—mostly. He was bound and determined to last longer than three seconds the next time he entered a rodeo, and that seemed like a reasonable goal to Casey.

She still hated the idea of her son on the back of a bucking bronco, of course, but she kept that to herself—**mostly.**

While the band played, Opal and her new husband danced on the floor specially constructed for the occasion, smiling into each other's eyes, surrounded by friends and family, immersed in the glow of their love.

Walker stepped up behind Casey, slipped his arms around her and rested his chin on top of her head. "Pretty romantic," he said, turning her gently around to face him, handing her a small velvet box.

Casey, not expecting a gift, was taken aback. "What's this?"

"Open it and see," Walker said.

She lifted the lid, peered inside the box and saw a beautiful heart-shaped pendant in tones of gold and silver, with two tiny charms suspended in the center—two Western hats, one to represent each of them. "Thank you," she murmured, overwhelmed with love for this man she'd married.

Fingers trembling a little, she removed the necklace from its case and handed it to Walker, so he could drape it around her neck and fasten it.

He did that, squeezed her shoulders lightly. "I think we ought to go straight home and celebrate."

Casey laughed, turned in Walker's embrace and smiled up at him. "That's not a bad idea, cowboy," she said. "Not a bad idea at all."

* * * * *